GIANT
PUMPKIN
SUITE

GIANT PUMPKIN SUITE

MELANIE HEUISER HILL

CANDLEWICK PRESS

First edition 2017

Library of Congress Catalog Card Number pending
ISBN 978-0-7636-9155-4

17 18 19 20 21 22 BVG 10 9 8 7 6 5 4 3 2 1

Printed in Berryville, VA, U.S.A.

This book was typeset in Sabon.

Candlewick Press
99 Dover Street
Somerville, Massachusetts 02144

visit us at www.candlewick.com

For Caleb and Marta,
my favorite ones to read with

In memory of Anne,
kindred spirit, bosom friend

For a seed to achieve its greatest expression, it must come completely undone. The shell cracks, its insides come out, and everything changes. To someone who doesn't understand growth, it would look like complete destruction.

—Cynthia Occelli

Chapter 1
May Day

Rose's bow zinged off the cello strings. Thomas hit the button on his stopwatch and grinned.

"Three minutes exactly!" he said. "Five whole seconds faster than Yo-Yo. Your bow was *flying*."

Rose tucked a stray curl behind her ear and tried not to smile. She could hear the admiration in her brother's voice. Thomas didn't know much about music, but he was impressed by speed.

"Bach's Cello Suites are not a track-and-field event," she said. Still, Suite no. 3's gigue wasn't easy . . . *and she had just played it five seconds faster than world-renowned cellist Yo-Yo Ma!* The important thing was how *well* she played it, however—not how fast. But she had just played it very well, she knew. *And* fast, which was immensely satisfying.

"Don't worry," said Thomas. "It sounds good, too."

Thomas stood in front of her, his big toe on the cello's endpin. When Rose sat and Thomas stood, they were the same height. She lost seventeen inches just by sitting down. She grabbed her pad of sticky notes and wrote SIT MORE! on a bright lime-green square. She folded it over so the sticky part was covered, and then shoved the note into her pocket, down along with the other goals crumpled in the pocket's depths. She already sat two to three hours a day while she practiced, so this would be an easy goal to achieve; she'd be practicing more, not less, in the coming weeks.

Rose liked achieving goals—small ones, like SIT MORE, but larger goals, too. Currently, the largest goal in her pocket was WIN BACH CELLO SUITES COMPETITION. That sticky note was soft and worn and had lost much of its bright-pink color. She'd been carrying it around for more than a year. Soon it would be achieved. At least she hoped it would.

"Any special numbers in that one?" Thomas asked as he wriggled his toe against the endpin.

Rose scanned the music in front of her, looking for

a pattern or sequence she might have missed. Bach could be tricky—she could've been looking at it for months and missed it. "I don't think so," she said finally. "Bach doesn't always do it. And the numbers are *significant,* not special."

"Special" sounded like she'd made it all up, and she had not. Bach liked math and puzzles and ciphers, and he included them in the notes and structures of his music. It sounded silly when she tried to explain it, but it wasn't—scholars of Bach studied how he used numbers. Harris Waldenstein, judge of the upcoming Cello Suites Competition, wrote a book about it, in fact. Her favorite chapter was on Bach's musical use of the number fourteen.

Rose flipped back in the music to Suite no. 1 and started the prelude. If you assigned a number to each letter of the alphabet—a somewhat common practice in Bach's time, apparently—J. S. Bach's last name added up to fourteen:

$$B (2) + A (1) + C (3) + H (8) = 14$$

He used the sum of the letters in his name in creative ways in his compositions. Harris Waldenstein said it was Bach's way of building in a cryptic "signature." It was interesting that Yo-Yo Ma's last name *also* added up to fourteen:

$$M (13) + A (1) = 14$$

Which obviously was significant, given how beautifully he played Bach's Cello Suites.

"This is the one that has forty-one measures, right?" said Thomas. He stood behind her and looked over her shoulder at the music. Rose had numbered the measures in pencil—it was helpful at her lessons.

She nodded and kept playing. Forty-one—the mirror of fourteen—was another number that appeared in Bach's music with unusual frequency. Fourteen and forty-one were Bach's favorite numbers, according to Harris Waldenstein. Along with five, because the digits in those two numbers—one and four—added up to five.

It was all *so clever*. Bach was a musical genius, but he didn't stop with beautiful music. He had all these jokes and numerical riddles running in the notes— forward, backward, and upside down sometimes. Two of her favorite things in one package: math and music! Oh, how she loved Bach!

"What about that last chord?" asked Thomas. "Isn't that measure number forty-two? That doesn't seem very *significant*."

Rose ignored him and kept playing. Thomas thought Bach's number games were ridiculous. And he was right about the prelude—there was a final measure that added up to forty-two, but it was just one chord, and Rose didn't count that. It was like "The End" in a story. In her mind, Suite no. 1's prelude—the glorious opening of the entire suite cycle—was a forty-one-measure piece. And that was significant.

"I'm heading to Mr. P.'s," said Thomas as measure forty-two's chord faded. "Do you want to come with?"

"Suite number four needs work," said Rose.

"Okay. I'll leave the stopwatch here." He hung the strap on her music stand. "In case you want to time it yourself."

"You can take it," Rose said. "I'll be starting and stopping a lot. Say hi to Mr. Pickering."

"Come over when you're done!" Thomas called as the storm door clattered shut behind him.

Probably not. She needed to tighten up the trills in Suite no. 4's courante movement. Mrs. Holling, her cello teacher, said her trills were too loosey-goosey. Bach was *never* loosey-goosey.

Rose closed her eyes and started Suite no. 1's prelude one more time, to put herself in the right frame of mind for working on Suite no. 4. When she closed her eyes, it felt as if the music played through her—as if she, not the cello, were the instrument. She adored the first forty-one measures of the suite cycle. It was probably the most well-known movement of the Bach Cello Suites. She'd been playing it since she was little—she had played it when she auditioned for Mrs. Holling, in fact, when she was just six years old. And soon she would play it for Maestro Harris Waldenstein!

Just as she reached the forty-second measure for the second time, Thomas crashed through the back door. Her bow screeched across the cello's strings and her eyes popped open to see the alarmed face of her brother in the kitchen doorway.

"What's wrong?"

"Mr. P.!" said Thomas. "Come help!"

He was gone before she could reply.

As quickly as she could, Rose placed her bow on the music stand and leaned her cello on its side on the floor. It was Mrs. Holling's cello—not the one she currently played, but the one she played through college and graduate school and even after. She let Rose use it because it was a nicer instrument than anything Mama and Gram could afford to buy or rent. It was important to have a nice instrument.

As soon as she was sure the cello was stable, Rose ran out the back door and across the yards to Mr.

Pickering's house. She hurried up her next-door neighbor's back steps and into his kitchen.

Everything was quiet.

"Thomas?"

"Down here!"

Rose moved to the tiny landing at the top of the basement stairs. The bare bulb at the bottom of the stairs showed Mr. Pickering in a crumpled heap on the floor.

"Ah . . . my second rescuer," Mr. Pickering said in a small voice.

Thomas waved her down impatiently. Rose grabbed the handrail and started to descend the steep stairs. She felt like a daddy longlegs. Her feet hung over the edge of each step and her legs shook as she rushed. She slowed down just a little. She couldn't trip—she'd land on Mr. Pickering.

"Thank goodness." Mr. Pickering sighed. His skin was the same color as his shirt. Lint color.

"Mr. Pickering, *what happened?*" Rose asked. Twice she tried to fold up her long legs to get down on the floor, but her legs were still shaking, so she stood looking down at her brother and their neighbor.

"He fell down the stairs," said Thomas. "He didn't

answer when I knocked, so I just came in like usual. He can't get up, and I can't move him."

"What's wrong with . . . your shoulders?" Rose asked Mr. Pickering. They were crooked. So was his left foot—it looked like a paper-doll foot that had been glued on wrong.

Mr. Pickering winced. "Actually, Rosie," he said, "I believe I've broken a thing or two. . . . And while I am lucky—very lucky"—he took what looked like a painful breath—"that you two have come, we need more help. Thomas tells me your mama and gram aren't home?"

"No, Mama's still at work, and Gram's at church," said Rose. Mama was a nurse at the hospital, which seemed ironic given the circumstances. Rose hoped Gram would be home soon—the more she looked at Mr. Pickering, the more nervous she felt.

"Should we call an ambulance?" asked Thomas.

"I think that would be best," said Mr. Pickering. His voice was filled with relief and pain—a contrasting sound, like a cello could make. "You won't be able to get me up and out of this wretched basement, even with your gram's help."

"Can we help you . . . rearrange yourself or something?" said Rose.

"I think we better let a trained professional figure out how to move me," said Mr. Pickering. "Now, which of you would be willing to go call an ambulance?"

"You go," Thomas said to Rose. "I'll stay with Mr. P."

As Rose turned to head back up the stairs, Thomas said, "What were you doing down here, anyway, Mr. P.?" It was a good question. Unlike their basement, which was crowded with stuff, Mr. Pickering didn't really have much in his. A few old boxes against the back wall, but that was it.

"Came down to water the seed. I was so excited to check on it that I forgot to pay attention to my footing on those awful steps."

"What seed?" said Thomas. Rose paused, a foot on the bottom stair.

"Just planted," said Mr. Pickering with a wince to his voice. "A very special seed."

"A special seed?" echoed Thomas.

"Yes," said Mr. Pickering. He sighed, which sounded like it hurt. "Could you water it if I don't get back home tonight? I think I might not. I believe I've messed myself up good here."

Rose flew up the stairs much faster than she'd come down.

Chapter 2

To the Rescue

Rose had never called 911 before. She was surprised by how quickly the operator answered and how calm she sounded. Her own voice was high and squeaky, like a poorly played violin, as she explained the situation.

"Yes, it sounds like an ambulance is needed," said the operator. "What is the address, please?"

Rose broke into a sweat. She tried to visualize the front of Mr. Pickering's house. Did he have a house number?

"I can look it up," said the operator. "No worries. Why don't you give me *your* address as a cross-check."

Rose's mind went blank. She couldn't remember her own address! She hated feeling nervous. Bach—that's what she needed! Rose breathed out the way Mrs. Holling had showed her—it was supposed to be calming—and then gathered the comforting prelude from Suite no. 1 into her mind and heart. Her left hand fingered imaginary cello strings on the telephone pressed against her ear. Yes. Much better. Her tense shoulders lowered into a posture proper for playing. Her house number was 3308. The digits added up to fourteen—how could she have forgotten?

"Hello? Are you still there?" said the operator.

"Yes, sorry. I'm here," said Rose. The suite continued softly inside her. "Our address is three three zero eight Library Lane. Mr. Pickering, the patient, lives next door to us. His house number must be something like three three one zero?"

"Excellent." Rose could hear the operator's smile. She hated it when adults found her amusing, as if she were just a small child. If the operator could *see* her, she'd know. "Is somebody with your neighbor?" the operator asked.

"My brother is," said Rose.

"Okay, honey, the ambulance is heading out now. Go tell your neighbor and brother that help is on the way."

Rose hung up the phone and went to the top of

the basement stairs. Thomas had put a towel under Mr. Pickering's head. The old man's eyes were closed. He looked—

"Mr. Pickering!"

He didn't open his eyes, but his voice was strong. "Are they on their way, Rosie?"

"Yes." Rose exhaled. "I'll wait on the porch for them." She didn't want to go down those stairs again.

"Good. Thank you. Thomas is doing a fine job here. I'm lucky to have you two to watch over me."

They watch over *him*? The other way around, really. Rose took a big breath, and as she exhaled, she felt the allemande, the second movement from Suite no. 1, begin its sixty-four-measure (two repeating sections of sixteen measures each—not especially significant but a lovely movement nonetheless) dance through her. When Rose needed Bach's suites, she could always call them up, but sometimes they played on their own—her own personal soundtrack. Her heart and breath slowed to the allemande's comforting rhythm as she made her way to the front porch to wait.

The steps were gritty with leftover winter grime, but remembering her most recent goal, Rose sat down anyway. No need to stand like a flagpole for the whole neighborhood to see. The yards on Library Lane wore the dirty grayish brown of early spring, but the breeze was fresh and . . . hopeful. For the first of May in Minnesota, the weather was unusually warm.

The first of May. It was May Day! When they were little, she and Thomas always made May baskets from construction paper and filled them with tissue-paper flowers. They'd sneak over to Mr. Pickering's front porch, hang the baskets on his doorknob, then ring the doorbell. Before Mr. Pickering answered, they would run home. Mr. Pickering always pretended not to know who had left the surprise.

They were too old for such things now, of course. She and Thomas were exactly twelve years, two weeks, and three days old. She was actually two minutes (and *fourteen* seconds) older than Thomas, having been born first, but he hated when she mentioned it, so she tried not to.

She didn't have time for May baskets anymore, and Thomas probably wouldn't even remember it was May Day. She shrugged off a twinge of sadness. Besides, it was a very different kind of May Day this year—more like the distress call: "May Day! May Day!" Mr. Pickering didn't need a May basket. He needed an ambulance.

Rose strained her ears, listening for sirens as she

shifted her legs, finally folding them to the side in what she hoped was a graceful position. It was hard to tell what might be graceful. Mama said she was still getting used to her height. If she could just *stop* growing, she might be able to get used to it, but since school had started in the fall, she had grown seven inches. Thomas had grown half an inch. He said he was stuck. Mama said they were simply on different schedules. They always had been.

At age twelve (and two weeks and three days), Rose was almost a foot and a half taller and four grades ahead of her twin. Thomas had been sick a lot in first grade and had been held back, while she'd skipped a grade a couple of times and had started high school this past fall. She was left-handed; Thomas was right-handed. She loved to read. Thomas hated it. She went to the university for math, but Thomas had never passed his multiplication tables. Nearly everyone had forgotten they were twins. Except Mr. Pickering, who seldom mentioned it. And Calamity Jane. Who mentioned it all the time.

Rose took down her hair and rewound the curls into a bun at the back of her head. As she did so, sirens howled around the corner. Finally! The ambulance slowed coming down Library Lane, its lights flashing.

The wail of the sirens was out of sync with the flashing lights, which was disconcerting. It wasn't an interesting syncopated rhythm—just off. Rose plugged her ears—sirens were a harsh sound for a musician's sensitive hearing—then unfolded her legs and stood, just in time to see Gram's car turn the corner.

Gram was out of her car before the paramedics were out of the ambulance.

"Rose! What happened?" She hurried up Mr. Pickering's front steps, clutching her purse. Gram could move pretty fast when she was terrified. "Are you all right? Is it Thomas?" Her eyes were wide and wild.

"It's Mr. Pickering," said Rose, opening the front door for the paramedics, who carried a stretcher. "He fell down his basement stairs." She and Gram led the paramedics through the living room and kitchen to the stairs.

Rose tried not to listen to the sound of Mr. Pickering's pain coming up the stairwell as the EMTs moved him onto the stretcher. Gram's look of fear settled into concern for her longtime neighbor.

"Those stairs are horrid," said Gram as they went back out to the front porch. "He shouldn't be on them at his age. What was he doing in the basement, anyway?"

"He went down to water a seed," said Rose.

"A seed?" said Gram. "Otis doesn't grow things."

"Well, he does now, I guess," said Rose with a shrug.

Mr. Pickering's face was a color worse than lint as the paramedics carried him to the ambulance. They'd put an oxygen mask on him, and his eyes were closed. But he lifted a hand in a halfhearted wave as Gram called out, "You'll be in our prayers, Otis. We'll check on you later this evening."

Thomas leapt back up the porch steps once the ambulance doors shut.

"Mr. P. says you'll be able to reach the seed—it's on top of the water heater."

Rose rolled her eyes—as if they needed to be thinking about a seed at a time like this. "We'll get it later."

The ambulance pulled away slowly, lights on, siren silent. Gram walked across the street to talk to Mrs. Kiyo, who was standing on her front stoop watching the events at Mr. Pickering's. Library Lane wasn't an unfriendly street, but people didn't spend much time outside. They knew most of their neighbors, but they didn't know much about them. And there was the empty house across the street and down a few houses—it'd been empty for almost a year, which Gram said was not good for the neighborhood.

Thomas waved. Mrs. Kiyo did not wave back. She never did. She maybe nodded her head, which was something. But it was hard to be sure. She moved very slowly. Gram said she was lonely. Mrs. Kiyo was Japanese, but she had married an American soldier after World War II—which made her super old, the oldest person on the block for sure—and came to live in Minnesota. She was something called a war bride, which Rose thought sounded romantic. Gram said it was more complicated than that. Kiyo was her first name, not her last name. Her last name was something like Andersen. But everyone called her Mrs. Kiyo. Rose wondered if she minded.

Señor Ocampo hurried up the street toward them. Señor Ocampo owned the hardware store down the block across from the library. Mr. Pickering helped Señor Ocampo with his English, and Señor Ocampo helped Mr. Pickering with his Spanish. Señor Ocampo looked very worried as he watched the ambulance carrying his friend turn the corner. Thomas ran down the sidewalk to tell him what had happened.

Across the street from Rose and Thomas's house, to

the right of Mrs. Kiyo, lived the Jacobis. Calamity Jane and her brothers were definitely not home—they'd be out in the middle of things if they were. Mrs. Jacobi would be at her second job at the sub sandwich shop now, so Jane and the boys were probably at the library under the watchful eye of Mrs. Lukashenko.

Gradually the neighbors drifted back into their houses, and Gram walked back across the yards to their own front porch.

"Should we call Mama and see if she can check on Mr. Pickering before she comes home?" Rose asked.

"Good idea," said Gram. "I'll see if I can catch her before the end of her shift." She shook her head in worry. Gram and Mr. Pickering had been neighbors for almost forty years. He was family, really. "Despite the circumstances, we might as well go to the library."

Friday was library day in the Brutigan household. Gram loved routine. She had taken her grandchildren to the library on Friday afternoons for nine years, and she could not be persuaded to change days, nor would she let her grandchildren skip a Friday.

But maybe Gram would make an exception today. "I think I'll stay home and practice," Rose tried. "The competition is coming up."

"You can practice when we get home."

"But I'm still reading the books I got last week," Rose tried again.

"I believe you need to return *Charlotte's Web*," said Gram. "So Jane can have it?"

"No," said Rose, her voice sharper than she intended. "It's *my* week coming up. I'll go and see if *she* has returned it yet." Calamity Jane was famous for returning it at the very last minute.

"We won't stay long," said Gram. "It's about time for me to start supper."

Staying at the library was not the problem. Rose could live at the library. The problem was the Jacobi boys outside the library.

Chapter 3
Free Fallin'

Rose stood in front of the bathroom mirror, wielding her hairbrush like a weapon. She would need the tightest bun she could muster for the library trip.

"Does your head ever hurt because your hair's so tight?" Thomas asked when she joined him in the living room with the stack of library books she'd finished. "And don't you ever get tired of reading *Charlotte's Web*? Charlotte's always going to die, no matter how many times you read it."

Rose glared at her brother. Thomas's curls sprawled all over his head, but that fit him. She needed more control of hers. And no, she never got tired of *Charlotte's Web* — and certainly not the ending, though it did make her throat tight and her eyes burn when she read it. *Charlotte's Web* was like Bach's music—it spoke to something in her in a way she could not explain but also could not do without.

"You should let your hair down occasionally, Rose," said Gram, holding the door for both of them. "It's so pretty when the curls are loose."

Rose decided to ignore this reprise of a conversation. Her hair was a mess when the curls were loose. That's why she wore it up all the time. She was a serious student of the cello—she did not need crazy curls in her way.

Rose and Thomas walked on either side of Gram down the street. Gram was smiling, which made Rose smile in spite of herself. It was wonderful to live on Library Lane. She got a secret thrill every time she wrote her address—*Library Lane*! To be able to walk to the library anytime you wanted was a truly great thing. Which was why she resented that her family's Friday afternoon routine had been ruined by the Jacobi boys. The Jacobi twins, to be exact. Unlike Rose and Thomas, Jesse and James Jacobi were identical. Same dark hair and eyes, identical goofy grin, exact same height. They were replicas of each other.

Every Friday—almost as if they knew she was

coming—Jesse and James posted themselves on the corner across the street from the library and . . . sang. The same song, over and over again. One of the boys—whichever one it was—played the guitar. Badly.

They'd started the singing when the three of them—Jesse, James, and Rose—started high school in the fall. They seemed to have forgotten that Rose was Thomas's twin and closer to their little sister's age than theirs. They teased her and talked with her like she was a high-school girl. It wasn't mean. Just embarrassing.

She heard the familiar strains when they were still halfway down the block. Something about a "good girl" who loved her mama and Jesus.

It was impossible to know which one was singing. She'd been able to tell them apart only once: the year Jesse stuck silver duct tape to his face at Halloween, trying to be the Tin Man from *The Wizard of Oz*. When he took the duct tape off, his eyebrows came with it. That distinguished him for months, but that was several years ago. The two boys had matching thick dark eyebrows again, and now they were growing identical fuzzy hair on their upper lip. Rose turned her head and pretended to watch something else. But nothing else was happening. Why did nothing *ever* happen in their neighborhood? Or if it did, it was something awful like an ambulance coming for Mr. Pickering. She shifted the library books she was carrying to her other arm in an attempt to look nonchalant.

They sang about the good girl being crazy about Elvis. Were people *really* still crazy about Elvis? Elvis couldn't possibly have the longevity of Bach. She knew that the song they sang was "Free Fallin'" by Tom Petty. She'd looked it up on the library's computer. Apparently, it was a "classic." It was hard to know why. It was the same three guitar chords over and over again, and Mr. Petty did nothing interesting with them. Rose preferred the clever sophistication of Bach.

Gram put a few coins in the Jacobi boys' open guitar case as they passed, which put the cherry on top of the whole mortifying situation. One of the boys pretended to tip a hat he was not wearing in thanks, and they launched into the chorus. Rose concentrated on crossing the street, one long foot in front of the other, taking extra care not to trip.

The chorus was the song's title — over and over and over again: *free fallin', free fallin', free fallin'* — with the *ee* of *free* drawn out way too long. It was their favorite part. They belted it out, unaware that their voices and the guitar were in different keys. The guitar had probably never been tuned.

They referred to themselves as a band. The band's name was *Jesse James*, which they'd painted in white paint on their guitar case. The real Jesse James was a famous bank robber. The Jacobi family had a lawbreaker theme. Eddie Jacobi, the Jacobi kids' dad, had spent a lot of time in jail for various nonviolent "white-collar" crimes. Gram said he was a con man—unless she was trying to "explain his actions in the kindest of ways," which she always encouraged. Then she said he was a "gregarious man who fooled a lot of people by misusing his charismatic gifts." Which was the kindest way of saying he was a con man.

Rose had met Mr. Jacobi once between jail stints. He was very handsome. The twins looked more and more like him the older they got. He seemed friendly and fun. He didn't seem like a dad, though. Gram said that's because he really wasn't; he was never out of jail long enough to parent. (It was hard to phrase this in a kind way.) Before Mr. Jacobi went to jail the first time, he named his twin boys Jesse and James. And then, when Mrs. Jacobi named their baby girl Jane, Mr. Jacobi insisted (from jail) on calling her Calamity Jane, after one of the wildest female outlaws of all time.

Rose heaved open the library door and held it for Gram and Thomas. Jesse and James hit the chorus again and sang louder. She stole a glance across the street. The boys smiled identical smiles and sang even louder. Rose turned into the library, hoping the door would shut fast behind her so she could be done listening.

Mrs. Lukashenko, who worked in the back room, came out singing.

"Hello, Rosa! Well, hello, Thomas! It's so nice to have you back where you belong!" Friday afternoons were sometimes unbearably musical. Tom Petty outside the library, and old musicals inside. Mrs. Lukashenko sang this song — loudly — every time they came into the library, and Rose was past being embarrassed about it. It was a variation on the title song from the musical *Hello, Dolly!* Rose hadn't seen the musical, but she knew it was one of Mrs. Lukashenko's favorites.

"Hi, Mrs. Lukashenko," she said.

"Hello, hello! How are my other favorite twins?" said Mrs. Lukashenko. Only it sounded more like "HallO, hallO! HOW are mY oZer favorITE twinZ?" Mrs. Lukashenko was originally from Ukraine, and she hit certain letters — pretty much any letter at the end of a word, and some others besides — hard.

"We're fine," said Rose, "thank you." Thomas waved, then disappeared into the comic-book section.

Mrs. Lukashenko sat down heavily on the chair at the circulation desk. "My bazooms . . . they need a rest," she said. She meant *bosom,* which was embarrassing enough. She heaved her large bazooms onto the desk to "rest." Rose busied herself putting her borrowed books on the conveyor belt that took them to the back to be checked in.

The sound of tap shoes announced the imminent arrival of Calamity Jane. Rose was glad only because if Jane was already at the library, it was possible that *Charlotte's Web* would be on the shelf.

"Tell me again," said Calamity Jane as she tap-danced around the desk. "How are you and Thomas twins? I can never remember."

"We are *fraternal* twins," said Rose. Calamity Jane couldn't seem to grasp the difference between fraternal and identical twins. Rose focused on Jane's sleek ponytail, which hung in a perfect silky stream down her back. Did she know how lucky she was to have hair like that?

"We're not identical twins like your brothers," she said. She tried to make her voice kind and patient, like Mrs. Holling's.

"But that's not really being twins," said Calamity Jane. She tap-danced in place, little shuffle taps, her forehead wrinkled in puzzlement, her silky ponytail bouncing in rhythm. Calamity Jane tap-danced when she was trying to think.

The letters in Jane's name added up to thirty. And Jacobi added up to forty. Numbers with a zero were just so . . . like a zero. Together, Jane's first and last name added up to seventy. *Three zeros.* You could tell a lot about a person by the sum of the letters in their name.

The door to the library opened up as someone else came into the library. The Jacobi boys were still singing the chorus.

"Those boys always sing loudest when you come, Rose," said Mrs. Lukashenko. "You are the boys' shipoopi, maybe?"

Shipoopi?

Calamity Jane burst out laughing and tap-danced in a circle around Rose. "It's from *The Music Man!*"

Mrs. Lukashenko had learned to speak English by watching old American musicals. She had a song for every occasion. When she shelved books, she sang "My Favorite Things" from *The Sound of Music,* and she sounded just like Maria. Maria with a lower voice, anyway.

Mrs. Lukashenko and Calamity Jane sang a line

together. Jane's tapping took on a different rhythm—
she pulled her knees up in quick jerks and kicked her
legs out to the side in rhythm.

"'Shipoopi' song is about the men's girlfriends,"
Mrs. Lukashenko explained, letting the *s* in *girlfriends*
buzz extra long. "Or rather, girls they *hope* will be their
girlfriends." Her dark eyes twinkled.

"Marcellus sings 'Shipoopi,'" Calamity Jane
explained. "But the whole town dances and sings
behind him."

Of course they did. Musicals were like that. People
broke into song over nothing, and everyone joined in
the song and dance. Cello suites were about a thousand
times more . . . refined.

Jane had watched *all* the musicals with Mrs.
Lukashenko many, many times. Mrs. Lukashenko was
Jane's godmother, which was a little weird because Mrs.
Lukashenko was Jewish and the Jacobis were
Methodist, like Rose's family. But Pastor Nancy said
anytime a family could be made bigger through love—
anytime the definition of family could be broadened—
she was all for it. So, a year ago, they added some
Hebrew to the usual baptism service and Mrs.
Lukashenko sang "Sabbath Prayer" from *Fiddler on*

the Roof, and she became Jane's godmother. It had been equal parts lovely and weird.

"I am *not* their shipoopi, Mrs. Lukashenko." A curl sprang from her bun. She tucked it back in.

Mrs. Lukashenko smiled. "Oh, I don't know, Rose. When you are older, maybe you will go to a dance together with Jesse or James. . . ."

Rose didn't have time for dances. Besides, her legs were too long. And if she were to go to a dance, which she would not, she certainly wouldn't go with either of the Jacobi twins. But she was not going to be drawn into such a ridiculous argument.

"You should come to my tap class!" said Calamity Jane, as if the idea had just occurred to her and she hadn't already asked Rose to come to her dance class forty-eight jillion times. Rose didn't bother to respond to that, either. She just walked back to the shelf that held *Charlotte's Web,* took it down, and went to check it out.

Forget about living at the library. Right now she couldn't wait to return home to her cello. She needed Bach.

Chapter 4

The State of Mr. Pickering

At suppertime, while they were telling Mama about their crazy afternoon, the phone rang. Gram rose to answer it.

"Yes!" Gram mouthed the word *hospital*. "Good of Otis to know we'd be concerned—and good of you to give us a call. I know you must be very busy."

She repeated things for their benefit: "Badly broken left ankle, broken collarbone, right side. Broken ribs, both sides. Assorted bruises. Well, I should think so! He fell down a terrible flight of steps, after all. . . . No indication of head trauma. There's a grace! . . . Surgery to begin in thirty minutes! It can't wait until tomorrow?

We were hoping to stop by to visit him." She looked at Mama with worry on her face. "I see. Risk of infection. Okay. Well, I do thank you for calling. Give him our love, please, as he goes into surgery. Thank you again."

Gram hung up and joined them at the table. "Poor Otis. Sounds like he's in rough shape."

"I'll go in early for the evening shift and check on him," said Mama, patting Gram's arm. Mama looked so tired. She'd stayed late at her first shift and would be going back in for the night shift after they went to bed. Mama had been picking up extra shifts for the better part of a year now. Whenever Rose or Thomas complained about missing her or expressed concern about how tired she seemed, she responded with something about overtime pay being too good to pass up.

"And on that note, I think I'll go lie down for a bit before I head back in. Play me a little Bach, honey? A little of that first suite?" Mama's favorite was the prelude to Suite no. 1, too.

"Sure," said Rose. She stood to take her dishes to the sink. She could tell Mama would be asleep before she'd finished the prelude.

"Can we go get that seed Mr. P. wants us to take care of first?" Thomas asked.

"That seed is the least of our worries," said Gram.

31

"He said it was an important seed," Thomas insisted. "*Special.*"

"You can look tomorrow," said Gram.

"Why not tonight?" asked Thomas.

"Because Rose has cello to practice, and both of you have homework."

"It's Friday!" said Thomas. He did a little dance in his chair. "We've got the whole weekend!"

Gram smiled; Thomas's sense of fun was contagious. "The homework can wait until tomorrow, I guess, but Rose needs to practice. Her session this afternoon was interrupted by the accident."

Thomas's face clouded over, which it did only when Rose's cello practicing got in the way of something he wanted to do.

"Just go get it and bring it over here," Rose said, rinsing her plate.

"I can't reach it. It's on top of the water heater, remember? But *you* could reach it!" said Thomas. "It'll just take a minute. Please, Rosie?"

Gram moved to the sink to start the dishes. Thomas clasped his hands dramatically and pleaded silently with Rose. Rose rolled her eyes and walked to the back door. Thomas scurried after her.

"Mr. Pickering's door is locked," said Gram over the sound of running water.

"Locked?" said Thomas. "Mr. P. never locks his back door."

"Well, I did," said Gram. "That man is foolish to leave his home open to whomever whenever."

"He just leaves it open for me and Rosie," said Thomas. "Mostly me. Rose is always too busy."

Rose shot him a look. Thomas had easy fifth-grade homework and no instrument to practice. What did he know about obligations and time pressures?

"Well, you shouldn't walk in and out of someone's house uninvited," said Gram.

Thomas shrugged. "Mr. P. says we're always invited."

Gram's face softened. "I know. Our friend has done a lot for us over the years." She rummaged in the junk drawer by the phone and handed Thomas a key. "Go get the silly seed. Don't dawdle. Rose needs to get back."

As they walked across the yard to Mr. Pickering's, the brown-gray grass crunched faintly beneath their feet. The evening had cooled off quite a bit. Rose shivered.

Thomas slid the key Gram had magically pulled

from the junk drawer into the lock of Mr. Pickering's back door and turned it. He seemed surprised when it worked.

They walked into the hushed quiet of Mr. Pickering's kitchen. His kitchen was so different from theirs. For starters, it didn't smell like anything. Their kitchen always smelled like whatever Gram had just baked or was getting ready to make for their next meal. Also, there was nothing on Mr. Pickering's table or counter. Well, almost nothing.

"Hey, look!" said Rose, pointing at a bowl of lemons. She hadn't noticed them when she'd called 911.

"A sign of spring!" said Thomas. Mr. Pickering made hand-squeezed lemonade in spring and summer. It was the only thing he made, but it was really good.

They went to the top of the basement stairs. At the bottom of the long, treacherous stairway and off to the right was a faint, strangely colored light.

"Come on," said Thomas.

Rose really didn't want to go down the horrible stairs again, but she turned on the light over their heads, took a deep breath to steady her wobbling legs, and followed her brother. Thomas was much quicker on his feet and less afraid of falling, so he made it to the bottom before she'd managed three steps.

Thomas jumped to pull the string on the lightbulb on the ceiling of the main room. The light was pitiful. A yellow, tired-looking light in a gloomy tired-looking basement. He led the way into the room with the strange light, off to the right. Rose wasn't sure she'd ever been in the room or what it was exactly. Maybe it was the laundry room before Mr. Pickering had a stacked washer/dryer moved in upstairs. Skeletal-looking pipes ran across the ceiling and up the walls. In the back corner was the water heater, which was small and hung high on the wall. It was one of the eco-varieties that heated smaller amounts of water on demand.

The new appliance shimmered in the otherwise dim room. Above it, attached to the rafters in the ceiling, hung the source of the strange white light. It made the corner glow like something from outer space.

"There it is," said Thomas, pointing to a dirty paper cup on top of the shiny water heater. "What's with the weird light?"

"It must be some kind of grow light."

"What's a grow light?" said Thomas.

"It fakes sunlight, I think."

"Maybe I should go stand under it," said Thomas with a goofy smile.

"Maybe I should move away from it," said Rose, smiling back. She stood on her tiptoes and reached for the paper cup. The side of the water heater was pleasantly warm. She took the cup down and looked inside. She was surprised to see it was filled with dirt. It looked like a piece of forgotten trash sitting up there.

"Let me see," said Thomas.

They peered into the cup together, Thomas's head blocking Rose's view. She shook the cup gently. A pale-green loop flickered in the dry black dirt.

Thomas looked up, bumping Rose in the nose. "Anything else up there?"

Rose rubbed her nose as her eyes watered. She stood on her tiptoes again and ran her hand over the top of the water heater. A folded piece of paper floated down to the floor. Thomas picked it up and unfolded it. He glanced at it and handed it to Rose.

C. *maxima* Seed

Plant seed in a cup of soil, water generously,

and place under grow light.

Direct sun not necessary until after germination.

Consistent warmth is a must for germination.

Once plant emerges, place in a sunny window.

Give one swallow of water three times a day.

Rotate ¼ turn each time plant is watered.

PREPARE TO BE AMAZED!

"What's that?" said Thomas, pointing to the words C. *maxima*.

"The name of the seed, I guess," said Rose with shrug. "Better bring it to our house and give it some water. It looks pretty dry."

Chapter 5
Prepare to Be Amazed

That's exactly what Mr. Pickering said last night," said Mama the next morning when Thomas showed her the care instructions. "'Prepare to be amazed! Prepare to be amazed!' He was quite worked up. Not our usual calm Mr. Pickering." She laughed. "Sometimes older people are a little loopy when they come out of anesthesia. But there's no doubt he's excited about this seed. It's good of you two to take care of it while he's in the hospital."

It wasn't really the *two* of them caring for the seed, just Thomas. But then, a seed really didn't need two people to look after it.

Thomas's stopwatch beeped. He jumped up. "Time to water it again! One swallow coming up!" Thomas took the watering-and-rotating-one-quarter-turn job very seriously.

"How much *is* a swallow, do you think?" Rose asked as she stretched her arms up and over the back of her head to check the security of her bun, a pre-practice warm-up to help her shoulders stay loose and her bun tight. A swallow seemed like such a specific measurement . . . yet hard to measure.

Thomas grabbed a glass from the counter, filled it halfway with water, took a mouthful, and leaned his head back.

"Aghbout thiggsth muach," he gargled.

He dumped the rest in the sink and spit the swallow back in the glass. He looked in, smiled, and held it up to Rose.

"About this much!" he said again, pouring the swallow onto the green loop in the seed cup.

"Gross!" said Rose, but she laughed.

"It's definitely growing!" Thomas announced. He tilted the cup so Rose could see from her cello chair. The green loop had risen out of the dirt overnight with its first swallow of water. It was still unfolding itself, but you could almost see it stretching upward. Did all seeds grow that fast?

Thomas stretched over the sink, his feet coming off

the floor as he put the seed cup back in the window—
adding a quarter-turn spin as he set it down.

"What kind of plant do you think it is?" he asked,
going to stand in front of Rose, his big toe up against
the cello's endpin. "Is *C. maxima* the name of the seed
or the plant, do you think?"

"I don't know anything about plants, Thomas."
She placed her bow on the cello's strings, hoping her
brother would take the hint. "I'm a musician, not a
gardener."

"You studied them in biology, didn't you?"

"Yes, but we didn't identify plants." She sighed and
lowered her bow. "*C. maxima* is probably the Latin
name of the plant. You could try researching that." She
should really learn Latin—learned people knew Latin.
Maybe during the summer if—no, *when*—she started
working with Harris Waldenstein. She picked up the
pack of blue sticky notes on her music stand and wrote
LEARN LATIN on a square, peeled it off, and shoved it
in her pocket.

"Will you help me research it?"

"I just told you everything I know," said Rose, trying keep the exasperation out of her voice. She lifted
the bow again.

Thomas grabbed her sky-blue sticky notes and a

pencil from her stand. "Hurry up and practice so we can do more research."

"I've got a lot to get through today." There were only forty-three more days until she would meet Harris Waldenstein. And if you added the digits of forty-three together—4 + 3—you got seven, and if you multiplied seven by two (Harris Waldenstein and herself!) . . . well, obviously, today was a significant day to practice.

"We need this plant," said Thomas, almost to himself.

"*I* don't need this plant," said Rose. "I need to practice."

"YOU, *especially,* need this plant," said Thomas.

Rose frowned, then closed her eyes to better concentrate on Suite no. 3's allemande movement. When she finished the movement and opened her eyes, Thomas was gone, but there was a sky-blue sticky note over the first line of the allemande.

PREPARE TO BE AMAZED! was written in Thomas's messy handwriting.

Chapter 6
Clues

Gram struggled with the lock on Mr. Pickering's door while balancing the casserole of chicken-peas-carrots-'n'-wild-rice and her purse on her other arm. Thomas carried salad, and Rose stood patiently behind him with a fruit crisp. It smelled unbelievably good and her stomach rumbled. She'd forgotten to have a snack after school—she'd just gone right to her cello chair.

Gram set the casserole down on the steps and used both hands to get the door open. She often cooked for people at church who were in crisis, and cooking for Mr. Pickering seemed like a natural extension of this. "I'll just bet that Otis Pickering has next to nothing in his refrigerator," Gram had said yesterday afternoon as she opened up their own well-stocked refrigerator. "And that is no way to begin recovering."

Gram was a great believer in the healing properties of a healthy diet. Her goal was to feed their family ten different fruits and vegetables each day. She managed this feat most days. Everyone felt her disappointment on the days the quota wasn't quite met. Mr. Pickering would be a challenge. The only fruit Rose had ever seen him eat came in the form of the fresh-squeezed lemon juice in his lemonade, and he only ate vegetables when he ate at their house and Gram passed them around the table and watched to make sure everyone took some.

"Good thing we have a key," said Thomas as Gram picked up the casserole again, "because I doubt Mr. P. does."

Once they were inside, they set everything on the clean countertops, and Gram opened Mr. Pickering's refrigerator door.

"See!" She pointed into the almost-empty refrigerator. "What does the man eat?"

Thomas shrugged. "Ketchup?" He scanned the kitchen. He was obviously looking for something— probably hoping to find a clue about the mystery seed. He was obsessed.

Gram busied herself making a list in the notebook she carried in her purse. She never went anywhere without her purse, including next door. By the time Mr. Pickering came home, his refrigerator and freezer would be filled with more than he could eat.

When Thomas wandered into the living room, Rose took the opportunity to slip out the back door. She needed to cement the runs at the beginning of Suite no. 3's prelude and make them sound as effortless as Yo-Yo Ma did. She was close, but she didn't want to leave any room for nervousness around Harris.

"Hey, Rose!" Thomas called from the living room. "Look at this!"

Rose paused on the threshold of the back door. Gram didn't seem to have heard Thomas, so Rose decided to pretend she hadn't, either. She closed the screen door softly behind her and walked quickly back across the yards to their house.

After the supper dishes were done, Rose and Thomas sat down at the kitchen table to do their homework. Mama turned on Minnesota Public Radio's classical music station on her way out of the kitchen. Music filled the room. It sounded like Beethoven—a symphony, probably, with lots of instruments, lots of drama. Rose enjoyed Bach more than Beethoven. Beethoven was so . . . extreme.

Thomas set the kitchen timer to police his thirty minutes of required reading. He sat down and picked up his book with a smile—which was a first.

"Good book?" Rose asked.

"Not really," said Thomas, still smiling. He slumped over his book in the usual way, chewing on the gum Gram gave him as a "concentration aid" during reading time. Then he looked up and winked at Rose— winked! Good grief, her brother could be so weird.

Rose opened *Charlotte's Web*. She read for Thomas's thirty minutes, too—not because she was required to, but because she wanted to. She let the book fall open wherever it would; she'd read *Charlotte's Web* so many times that it didn't matter where she started. It opened to the chapter in which Avery falls on the rotten goose egg that the rat, Templeton, has added to his collection. The stinky chaos was one of the funniest scenes in the book, but not even this comic scene could hold her attention tonight.

Her practice session had not gone well. The runs in Suite no. 3's prelude were still not foolproof. This made her nervous. What if she didn't win the chance to study with Harris Waldenstein? She believed so completely in positive thinking (and hard work, of course) that she seldom let herself slip into this thought pattern. *But what if she didn't win?*

Thomas slid an odd envelope across the table, a grin spreading across his face as he did so. Rose picked it up, happy for the distraction.

The smallish envelope was square and made of stiff brown paper that was coated in a waxy substance. It was addressed in small precise block letters to OTIS B. PICKERING and was covered in blue and orange stamps.

Usually, Rose thought of Mr. Pickering as a ninety-two—the sum of the letters of Pickering. It was a good number—it meaningfully produced a seven if you subtracted the two from the nine, and seven was a factor of fourteen, of course. When you added in his first name, Otis, he was a 155, which had no special significance, really, other than the digits adding up to a prime number. (1 + 5 + 5 = 11.) But the *B* made him a 157! A large and satisfying prime number in and of itself. Mr. Pickering was "a good egg," as Gram would say—even the letters in his name proved it.

She peeked inside the envelope. There was a folded piece of paper inside. She pulled it out and unfolded a magazine picture. A man stood beside an immense . . .

something . . . in what looked like a field. Enormous leaves stretched out into the distance. Scrawled across the giant . . . whatever it was . . . in red pen were the words *Good luck, Otis!* The caption below the photo read, *Jonathan Gunderson in his garden.* Who was Jonathan Gunderson? And what the heck was that crazy plant? It looked like a gigantic beanbag chair!

Rose squinted at the postmark over the stamps. New Zealand? She flipped the odd little brown envelope over. Across the top, written in that same red pen, was *Prepare to be AMAZED!* Across the bottom: *Contents: 1 AMAZING C. maxima seed! Good luck!*

She looked up at Thomas. His eyebrows were zigzagging. They'd perfected silent methods of communication over many nights sitting at the kitchen table doing homework.

Noiselessly, Thomas stood on his chair and made a giant letter C with his skinny arms. It was backward as Rose looked at it, but then he fixed it.

Next he held his arms out as if he were measuring. He moved them wider, then wider still. The Beethoven on the radio crescendoed with his arm movement, as if he were conducting the piece, and Rose struggled not to laugh.

Mama appeared in the kitchen doorway, her

knitting under her arm and a warning look on her face. Thomas jumped down off his chair. The phone's ring saved them. Mama turned to answer it.

Rose suspected Thomas was right. Undoubtedly, *Maxima* meant *maximum*. . . . Huge, large, as big as it can get. Thomas was both a good guesser and good at figuring things out. She only knew what she *learned*.

"But what's the C stand for?" Thomas whispered, pretending to read his book.

"How should I know?" She tried to think back to her botany unit. What was the maximum C? *C. largest?*

Thomas brought out a small stack of books from his backpack and slid it across the table. He gestured in the direction of Mr. Pickering's house.

Rose picked up the first book. *Growing Things in Minnesota*. The words sprawled across a faded picture of a vegetable garden that was so big it spilled off the cover of the book. She thumbed through pages of flowers and vegetables, pages that were rippled and smudged with dirt. Someone had used the book hard. She looked inside the front cover. In small block letters it said JONATHAN GUNDERSON.

The mystery continued. Why did Mr. Pickering have Jonathan Gunderson's gardening books?

She flipped through the vibrant pictures in another book: *Growing All Your Food in a Minnesota Summer.* Really? Minnesota summers were not very long. The days were long—it stayed light until nine thirty or later in June and July because they were so far north—but by September the sun went down earlier. They'd had snow in both September and May before, and their own yard was still grayish brown. It could be another few weeks before green grass was brave enough to show itself. But this book made Minnesota look like a year-round rain forest with so much green and so many bright colors. It seemed a little misleading.

"Who's Jonathan Gunderson?" she whispered.

Thomas shrugged and pointed to the magazine picture. "More important, *what is that plant?*"

"Homework, you two," said Mama, hanging up the phone. "I'm going to pick Mr. Pickering up in thirty minutes. He refuses to stay one more night in the hospital."

"Can we go?" Thomas asked.

"See what you can get done in the next fifteen minutes," said Mama. "Focus."

Thomas waggled his eyebrows at Rose. The mystery would soon be solved.

Chapter 7
C. Maxima

Mama pulled into the drive-through loop at the front of the hospital, parked the van, and turned to look at Thomas in the backseat.

"No questions about the mystery seed. The move won't be easy for Mr. Pickering. You can talk about the seed tomorrow. Understand?"

"Absolutely," said Thomas.

A hospital worker pushed Mr. Pickering out in a wheelchair. Thomas jumped from the car before Mama had unfastened her seat belt.

"Hey, Mr. P.! What does the C in C. *maxima* stand for?"

Mr. Pickering's face lit up.

"Thomas James!" Mama snapped. "What did I *just say?*"

"Sorry—it just slipped out!" said Thomas. "And Mr. Pickering doesn't mind."

Mr. Pickering looked delighted, in fact.

"*Maxima* means *maximum*," continued Thomas. "That was easy. But we can't figure out the C part."

Mama's lips were in a thin line. Rose decided to change the subject. "How are you feeling, Mr. Pickering?"

Mama nudged Thomas and raised her eyebrows, as if to say, *See! Manners!*

"Well, all things considered, not bad," said Mr. Pickering. "Not bad enough to stay another night in the hospital, anyway. You nurses don't know how to let a man *sleep*." Mr. Pickering smiled at Mama. "Telling them you lived next door helped." He took off his cap and gingerly reached up and rubbed his hair. "Thank you, Tess."

Mama smiled. "You're welcome, Otis. Let's get you home, now."

Mr. Pickering's smile faded as Mama and the hospital worker tried to get him into the front passenger seat of the van. He didn't bend well, his right arm was in a sling, and he couldn't put weight on his left foot.

"This is like trying to get Rose's cello in," said Thomas.

Which is how they got the idea to move Mr. Pickering to the backseat, where they put the cello. This was still difficult, but they got him in at last. By the time he was situated, though, Mr. Pickering was sweating and his smile was gone.

Rose climbed in the front seat, and Thomas ran around to the other side of the van and piled in the back with Mr. Pickering.

"How is it?" Mr. Pickering asked while Mama finished talking to the hospital worker. "Is it growing?"

"You can almost *watch* it grow, Mr. P.!"

"Whoo-wee!" Mr. Pickering awkwardly clapped his hands together, wincing. "Dang collarbone . . ." he muttered. "I knew it was a good seed when I put it in the dirt," he said. "I could just *feel* it!"

Mama climbed in the front seat. "Seat belts, everyone. Thomas, help Mr. Pickering, please." Mama and Rose turned to make sure Thomas had things latched properly—just like they did when he buckled in the cello.

"It will be wonderful to have you home again, Otis," said Mama.

Rose nodded. "We missed you."

"And you have no idea how much I've missed you all," said Mr. Pickering. "I've been quite anxious to get home and . . . see how things are." He winked at Rose—and looked very much like Thomas when he did so.

It occurred to Rose that perhaps a desire for a good night's sleep wasn't the *only* reason Mr. Pickering had asked to check out of the hospital early.

When they arrived home, Mama and Rose helped Mr. Pickering out of the van and up the steps to his back door. Thomas held the door open as Mama eased Mr. Pickering through it.

"Go get the plant, Rosie," said Thomas. Rose made a face over Mr. Pickering's shoulder. She was hoping to run through a portion of Suite no. 4's bourrée, which was giving her fits, before bed. And she still had some math to finish. But Mr. Pickering was home. She'd help get him settled in first.

Rose let herself in their back door and went to the kitchen to retrieve the paper cup off the windowsill. The plant looked as if it had grown since supper. Was that even possible? The cup teetered against the window, its larger leaves throwing it off-balance.

She grabbed the strange square brown envelope off the table and slid it into her pocket next to her sticky-note goals. Carefully, she carried the cup with the crazy mystery plant across the yards, hunching over it to protect it from the chilly evening air. The sun was almost down, but she heard birds chirping. They sounded excited.

Mr. Pickering had settled into his reading chair when Rose walked in. Mama turned on all the lights and asked if he wanted some supper. She explained the bountiful options Gram had left in the refrigerator and offered to make him a plate.

"That would be wonderful, Tess," said Mr. Pickering. "I could use some home cooking."

Thomas was perched on the arm of Mr. Pickering's chair. Rose handed Mr. Pickering the paper cup, and Thomas leaned over his shoulder to peer at the plant.

"It grew while we were gone!" he said.

"Also, Thomas found this envelope," Rose said. She felt like she was confessing something.

"We wanted to know what the plant is because it's growing like crazy and it drinks all the water I give it immediately. Like it's *thirsty*," said Thomas. "So I looked on your bookshelf for some research materials. That's where I found the envelope."

"And Jonathan Gunderson's gardening books," Rose added.

Mr. Pickering didn't look like he was listening. He stared at the plant, a ridiculous grin on his face. Mr. Pickering was not usually a grinner. He turned the cup all the way around and held it up to the light and examined the underside of the plant's leaves.

"I do thank you two for taking such good care of it. It's growing just as Jonathan said it would. Looks like we'll have to get it into a bigger pot right away. I believe we are in for a treat, dear neighbors!"

"Who's Jonathan, anyway?" Thomas asked.

"My brother-in-law," said Mr. Pickering. "He grew up here in Minnesota but retired to New Zealand. He died last fall, but he left me this seed in his will."

"He left you . . . a seed?" said Rose.

"Not just any seed," said Mr. Pickering. "A C. maxima seed! Cucurbita maxima. Cucurbita is the genus of the plant," Mr. Pickering explained. "Plants in this genus are typically characterized by their vining nature. They grow edible and sometimes ornamental fruit. But we won't want to eat this one! We couldn't eat this one!"

He chuckled as if he'd made a wonderful joke. His glasses slid to the end of his nose.

"They are very tender plants that can't grow on their own," he continued, rotating the small paper cup dwarfed by the plant it held. "They *require* human care. *Maxima* is the species within the genus," he added. He sounded like a botany book.

"But what *is* it?" Mama asked as she brought in Mr. Pickering's supper plate.

Smiling, Mr. Pickering looked at Mama, then Rose, then Thomas. "What we have here, friends, is a giant pumpkin plant."

Chapter 8

Fooling Around

Rose and Thomas went straight to Mr. Pickering's after school the next day. Thomas always ran outside after school—sometimes he didn't even go *inside*—but this was a change for Rose.

"Some kids just need to fool around," Mama said once when Rose asked her why Thomas ran outside every day after school no matter what the weather was.

She didn't have time to fool around. She went from school to cello practice to supper to homework to bed (sometimes with just a little more cello practice thrown in before she brushed her teeth), and then she got up the next morning and did it all over again. Besides, she only liked being outside when the weather was nice. Only when it was perfect, actually.

But today was pretty perfect. Sunny and warm again. The grass was starting to green up, and she wanted to check on Mr. Pickering before she started practicing. So she grabbed one of Gram's oatmeal-chocolate-chip cookies and followed her brother out the door.

That she didn't come back until Gram called them in for supper surprised her. They didn't actually fool around—at least she didn't think they had. Mr. Pickering gave them money to go to Ocampo's Hardware and get potting soil and a bigger pot for the pumpkin plant. They repotted it under Mr. Pickering's direction. The plant seemed to stretch up in thanks. It was kind of crazy how fast it grew. Rose was starting to suspect that if you stared at it long enough, you might be able to *see* it grow.

They moved all of the stuff in Mr. Pickering's yard—old pails and junk, a small rickety picnic table, lawn chairs that sat out all winter—to his garage. There was plenty of room, since his garage was more of a workshop than a garage; he parked his car in the alley. After that, Mr. Pickering instructed them in the art of squeezing lemons—his collarbone injury prevented him from squeezing—and they made the first lemonade of the season.

Rose tried to make her exit at that point; she could practically hear her cello calling for her. But then Thomas retrieved one of the sturdier lawn chairs from Mr. Pickering's garage, and it took both of them to help their neighbor move to the back stoop. And then Thomas carried out three glasses of lemonade, so she agreed to sit for a few minutes in the late-afternoon sunshine and drink a toast to spring. As they drank, Mr. Pickering told them what they might expect from the giant pumpkin plant in the next few weeks. It sounded amazing, all right. Also like a lot of work.

When Gram called them in for supper, Rose was horrified. She had missed her entire after-school practice time! She hurried across the yards and up the steps to the back door. She stopped, catching her reflection in the window next to the door. Curls had slipped out of her bun and sprang out like unruly vines from her head. She was a mess!

"Would you chop those carrots, please?" Gram said when she came through the back door. "Oh, it's you, Rose. Best let Thomas chop them when he comes in. You tear the lettuce—can't have you accidentally cutting a finger."

Rose went to the bathroom to wash her hands. It took some doing to get the dirt out from under her fingernails. She smoothed back the wispy curls with her wet hands and stared at herself in the mirror. She had wasted all afternoon in the dirt and the wind.

When she came back into the kitchen, Gram looked at her over the top of her glasses. "I've missed the Bach while cooking, honey. I hope dinner turns out okay."

Rose sat down at the kitchen table and tore the lettuce into the salad bowl. It smelled like dinner was turning out fine. Spaghetti pie, one of their favorite suppers. Gram insisted on putting both spinach and squash in the pie, but it was still good. Most important, spaghetti pie meant Gram's garlic bread, which was the best thing this side—and probably the other side—of the Mississippi. Crispy crust, soft and squishy in the middle, lots of butter, and garlic you could still smell in the house the next day. Rose's stomach growled.

"How long till we eat?" Thomas asked, bouncing in the back door. "I'm starving."

"Wash your hands, finish that salad, and then, I believe, we're ready." Gram pulled the garlic bread and spaghetti pie out of the oven.

Thomas galloped to the bathroom and back into the kitchen in record time. He certainly still had dirt under his fingernails. He plopped down in the chair to the right of Rose.

"Gram, me and Rose helped—"

"Rose and *I*."

"Yup, *Rose and I* helped Mr. Pickering this afternoon, and he wants us to help him every day after school. So can we?"

When had that come up? "I can't do this every afternoon, Thomas," said Rose.

"Sure you can," said Thomas without even looking at her.

"What will you help him with?" Gram asked.

"Growing giant pumpkins. He needs help clearing his yard of rocks and stuff," explained Thomas. "He can hardly do anything right now because he's so banged up. And we need to get the pumpkin plant in the ground by Mother's Day."

"Mother's Day is this Sunday," Rose said. Her lesson was on Monday. She had a lot of work to do between now and then, starting with making up for this afternoon.

"Yup," said Thomas. He dumped chopped carrots on top of Rose's lettuce. Rose put the cutting board and knife into the sink. Gram placed a dish of steaming broccoli on the table, then sat down, unfolded her napkin, and put it on her lap.

"Thomas, would you please say grace this evening?"

Almost before they had a chance to bow their heads, Thomas had finished saying grace: "Thanks, God, for spaghetti pie and Gram's garlic bread. Thanks for spring and Mr. P. being back home again. Help our giant pumpkins to grow. Amen."

Gram pursed her lips. "Have some broccoli," she said, spooning the bright-green stalks onto Thomas's plate.

"There's lots to do after the plant is in the ground, too," Thomas continued breathlessly. "When the university tells us what his dirt needs, we can help give it . . . whatever it needs."

It was a little vague, Rose thought, what the dirt might need—fertilizers, maybe?—but Mr. Pickering was clear that there would be a lot of work to do. He'd already taken something called soil samples and mailed the dirt from his backyard to the university in a plastic envelope. The university's report was due back soon. Then, he said, the real work would begin.

Mr. Pickering's backyard was worse than theirs. They had some grass, at least. Mr. Pickering's looked like the moonscape in Thomas's space book. It was hard to imagine it covered with a jungle of pumpkin vines, but that's what Mr. Pickering said would happen. And fast.

Thomas went on. "Mr. Pickering said he's pretty sure the university will tell him his yard is full of dirt, and we'll have to make it into soil. Soil is dirt that has healthy stuff in it," he added. "Anyway, that's why he needs us—to help make soil for his giant pumpkins!"

"Please do not talk with your mouth full," said Gram. "And don't exaggerate."

"I'm not exaggerating," said Thomas after he swallowed.

"Pumpkins are pumpkins," said Gram. "There are bigger ones; there are smaller ones. There are pie pumpkins and jack-o'-lantern pumpkins. There are even orange pumpkins, yellow pumpkins, and white pumpkins. But I don't believe the good Lord created giant pumpkins. I think, my dears, that Otis Pickering is pulling your legs."

"He's not," said Rose. Gram looked at her in surprise. "We saw a picture of one. It was gray-green and *giant*, Gram." It also had lumps and bumps and warts, though she didn't mention those. She really hoped Mr. Pickering's pumpkin would be prettier.

"Mr. P. got the special seed from New Zealand," Thomas continued. "From his brother-in-law, Jonathan, who grew lots of them before he died. And he sent a seed from his biggest pumpkin to Mr. Pickering. He *willed* it to him."

"New Zealand? That's just silly," Gram said. She scooped more spaghetti pie onto Thomas's plate. "Señor Ocampo sells pumpkin seeds at the hardware store down the street. A seed from New Zealand probably won't even grow in Minnesota."

"The parents and grandparents of Mr. Pickering's seed are the biggest pumpkins New Zealand has ever grown," Rose said. She felt obligated to help Thomas make his case—maybe then he'd let her off the hook from doing the work. "Some of them weigh close to two thousand pounds."

"And the New Zealand seed *will* grow in Minnesota," Thomas added. "It has to do with that thing . . . latitude. It's about the number of hours we have sun in the summer. It's about the same as the number of hours New Zealand has sun in *their* summer. Plus, it's so cold in the winter here that a lot of the pests that would bother giant pumpkins die. Places like Minnesota and New Zealand grow giant pumpkins *best*."

Gram harrumphed. She did not look convinced. Or that interested.

"Mr. Pickering says our pumpkin could grow big enough for me to climb inside!" said Thomas as he reached for another slice of garlic bread.

"Just like Cinderella," said Rose. She meant it to sound like teasing, but it came out sounding annoyed instead. Mr. Pickering had not said the pumpkin would grow big enough to hold *her*. Somewhere between big enough for Thomas and not quite big enough for her was how big the pumpkin would be.

"Time will tell, I guess," said Gram.

"Does that mean we can help after school?" Thomas asked.

"Well, I think it is fine if you want to help, but there's no time in Rose's schedule. The Bach Competition is less than six weeks away."

"What if she practiced a little right before supper?" pressed Thomas. "And then some more after? You know, break it up."

"Thanks, Thomas," said Rose quickly, "but I've really got to stay focused." Gram smiled at her in approval and then turned back to Thomas.

"Maybe Jane Jacobi could help you instead," said Gram.

Rose cringed. Calamity Jane would trample the pumpkin vines with her stupid tap shoes.

"Rosie's pretty smart," said Thomas. He waggled his eyebrows at Rose. "We'll figure something out. Calamity Jane would be a disaster."

Chapter 9
Mrs. Holling

Rose butchered the fourth suite the following Monday at her lesson. Parts were too fast. Parts were too slow. Notes were missed, as well as straightforward rhythms and basic bowing techniques she'd had down for years. Her head, heart, and fingers were out of sync. And she was nervous. She was not well prepared for her lesson, and she was *never* not well prepared.

"Rose, dear," said Mrs. Holling after the last screech faded. "Did you clip your nails yesterday?"

Rose gripped her bow with her right hand and curled her offending fingers on the left. Clip her nails?

She could feel they were too long now that they pressed into her palms. She felt the grime under them, too.

"Um . . . I must've forgotten. There was a lot going on this weekend." She looked down at her scraggly nails.

Mrs. Holling gently took Rose's bow and placed it on the music stand. She held out her hands in invitation. When Rose had started cello, Mrs. Holling greeted her this way each week. Rose would lug in her cello—back when it was almost as big as she was—and sit down sweaty and out of breath, already frazzled and clumsy at six years of age. Mrs. Holling would hold out her hands and clasp Rose's fingers in her own as she asked about her week.

Usually, Rose didn't say much. It was as if Mrs. Holling's gentle hands cast some sort of spell over her. She'd forget all of the things she had wanted to tell her teacher and mumble something about the book she was reading or a fight between two boys on the bus. Mrs. Holling said she could feel what Rose did not say, however. She could feel Rose's worries and joys, her hurts and excitement, her confusion and anxiety. She said the music could feel these things, too.

This weekly exchange had served another purpose, as well. While she held Rose's hands and listened, Mrs.

Holling felt Rose's fingernails to be sure they were trimmed and ready to play. If they were not, Mrs. Holling would cut her fingernails for her with a tiny pair of gold scissors. The handles were etched with a lacy pattern of flowers and hearts. Carefully, and without judgment, Mrs. Holling trimmed Rose's nails with the beautiful scissors while they talked.

When Rose grew so tall and seemed older, Mrs. Holling suggested that this was a personal hygiene task Rose should be responsible for herself. And Rose was always responsible, so every Sunday afternoon before she practiced, she clipped her fingernails with the ugly green-handled fingernail clippers from the bathroom drawer. Sometimes she had to clip midweek as well; cello playing required the shortest of nails, and hers seemed to grow as fast as the rest of her.

Thomas had begged her to help in Mr. Pickering's yard on Saturday. She gave in, promising thirty minutes of working in the yard between one-hour practice sessions. But the first thirty-minute session turned into the whole afternoon—there was so much to be done and she just couldn't leave Thomas to do it all. She'd spent all afternoon in the yard on Sunday, Mother's Day, too, after she and Thomas made breakfast for Mama and Gram. She'd barely practiced all weekend, in fact!

"You seem a bit distracted today," said Mrs. Holling. She reached up and slipped a stray curl behind Rose's ear.

When she was younger, especially, Rose wanted to be like Mrs. Holling—a university professor, a kind teacher, a well-respected performer. She loved everything about her teacher: her soft-pink lipstick, the way she smelled, her strong hands, her beautiful white hair gathered in a bun. Mrs. Holling's bun was the reason Rose had started wearing her hair up. But her bun never looked like Mrs. Holling's. Mrs. Holling's bun was whipped icing on a cupcake. Hers was a mangled, overgrown shrub.

"I'm sorry."

"I'm just a little concerned. We are getting close to the Bach Competition. Now is not the time to be distracted. The suites were better last week." Mrs. Holling was always honest but never unkind. Why couldn't everyone be like that?

"I know. I just had a different kind of week," said Rose. "It won't happen again." She couldn't let it happen again. What had she been thinking? She would explain to Thomas that she just . . . couldn't help with the pumpkin right now. Maybe after the competition.

Probably not, though; she hoped that by then she'd be very busy studying with Harris Waldenstein.

"A different kind of week? Do tell!" Mrs. Holling's smile was genuine. "Something new and different can be good for an artist, Rose! Our lives are filled with discipline and repetition. Different can be *wonderful*."

Rose's eyes grew hot. Mrs. Holling had said *our* lives, as if they were *both* artists. Rose couldn't imagine that real artists dug in the dirt. How could they possibly have the time?

"Tell me about your week, Rose."

Rose took a deep breath, and the prelude of Bach's first suite started up inside her. Mrs. Holling produced the pretty gold nail scissors from the table next to the music stand and began to cut Rose's nails. She cleaned under them, wiping the weekend's dust and grime on a tissue as she went.

"It just included a lot of yard work, I guess." Rose blinked fast. Mrs. Holling looked up at her in surprise. But she smiled and quickly went back to Rose's manicure.

"Yard work?" She smoothed Rose's ragged thumbnail with a dainty silver nail file. "Tell me more."

It had been more than yard work, actually. The

results of Mr. Pickering's soil test had come on Friday. The dirt in his backyard was worse than he had feared. It barely qualified as dirt. "As far away from soil as we can get," said Mr. Pickering when he looked at the report from the university.

Over the weekend, Rose and Thomas dug six giant bags of compost from Señor Ocampo's hardware store into Mr. Pickering's dead yard. It had taken all of Saturday just to dig the compost into the hole Thomas made Friday afternoon while Rose practiced. What Thomas lacked in size and strength he made up for in energy; he had dug an impressive two-hour hole. But they'd had to dig more. Two full days more.

"It's not important," said Rose. She pulled her hands back from Mrs. Holling. "The compost is in the ground. Thomas can figure out how to help Mr. Pickering do the rest of the work. He's good at stuff like that. I'm probably in the way." The shovel was awkward, anyway—heavy and unwieldy. She felt ridiculous using it.

"How is Mr. Pickering?" asked Mrs. Holling. She took Rose's hands back into her own. "I haven't heard you talk about him in ages."

"He fell down his basement stairs and broke his ankle and collarbone. And a few ribs."

"Oh, my!" Mrs. Holling squeezed Rose's fingers.

"He has a"—Rose paused —"project he needs help with. He's moving slowly because of his injuries."

"You mentioned compost," Mrs. Holling said. "Is it a gardening project he needs help with?"

Rose's cheeks warmed. She nodded.

"I love gardening," said Mrs. Holling. "I can't wait for this spring to really get going so I can get back out to my garden."

"You have a garden?"

"Oh, yes," said Mrs. Holling. "I love to dig in the dirt. Tell me more about what you and Thomas did this weekend."

She rubbed something on Rose's fingernails that smelled like lemon and mint, patterned and peaceful somehow—like Bach. Rose took a deep breath, closed her eyes, and listened for the Bach inside.

"I dug two hundred and forty pounds of compost into hard, caked ground." She kept her eyes closed. Six forty-pound bags—a lot of compost. "Thomas broke up the dirt and I shoveled and mixed the compost in."

She waited for Mrs. Holling to gasp or drop the nail file in shock.

"The source of these almost-blisters, I imagine," said Mrs. Holling. She turned Rose's palms up. Rose looked down. The palms of her hands looked like they'd been burned.

"We *had* to get the pumpkin in the ground this weekend. It was outgrowing its pot." The Bach inside her played faster, providing less comfort. "It grows so fast it's almost scary. Mr. Pickering says it'll grow even faster once it's at home in the yard and the sun gets warmer. We had to build a plastic tent over it to protect it from the wind and keep it warm at night. We ran an extension cord out to the tent and plugged in a little space heater, too."

It sounded so weird as she heard herself say it. A *plant* took her off task in her competition preparation? Rose was suddenly ashamed. She stole a look at her teacher.

Mrs. Holling was smiling. She rubbed some of the lemon-mint salve onto Rose's tender palms. They felt better immediately.

"This sounds exciting, Rose! Did you say a pumpkin? I hadn't realized pumpkins required so much work."

"It's not a regular pumpkin. It's a *giant* pumpkin."

"A giant pumpkin! I've never heard of such a thing. What exactly does *giant* mean when one is speaking of pumpkins?"

"Big enough for Thomas to climb into."

"Really? Big enough for you to climb into. Imagine!"

The Bach inside her stopped abruptly. Rose pulled her hands away from Mrs. Holling's.

"Not big enough for *me*. Big enough for Thomas."

Mrs. Holling's gentle gaze held hers. Rose could feel her heartbeat throbbing in her head. The scent of lemon and mint pressed in on her. She looked away and focused on Mrs. Holling's cello—not the one she was lending Rose, but the one she played now. She kept it on a cello stand in the corner of her studio. It was lighter in color than the one she'd given Rose to use. Rose loved the darker sheen of hers.

"It sounds to me like Mr. Pickering and Thomas could use your help," said Mrs. Holling after a minute. "And I think digging in the dirt might be just the thing for you, Rose."

Mrs. Holling moved to her desk for a pen. "Tell me, how long does your homework take each night? On average. Just give me a guesstimate."

A *guesstimate*? Rose stared. Mrs. Holling waited.

"A couple hours."

"Sometimes more, I'm guessing, given your math load?" asked Mrs. Holling.

"Sometimes." Rose shrugged. It probably could be less if she did not feel obligated to do it all perfectly. She shrugged again.

"And you've been practicing at least two hours a day . . . ?"

"Yes. Like you told me to," said Rose. "But not this past weekend." Her face burned with the confession.

Mrs. Holling nodded.

"And for fun you . . . ?"

They stared at each other. Mrs. Holling seemed to want her to fill in the blank.

"Right," said Mrs. Holling. "Yes, something must be done. Let's see . . . finals at the university are in two weeks. Does your math final require a bit of extra study?"

"Not really." Math was inside her—kind of like Bach's music. She would study because that was the right thing to do, but she probably wouldn't study *extra*. She should be using any spare time for practicing.

Mrs. Holling nodded, as if all her suspicions were confirmed. She wrote a small list in the notebook in her lap. Rose couldn't see what it said.

"I believe a shift is warranted," Mrs. Holling announced. "You are old enough now, Rose, to learn more advanced methods of preparation for performance and competition. You would not be playing in the Bach Competition next month if I did not feel you were ready quite a while ago. Therefore, all that is necessary at this point is the maintenance of your readiness. There is a danger in going too far with practice, in fact," she added.

Rose knew she was staring again. But she was pretty sure Mrs. Holling was about to tell her she needed to practice *less*.

Chapter 10
For the Pumpkins

"I would like you to play through the Bach Cello Suites cycle for one hour each day," said Mrs. Holling. "Not a minute over."

One hour! "But—"

"Yes, I know you can't play the whole cycle in sixty minutes. You don't need to. Begin with the first suite tomorrow; you've played enough for today here at your lesson."

Rose gaped. She *always* practiced when she arrived home from her lesson.

"Tomorrow you will play through numbers one, two, and three," continued Mrs. Holling, scribbling in the notebook. "Probably into number four. . . . But then you'll be hitting the one-hour mark. Stop when you hit that sixty-minute mark. Midway through a suite—even midway through a phrase is fine. Use Thomas's stopwatch."

Midway through!

"The next day, begin with the second suite and play through whatever you can for one hour exactly. Don't rush. You should get through some of number five. On Thursday, begin with the third suite—one hour again. No need to play the sixth suite; I know you like the challenge, but it's not part of the competition."

Suite no. 6 had originally been written for a mysterious five-string cello-like instrument. Playing it on a four-string cello was very difficult. But she did like to *try*.

"Rose, dear, are you ill?"

"No. I just . . ." Maybe she *was* ill. She felt a little sweaty. "What about scales and arpeggios?" Mrs. Holling insisted she always begin her practice time with scales and arpeggios.

"A few minutes of scales and arpeggios is fine," said Mrs. Holling, as if it didn't matter at all. "You understand the instructions? I'm writing it down in your notebook."

Mrs. Holling waited for her reply. Rose realized she was staring, mouth open, at her teacher.

"I understand." She didn't really, though. She understood the instructions. What she didn't understand was *why*.

"Your task these next few weeks is to remember how to *enjoy* the suites," said Mrs. Holling. "Love them — and let them love you! You will be competing against musicians who are much older than you. The unique gift you bring to these pieces is that you are still a child, so you have the *heart* of a child. I have erred in not recognizing the importance of this distinction. Therefore, we will make some bold corrections, effective immediately."

Rose hugged her cello to steady herself.

"What am I supposed to do when I'm not practicing?" Maybe there was some other preparation she could make.

"Well, I think you might help Thomas and Mr. Pickering," said Mrs. Holling. "This pumpkin growing sounds like quite a project."

Quite a project, yes — but not one she wanted to be involved in, necessarily.

"One more thing, Rose." Mrs. Holling peered over her glasses at Rose, which she only did when she was very serious. "I want you to play the suites outside."

"Outside?"

"Specifically in Mr. Pickering's backyard—weather permitting, of course. Not only will the fresh air and sunshine be good for you, but Bach will be just the thing for that pumpkin plant. Did you know there are studies indicating that music helps plants to grow?"

She had to be kidding.

But Mrs. Holling sounded quite serious. "Play for one hour outside as I've outlined for you, then put your cello away and go help in the dirt. There's a lot of work to be done."

She handed Rose her cello notebook with the bizarre practice instructions.

"Your fingernails should show evidence of this activity when you come next week. If they do not, I fear you will not be ready for the competition."

Mrs. Holling stood up, her indication that the lesson was over.

"But wear gloves when using a shovel," she added. "Blisters are no fun. And if they get infected, they can be dangerous."

Rose stood up. Her legs shook.

"One hour of gorgeous Bach each day," said Mrs. Holling with a smile. "For the pumpkins!"

* * *

Mama opened the back door of the van and helped Rose settle the cello into the backseat. Rose buckled it in. When she and Mama were situated in the front seat, they started down the long spiral of the parking garage. Mama hummed as she went—she was smiling. She'd been smiling when she came out of Mrs. Holling's studio after their post-lesson meeting.

"What did Mrs. Holling say?" Rose asked.

Mama's smile grew. "Well, she told me about your very particular instructions regarding cello practice from now until the competition. Playing for the pumpkin plant! I think that sounds wonderful."

Rose cringed. "Only when the weather is nice," she said, thankful for once that Minnesota springs were so unreliable.

"And we discussed how we might lighten your homework load, to give you more free time."

"Lighten it how?" Rose asked.

Mama inched the car up to the parking garage attendee. She made polite conversation about the coming of spring with the woman in the booth. Rose thought she might explode before they pulled out of the garage.

"Actually, stopping the homework might be a better descriptor," Mama said as she turned out into the university traffic. "Mrs. Holling suggests we notify your teachers that you won't be doing any homework for the remainder of the school year."

"You can just tell them I'm not going to do it?"

"Yes, I can. I doubt they will argue with me, Rose. You do homework night after night that you really don't need to do; you've clearly mastered the work, and they don't have any more higher-level classes you can move to. Mrs. Holling thinks you should be outside more, playing with Thomas and helping Mr. Pickering with the pumpkin project. I'm inclined to think she's onto something."

They rode in silence for a while. When they turned onto Library Lane, Rose worked up the courage to ask the two questions she was afraid to ask.

"What if I *want* to do homework? What if I *want* to play cello for more than an hour a day?"

Mama pulled up in front of their house and shut off the van. She turned in her seat to face Rose.

"I think you should try Mrs. Holling's ideas, Rosebud. You are so tall and beautiful and accomplished . . . everyone forgets you are just twelve—even me, sometimes. Twelve-year-olds need a chance to be bored and wonder and explore. Twelve-year-olds should have sleepovers and go to parties and play with friends. . . ."

Rose wasn't interested in sleepovers and parties or any of the other things kids her age were into. She liked cello and math and Bach and books. . . .

"You are twelve and you're living the life of an intensely focused middle-aged woman," Mama said gently.

"I'm almost thirteen!"

Mama smiled. "Really just barely twelve, sweetheart. Let's not rush into the teen years. The point is, you're still a little girl."

"Not *little*."

"You are a *tall* little girl. Let's give Mrs. Holling's ideas a fair shot. She says you're ready, so let's loosen things up a little bit for the end of the school year. There's only a few more weeks, anyway. And you might like some margins to your days once you grow accustomed to them. Maybe you and Jane Jacobi can play sometimes."

"Jane's in Thomas's grade!"

"Yes," said Mama. "But she's less than a year younger than you. You played together when you were little."

Rose sulked. There was too much Calamity Jane in her life already, always poking her nose in where it didn't belong, asking Rose to come to her tap class.

Besides, Calamity Jane didn't do anything besides tap-dance.

"We don't have anything in common," she muttered.

"You both love *Charlotte's Web* so much—maybe that could reignite your friendship."

Rose changed the subject. "And what about Thomas? He'll hate it if I don't have to do homework but he does."

Mama sighed. She stared up at their house. Rose followed her gaze. The top of Thomas's head whizzed by the window.

"I don't know, Rose. Maybe we haven't done the right thing for Thomas, either." Mama sounded tired. They sat for a minute, both of them watching through the window of their house.

"Mama, why are Thomas and I so different? How come we're not more alike? Like Jesse and James— they're exactly the same."

"They're not exactly the same," said Mama. "I'm sure Jane and Mrs. Jacobi can tell them apart. You and Thomas are very different, it's true. But it's good you are so different. You complement each other and challenge each other. Gram and I wouldn't change a thing about either one of you."

She turned and opened the car door. "Before you come in, why don't you run down to the library? Mrs. Lukashenko called earlier and said she found a book for you. Is it your week with *Charlotte's Web*?"

"No." Though that would be nice. "I turned it in on Friday. It's Jane's week this week."

Maybe she could pick up some other books, though. She was going to have a lot of free time on her hands in the coming weeks.

Chapter 11
Serendipity

*H*ello, Rosa! Well, hello, Rosa!" Mrs. Lukashenko pranced out of the library's back room and up to the checkout desk.

"Hi, Mrs. Lukashenko. Mama said you found a book for me?"

"I did, indeed," said Mrs. Lukashenko. "The wonders of *serendipity*! I was looking for a cookbook . . . and I found *compost books*!" Mrs. Lukashenko was very into serendipity, which she called "the art of stumbling upon something you did not know you needed or wanted." Serendipity was probably something in a musical. Mrs. Lukashenko pushed a book across to Rose, a big smile on her face. *Composting for Dum-Dums* was splashed across a garish orange and black cover.

"Um . . . why did you think of *me* when you found this book?"

"I heard from Señor Ocampo that you have been buying lots of compost for a *secret project*," said Mrs. Lukashenko with a know-it-all kind of smile. "You should really make the compost if you'll be using so much. Even Señor Ocampo thinks so! These books tell you how. Not hard. My husband—*alav ha-shalom,* may he rest in peace—made a compost bin for us when we were newly married. You throw in your scraps and bits and nothings . . . and out comes black gold!"

She rested her bazooms on the desk and leaned closer. "What are you growing in Mr. Pickering's yard, Rose?" she asked in a stage whisper. "You can tell me—I won't tell a soul."

"It's not a secret," said Rose. Good grief—a secret giant pumpkin? "And *I'm* not growing it. Thomas and Mr. Pickering are growing it. I just helped a little this weekend. . . ."

She flipped through the book. It had lots of information, but the title was awful. Why couldn't it be *Composting for Smart People*?

"Are there any . . . other books on composting?" she asked. She could pick something up for Thomas; maybe he'd count it as helping and give her a break on the other stuff, like digging.

"Yes!" said Mrs. Lukashenko. "You can take a look yourself. Straight back to the bathrooms—turn right at the *Charlotte's Web* shelf. Top shelf on the right."

Rose made her way through the familiar shelves of books. She found two other composting books quickly. *Composting 101* had fewer pictures but a much better title. It also had detailed plans for building your own compost bin, which Thomas would probably want to do. *Compost Happens* looked pretty good, too. She decided to take both of them. She put *Composting for Dum-Dums* back on the shelf, and out of habit she made her way through the kids' chapter books on her way to the front to check out. She planned to walk right past the shelf that held *Charlotte's Web;* no sense in looking since it was Jane's week.

The rule was this: *Charlotte's Web* had to be turned in on Friday, and Mrs. Lukashenko had to put it back on the shelf before the next person could check it out. Rose was allowed to have it for one week, Calamity Jane the next, and then it had to sit on the shelf for a week "in case someone else wants to read it," a rule

Mrs. Lukashenko was firm about—which was silly, since there was a perfectly fine paperback edition of the book on the shelf, too. The odds that *two* someones would want to check out *Charlotte's Web* at the exact same time seemed small.

Early on, however, Rose and Jane forged an alliance around the third week. They agreed to poke it back on the shelf so it wasn't visible if someone was simply scanning the shelves for a good book (a serendipitous behavior Mrs. Lukashenko encouraged all the time). If someone besides Calamity Jane or Rose checked it out, that person could borrow it for the usual three weeks, and that would throw off the agreed-upon schedule. Neither of them wanted to risk that. In two years, nobody had found their hidden copy.

Rose had her own copy of *Charlotte's Web*—Gram had seen to that—but it sat unread on her bookshelf at home. It was the library copy she loved. Its corners were worn to a comfortable gray. There was a small hot chocolate stain on page thirty-six by the picture of Wilbur meeting Charlotte for the first time. She could almost taste the chocolate whenever she saw that faded brown drop. She loved the picture on the cover—the tired red ribbon in Fern's ponytail, the old sheep's kind eyes, the daintiness of Charlotte dropping down from the C in the title.

She didn't know what Jane's fascination with *Charlotte's Web* was. Probably she just didn't want Rose to have it. Although, to be fair, Rose didn't know what *her* fascination with the book was either. She simply loved everything about it. The story, of course—the friendship between Wilbur and Charlotte, the details of life on the Arable farm, the personalities of the animals. She'd read it so many times, she really didn't have to read it anymore. It was as much a part of her as Bach's Cello Suites. She read it again and again anyway—every three weeks for the last couple of years—because of the *words*. Individually and all together, she loved the words and how the author, E. B. White, strung them together.

Rose scanned the titles of the chapter books as she wandered down the row. She'd read most of them and already had a stack at home, but maybe there'd be something new. Eventually, she wound up in front of the *Charlotte's Web* shelf, slowly running her fingers over the familiar spines of the books that led to the space designated for *her* book. . . .

There it was—right under her fingers! Rose's heart

fluttered in her chest. *Charlotte's Web* was on the shelf! Not the paperback—it was gone, in fact—but *her* copy was just sitting there in the open, where anyone could take it. Rose stared in disbelief. Could Jane have forgotten it was her week?

She pulled the book off the shelf and brought it to her nose and inhaled. It had the most fantastic smell. It lacked the plasticky smell of most of the books at the library, which were covered in a clear protective cover. *Charlotte's Web* smelled slightly woody, old but not musty, dry and comfortable—in short, very much like her cello. It was a steadying smell.

She opened to the very first page of the book, the blank page before the title page. There the initials E. B. were scrawled in green crayon. Mrs. Lukashenko said it was not an "authentic" autograph. She said authors only sign on the title page, seldom with a green crayon, and usually include their last name. Calamity Jane insisted it was real, though—as if she knew something Mrs. Lukashenko did not, which was hard to believe. Rose traced the green letters with her finger. E (5) + B (2) = 7. Naturally, the author of *Charlotte's Web* would have a nice prime number (and a factor of fourteen!) associated with his name.

Rose slipped the book back in its space. She leaned

against the shelf, her fingers unwilling to leave the spine of the book. It was Monday, late afternoon. If Jane had forgotten it was her week, she'd *really* forgotten. She'd had the weekend and all of Monday to remember. Rose couldn't check it out, because Mrs. Lukashenko would check the schedule and see that it wasn't her week. *But what if she borrowed it . . . without checking it out?* Was that cheating on their agreement? Probably. Definitely, if she was honest. But . . . if Jane really had forgotten it was her week, then Rose could keep it for three weeks: the remainder of Jane's week, the week it usually hid on the shelf, and then her scheduled week. Three weeks would almost get her through the end of school. It would be so wonderful to have *Charlotte's Web* with her now that she wasn't allowed to do homework and Bach was limited to one hour a day.

It would be safer to come and visit it at the library, though. Taking *Charlotte's Web* was a little too much like stealing. She'd just have to be sure that Jane didn't see her, or she might be reminded it was her week. Rose poked the book back into the shelf and pulled another book over it to hide it.

"Ah! You found more compost books—good!" said Mrs. Lukashenko. She smiled as she checked out the books to Rose. "You don't need any other books?"

"No, I still have the ones I checked out on Friday."

"Is it your week with *Charlotte's Web*?"

"Nope. Jane's."

"And then finally someone else can have a chance," said Mrs. Lukashenko. She smiled again. Rose tried to smile back.

"Are you okay, Rose?" Mrs. Lukashenko asked. "You look a little peaked. . . ."

"I'm fine," said Rose. But her stomach was flip-flopping. She really wanted *Charlotte's Web*. Needed it. She'd be stupid not to borrow it. Mrs. Lukashenko thought it was with Jane, and next week was the week it was supposed to sit on the shelf. Nobody would be looking for it.

"Maybe I'll just get a drink and use the bathroom before I go home. . . ." Rose said, inching toward the shelves.

"Good idea." Mrs. Lukashenko nodded approvingly. "Splash some waters on your face. You will feel better!"

As soon as she was around the corner and out of Mrs. Lukashenko's sight, Rose flew down the long rows of books that led in the direction of the bathrooms, stopping when she got to *Charlotte's Web*. Her hands shook a little as she placed the book between

Composting 101 and *Compost Happens,* but as soon as she pulled the stack of books close to her, she felt better. No face splashing necessary.

She would go home and make three sticky-note goals:

1. SKIP HOMEWORK

2. PRACTICE ONLY ONE HOUR

3. PRACTICE OUTSIDE

Then she would read some *Charlotte's Web* to take her mind off of the craziness of these three goals.

She wasn't stealing, she told herself as she exited the library. She was just borrowing the book without the formalities. Nobody would even know.

Chapter 12
Leaves

Thankfully, the rest of the week went by without any opportunities for outside cello playing. It rained Tuesday and Wednesday, and it was too chilly and damp Thursday and Friday. The pumpkin plant needed the sun and the warmth, but Rose dreaded the day the skies would clear.

"It's a typical Minnesota spring," Gram said. "Otis was a fool to put that pumpkin in the ground so early."

"It had to get out of its pot, Gram," Thomas explained. "It's doing stuff underneath the ground we can't see. It needs space. And sun." Thomas worried about the lack of sun.

They ran the space heater in the pumpkin tent even during the day because it was so cold. The heater warmed the tent well, but they couldn't leave it on too long or it got *too* warm. Of course, they also couldn't leave it *off* too long or it got too cold. The up and down temperature changes themselves were not good for the pumpkin plant, either, but not much could be done about that. They put an old thermometer in the tent and Mr. Pickering checked it every hour, trying to keep the temperature as steady as possible.

Jonathan had written in a letter that came with the seed that the pumpkin plant would begin to vine within a week or so of being planted in the ground. There was a lot of work to be done before then. According to Jonathan, the vine could grow three feet or more a week—which was hard to believe, but Mr. Pickering said Jonathan had not been prone to exaggeration—and it had to be anchored to the ground so it would put down roots and grab nutrients from the soil. Mr. Pickering's yard was still mostly dead dust—dead mud, really—and not at all ready for a hungry vine. More compost was needed, and digging in the mud was a lot harder than digging in dusty dirt.

Thomas, too, had been given a reprieve from homework for the last few weeks of school. He did not ask any questions about how this wonderful fortune came to him. He just cheered, did a little dance in the kitchen, and then went to Mr. Pickering's backyard and built a compost bin from plans in the books Rose had checked out from the library. He was reading more than ever — he had practically devoured the compost books — and this made Gram a much bigger fan of the pumpkin project. She ordered *Growing Giant Pumpkins,* Volumes I–IV — their library system didn't even carry them — to add to the stack of research books at Mr. Pickering's. In addition, Gram took very seriously her role in feeding the newly started compost pile with fruit and vegetable scraps. They had a stir-fry or smoothie — sometimes both — every day to keep up with the quota.

"How much compost do you think you will need?" Gram asked as she chopped bananas, apples, and carrots for their breakfast smoothie. She raked the ends and peelings into a big bowl that had become a permanent fixture on the kitchen counter.

"Lots," said Thomas. "It has to be dug in ahead of the plant. The vine sends down roots as it spreads, and we need those roots to go into good soil."

"Well, how far will it spread?" Gram asked.

"The whole yard," said Thomas. "Might spill into ours, too."

Gram stopped chopping. "Really?"

"Yup," said Thomas.

Gram pulled out more carrots from the refrigerator.

"What are you going to do about brown leaves?" Rose asked Thomas. He'd read in *Composting 101* that compost piles needed good amounts of "brown matter"—fall leaves—to make the compost process work efficiently. It was a problem; the leaves were just coming out on the trees in tight bright-green buds. It would be months before there were any leaves to be raked. He'd been worrying about it for days.

"What about Mrs. Kiyo's backyard?" said Gram. "She hasn't raked her leaves in years. It practically *is* a compost pile."

"Great idea!" said Thomas. "Rose can ask her. I don't think she likes me."

"She doesn't like me, either!" protested Rose. "Besides, I have to practice."

Gram stopped chopping the carrots. "Why in the world would Kiyo not like you?"

"I don't know." Thomas shrugged. "She just . . . looks at us."

"She never smiles," agreed Rose. "Not really, anyway."

"What do you mean she never smiles?" said Gram.

"She hardly comes outside, unless it's to sit on the bench at the end of her yard and stare into space," Thomas said. Rose had seen her do that when it was warm. She'd watched Mrs. Kiyo through the window just the other day, in fact, while she practiced. She just sat there, even when it started to rain.

"If you say hi, she doesn't say anything back," said Thomas.

"Kiyo is not a chatter, that's true," said Gram.

"Does she speak English?" Rose asked.

"Does she speak English!" Gram dumped the carrots into the blender and turned to her grandchildren. "I think it is time you two became acquainted with Mrs. Kiyo. Smoothies first, but then you get over there and get to know our neighbor, please. You can practice when you get home, Rose." Gram shook her head and muttered, "Does she speak English!"

On the way across the street, they agreed that Thomas would knock and Rose would make the request for the decomposing leaves. But Mrs. Kiyo opened the door just as Thomas raised his hand to knock. She said nothing, and her lips stayed in their usual thin straight line. She tilted her head back to look up at Rose.

"Good morning, Mrs. Kiyo," said Rose in her best

polite-to-adults voice. She called up Bach's first suite to steady herself, and after the first two comforting measures, she launched into her explanation about the pumpkin project and the leaves.

Mrs. Kiyo's wrinkled face didn't change at all. Rose tried to speak slower, which for whatever reason made her speak louder, and then she started giving more information than was needed. Tiny Mrs. Kiyo did not even blink while Rose rattled on about microbes and nutrients. Rose felt huge—even down a step on the front stoop.

"Can we rake your leaves," Thomas interrupted, "and use them for our compost? Gram says your backyard is pretty full."

Mrs. Kiyo blinked and turned to Thomas as if she'd just noticed he was there.

"You want to use my leaves?" she asked with no trace of accent.

Thomas nodded.

"I haven't been able to rake my yard for three years now," said Mrs. Kiyo. "But perhaps I was just saving the leaves for you two." Her lips turned up slightly at the corners, which was enough to make her wrinkles ripple out into her short gray hair. It was the kind of smile that you might not notice if you were seeing it from across the street. But it was most definitely a smile.

"Thank you," said Rose, which seemed like a dumb thing to say, but she was dumbfounded. Mrs. Kiyo spoke perfect English! She felt terrible for having assumed she didn't. "May we start raking now?"

"Don't you have to practice?" Mrs. Kiyo asked Rose.

"Yes. I'm just . . . going to rake a little first," said Rose. How did Mrs. Kiyo know she needed to practice? Or that she practiced at all, for that matter?

"As you wish," said Mrs. Kiyo with something that looked more like a real smile. "But I hope you have your own rakes, because I gave mine away years ago."

Chapter 13
Composting

It took longer than expected to rake up Mrs. Kiyo's backyard of leaves and cart them to their new compost bin. It wasn't even a large yard—there were just *a lot* of leaves. They were a foot deep where they'd blown around the edges of the yard. Mrs. Kiyo kept watch from her kitchen window. She did not smile, but somehow she looked happier than she usually did. Or maybe Rose just knew how to read her expressions better.

"These leaves are half composted already," Thomas said as he shoveled the first wagonload of the mess into the compost bin in their backyard.

"Perfect!" said Mr. Pickering. "Leaf mold—most excellent stuff. Lemonade, anyone? First batch I've made myself! Took me half the morning, squeezing with just one hand, but I managed." The day had turned warm—warmer than it had been all week. Thomas was wearing shorts. Rose was hot in her jeans. They both nodded.

"I think we should mulch with the compost, rather than digging it in," Rose said as they sat on the back-porch steps.

"What does that mean?" Thomas asked.

"Just put the compost on top of the dirt all around the pumpkin vine, then let the worms dig it in." She'd read about it in the compost books. Apparently Thomas had skipped that part. "It's supposed to be better for soil making. Worms are gentler and more thorough, apparently." It would be much easier than doing it themselves. Easy enough that Thomas could do it on his own, in fact. Which would be good.

"Where do we get the worms?" Thomas asked. "Because I haven't seen any."

"I think you can order them," said Rose. She knew you could, actually; she'd left *Composting 101* open to the proper page on Mr. Pickering's kitchen table.

"Really?"

"Yes," said Mr. Pickering as he poured his fresh-squeezed lemonade into the usual red plastic cups.

"Believe it or not, there are worm farms that will mail you a box of worms. I read about them in one of those books you borrowed, Rosie. Probably a solid investment for us."

After their lemonade, Thomas jumped up and held out his hand to help Rose up.

"Better get back to it!" he said.

"Thomas, I've got to practice." She felt bad as soon as she said it.

Thomas's shoulders sagged. "Just another twenty minutes?" he pleaded. "If we're not done then, you can go practice and I'll finish up."

Rose sighed. "Fifteen minutes. Then I really need to practice."

It actually didn't take long to finish, and when they were done, Mrs. Kiyo's backyard looked like a different place. Rose stood in the middle of the yard with her rake and surveyed their progress. The grass was a matted soggy brown—who knew if it would recover, but at least it could breathe now and get some sun. Along the side of the yard, there were the remains of interesting landscaping—thin-limbed trees arching over stone birdbaths and benches. Bushes that looked thoughtfully placed. She could imagine that it could be quite beautiful. Soothing, even.

"Hey," Thomas said as he jogged up to her with the empty wagon. "I know you've got to go, but Mrs. Kiyo wants to talk to us."

Rose turned and saw their tiny neighbor standing on her back stoop watching them again. Rose glanced at Thomas, who shrugged. They balanced their rakes on the wagon and walked to Mrs. Kiyo.

"I am very grateful for this service you have done for me," said Mrs. Kiyo in her perfect English. "It has been years since I've been able to care for any of my gardens, except for the Listening Garden in the front. I do try to keep the pots tended there."

"What's the Listening Garden?" Thomas asked.

"It is the space with the bench in my front yard," said Mrs. Kiyo. "I go there to listen."

"To what?" asked Thomas.

"To the cello," said Mrs. Kiyo softly, looking up at Rose.

Rose felt her cheeks grow warm. Mrs. Kiyo listened to her practice?

"You can hear Rose play her cello from *across the street*?" said Thomas.

"Well, one must listen very carefully," said Mrs. Kiyo. "And when boys are playing basketball next door, it is very difficult." Her mouth settled back into its customary line, but Rose could now detect a shift in the wrinkles around her eyes that made it clear she was teasing.

Thomas grinned. "Sorry about that."

"I would like to invite the two of you for tea," said Mrs. Kiyo. "To thank you for what you have done for me and my garden."

"Aw, that's okay," said Thomas. He hated tea. Gram sometimes gave them chamomile tea before bed, but Thomas never drank his. He said it tasted like weeds. "We really needed those leaves, so it worked out for both of us, I guess."

"A special tea," said Mrs. Kiyo. "A Japanese tea. In my home. If you would come."

"Like a . . . tea party?" said Thomas.

"We would love to," said Rose quickly. A special tea. A *specialty*. "What can we bring?" she added. Mama always asked this question when they were invited somewhere. Rose felt grown-up remembering it.

"Gram's expecting us home for supper," Thomas said.

"That is fine," said Mrs. Kiyo. "I will need three days to prepare. And there is no need to bring anything."

"Three days to prepare tea?" said Thomas. Rose elbowed his shoulder.

"Many preparations must be made," said Mrs. Kiyo. "Are you free Wednesday between school and practice?"

"I have my math final on Wednesday," said Rose. "Would Thursday be okay?"

"Certainly—even better," said Mrs. Kiyo.

"Rose could bring her cello," said Thomas. Rose elbowed him again—harder this time. "What?" he said, rubbing his shoulder. "Mrs. Kiyo might like to hear it up close sometime."

"I would, indeed, like to hear it up close, as you say," said Mrs. Kiyo, "but not when we have tea. Please come at three o'clock. That is the traditional time of tea. Study hard for your final, Rose."

Rose nodded. She didn't really need to, but she probably would anyway.

They said their good-byes, then slowly crossed the street to their house.

"Maybe Gram will tell us we can't go," Thomas said when they were out of earshot.

"Why would she say that?"

He shrugged. "Maybe it'll take too much time?"

"Take too much time from what?"

"The pumpkin project? She seems to like having us help Mr. P. with that. And your practicing, of course."

"We can make time for this," said Rose.

"Oh, my," said Gram when they told her. "That is quite an invitation."

"Do we really have to go?" asked Thomas.

"Well, I should think so!" said Gram. "It would be very rude to turn down such a special invitation."

"A tea party? *Really?*"

"I suspect this experience will be much more than a tea party. The Japanese have a long tradition with tea. They do tea *ceremonies,* not parties. They even have special rooms just for having tea in."

Gram wiped flour off her hands. "Let's go try on your spring things and see what good clothes we have to work with."

"Aw, man—am I gonna have to wear a tie and belt and everything?" said Thomas.

Chapter 14
The Way of Tea

Thomas did wear a tie (a clip-on) and belt. And his good shoes that pinched. And Rose wore her Easter dress—the only dress she hadn't outgrown yet—and her white slip-on flats that made her feet look like skis, but at least did not add to her height. They both felt overdressed, but Gram would not let them out the door without looking their best.

"Are you sure you don't want to wear your hair down, Rosebud?"

"No," said Rose. All the preparations were making her a little nervous. She liked the security provided by her tight bun. Besides, her hair was so *large* when it was down, and she already felt enormous next to Mrs. Kiyo.

Gram sighed. "All right, then. Remember to be respectful. Be grateful. And ask questions if you need to. Better to ask than offend."

As they walked up Mrs. Kiyo's front steps, Thomas whispered, "Do you think we'll sit on the floor?" He knocked on the door. "Don't Japanese people sit on the floor at little tables when they have tea?"

"We'll do whatever Mrs. Kiyo does," said Rose. She hoped that didn't include sitting on the floor, though, because although she continued to improve in graceful sitting, wearing a dress would make it especially challenging.

The door opened partway. Mrs. Kiyo peeked around the door and smiled at them—a close-lipped smile but a real one. Even her eyes smiled. Then she opened the door fully and gestured for them to enter. She pointed to a mat inside the door, where two very small shoes, presumably hers, were placed precisely in the bottom-left corner. Rose removed her white slip-ons and placed them beside Mrs. Kiyo's. Her shoes were almost twice as long as her neighbor's. Thomas kicked his shoes off and left them catawampus on the mat. Rose quickly bent over and lined them up next to hers. Mrs. Kiyo smiled at her. Thomas's toes wiggled in his socks on the floor beside the shoe mat.

Mrs. Kiyo led the way down the hall. They walked through her kitchen toward two glass doors off the eating area. One was already open, but Mrs. Kiyo opened the other before indicating they should enter.

It was a screened-in porch, basically, but it had a very different feel from any porch Rose had visited before. The walls were paneled in a light wood, and there were large screened windows on three sides, which made them feel like they were more outside than in. In the middle of the room, there was a small rectangular table with simple wooden benches around it. Between two of the windows hung a white scroll with what Rose assumed was Japanese writing on it. There was nothing else in the room except for a very narrow table against the wall, which held a vase with a skinny branch coated in small pink flowers.

Rose looked out the window at the backyard. The trees that arched over the stone benches they had discovered when they raked Mrs. Kiyo's leaves were now covered in beautiful soft-pink flower buds—the same as the branch in the vase. Two of the windows were open, and they could hear birds at a new bird feeder that hung from a wooden post. Amazing the difference a few days made in the spring.

"Cool!" said Thomas.

And it was cool, though Thomas's voice seemed very loud.

"My husband built this room for me," said Mrs. Kiyo. "It is my favorite spot."

"Is this a special room just for tea?" Rose asked.

"Not just for tea. It's good for reading . . . and now that my backyard has been recovered, it's very good for birdwatching. But it's a nice place to have tea, yes."

On the table in the middle of the room was a medium-size pot—it looked a little like Gram's fancy soup tureen, but it was made of metal and had an ornate lid. The pot sat on a small bowl, and Rose could see a candle burning through an opening on the side of the bowl. Arranged beside the bowl were a series of wooden utensils. One looked like a ladle, another like Mr. Pickering's fat shaving brush, only with wooden bristles, and another like a very skinny knife with a bent tip. Beside the wooden tools, there was one small container with a lid, one medium-size empty bowl, and three mismatched rough-looking bowls. Two cloths— one white, one red—sat next to the bowls. Nothing about the setup looked like a tea party. There weren't even cups and saucers.

Rose and Thomas sat together on a bench — not the floor, thank goodness — facing the pretty backyard. Rose did not feel quite so large once she sat, and she was glad to have Thomas next to her.

Mrs. Kiyo sat down across from them and smiled again. Then she placed her hands in her lap and bowed her head down to the surface of the table. Thomas immediately did the same, which startled Rose. She quickly did so as well, but she knew her bow lacked the elegance of Mrs. Kiyo's — or even Thomas's. When Rose lifted her head, though, Mrs. Kiyo was smiling again, which made her feel better.

Mrs. Kiyo took the red cloth, folded it slowly in a series of precise geometric folds, and then used it to gently but thoroughly wipe the outside of the small lidded container and the skinny bent-knife tool. She set the fat brush with wooden bristles on its end and then wiped the wooden ladle.

Every move she made seemed choreographed, and Rose felt herself calm as she watched her neighbor's slow movements. Even Thomas sat still and watched. They could hear the birds chirping outside the window and could smell the warm sunshine on Mrs. Kiyo's drying yard. Maybe the tree's pink buds would open with the sun.

When she'd finished wiping the tools with the red cloth, Mrs. Kiyo bowed again, so Rose and Thomas did, too. She slid a plate Rose had not noticed before toward them. Three of the dearest treats Rose had ever seen were on the plate. In the gentlest shades of pink, lavender, and green, the sweets were molded to look like spring flowers—but not flowers like you'd see in Minnesota. Maybe Japanese flowers? She couldn't think what the treats could be, though. They were too soft-looking to be cake decorations, too pretty to be cookies.

"*Wagashi,*" said Mrs. Kiyo. "Please enjoy while I make your tea."

Thomas took one right away, but Rose continued watching Mrs. Kiyo, who removed the lid from the pot in the center of the table and smiled as a small waft of steam rose up over the edge. She picked up the long-handled wooden ladle and, without spilling a drop, scooped a small amount of water into one of the mismatched bowls. She used the wooden-bristled brush to stir the hot water around, then carefully dumped the water out in the empty medium-size bowl and wiped the now-empty bowl with the white cloth.

Rose was entranced—it was all so precise, so

measured. Mrs. Kiyo looked peaceful as she washed and wiped and arranged things. Next, she opened the small lidded container. It was filled with a bright-green powder. She used the skinny bent knife to scoop some of the powder out of the cup and into the freshly cleaned bowl — two scoops. She placed the tool back in the exact spot it had been, and then with great care ladled hot water onto the green powder. After placing the lid back on the big pot and balancing the wooden ladle on top, she picked up the wooden brush and whisked the green powder and water together.

Rose almost laughed then. Everything had been done so slowly, with such meticulous movements — and suddenly Mrs. Kiyo was whisking so quickly! In tight controlled circles, she whisked until the water in the bowl turned a brilliant shade of new-spring-grass green. Again, she placed the brush in the exact spot she'd taken it from, then handed the bowl to Thomas.

"Thank you," Thomas said quietly, setting the bowl down before him.

Mrs. Kiyo picked up one of the empty tea bowls and mimed how to drink from it. Thomas grinned; Gram never let them drink the rest of the cereal milk or the last drops of soup from a bowl, but that was exactly what Mrs. Kiyo seemed to want them to do. He tipped the bowl up and took a big slurp. The bowl came down and he looked at Rose with slight panic in his eyes. He seemed unsure of how to swallow. Then his eyebrows shot up and he gulped. His eyes watered, but he looked relieved and proud. Mrs. Kiyo laughed—a gentle laugh of pure joy.

"*Matcha* is *very* bitter," she said. "Let the sweet balance it."

Thomas popped the rest of his *wagashi* treat in his mouth and then took another sip of the *matcha*. He smiled.

"Better?" said Mrs. Kiyo.

"Better," said Thomas.

Mrs. Kiyo nodded, then picked up another bowl and repeated the whole process. When the mixture was properly whisked, she handed the bowl to Rose.

The bowl had surprising heft. It looked to be made of clay—much like the chili bowls they had at home but without a handle. Irregularly shaped and roughly glazed in a grayish-brown color, the bowl was not pretty so much as . . . satisfying. Rose turned the bowl in her hand. An irregular crack of bright gold traveled from the top of the bowl down the side and underneath.

It looked like a scar. A very beautiful scar. Rose touched it with her thumb, half expecting it to burn, as the gold was so bright against the dark clay.

She looked up at Mrs. Kiyo and was surprised to see the old woman's eyes sparkling with tears. Once again, Mrs. Kiyo bowed, and this time her bow lingered close to the tabletop. Rose wasn't sure how to bow while holding a bowl of hot tea, so she dipped her head and hoped it was enough.

"*Wagashi* first," Mrs. Kiyo reminded her when her head came up.

Rose put her tea bowl down and picked a pink *wagashi* off the plate. She took a small bite. The consistency of the treat was different from anything she'd eaten before. Soft but just a bit of texture, too. It was sweet, but she could not have said what the flavor was exactly. It was good, though. She set it down and picked up the scarred bowl and took a sip of the *matcha*. It was bitter, all right! But it went well with the sweet *wagashi*.

"Did you make those *wagashi* things?" Thomas asked.

"I did." Mrs. Kiyo nodded. "That's why I needed a few days to prepare. They are . . . quite labor intensive. It is a process that cannot be rushed."

"They are very beautiful," said Rose. "What are they made of?"

"Bean paste, sugar, and rice flour."

"Bean paste?" said Thomas. Rose could tell he was trying not to make a face.

"And sugar," said Mrs. Kiyo, her dark eyes dancing.

They watched as Mrs. Kiyo briskly, but with just as much care and attention as before, made the third bowl of tea for herself. She took a bite of the remaining *wagashi,* followed by several sips of the bitter green tea, which she seemed to enjoy very much.

When they were finished, Mrs. Kiyo began to clean their tea bowls with the white cloth and hot water. Again, she moved with precise, peaceful efficiency.

"How come Rose's bowl is cracked like that?" Thomas asked as Mrs. Kiyo rinsed it. "With the gold and everything?"

"That is *kintsugi,*" said Mrs. Kiyo. "A golden repair. In Japan we revere the art of mending broken things."

"Why not just superglue it back together?" Thomas had repaired more than his share of things with superglue.

"The gold reminds us that beauty is found in the

story of the object, its history," said Mrs. Kiyo. "The bowl is more beautiful, more valuable, for all that has happened to it."

Rose's gaze lingered on the bowl in Mrs. Kiyo's hands. "Did you bring the bowl with you from Japan?"

"Yes. My mother gave it to me when I left Japan to come to America and get married."

"It looks really old," Thomas said. Rose nudged him with her elbow.

"It is extremely old, in fact," said Mrs. Kiyo. "And very valuable."

"How old were you, Mrs. Kiyo, when you left Japan?" Rose asked.

"Twenty-one. Just barely. It's been almost seventy years now. . . ." She shook her head in wonder.

"Gram says you were a war bride," said Thomas. Rose wasn't sure if she should elbow Thomas for that comment or not; it sounded rude, but Mrs. Kiyo didn't seem to mind.

"Yes," said Mrs. Kiyo. "I suppose I was. But I was a war bride in love, which was not the case in every situation."

The old woman paused. Rose watched her neighbor steady her face. Maybe all of the memories were not happy ones.

"My marriage caused quite a rift in my family," continued Mrs. Kiyo. "My mother was the only one to come see me off, and it was hard for her to do so. That bowl was the most treasured thing she owned. Her grandmother had given it to her when she married—it was the last remaining piece of a set of tea bowls *her* mother had received when she married."

"Wow," said Thomas. "It should be in a museum."

"Yes," said Mrs. Kiyo. "It could be. But then I couldn't use it." She traced the gold scar—the golden repair. "I broke this bowl when I was a small child. It is my earliest memory. My mother wept. She saved for many years to be able to afford a reputable *kintsugi* artist to repair it. And she didn't have it long . . . before she gave it to me."

"Why did she give it to you if she loved it so much?" Rose asked.

Mrs. Kiyo considered this. "It was all she had to give. Japan was war-torn and we didn't have many nice things left—that the bowl had survived was a miracle. That *we* had survived was a miracle, too. I think she wanted to give me some of that endurance, that survival. And, probably, she wanted me to have it in case I needed something valuable to sell. But I could never sell it, of course. Fortunately, I never had to consider it."

She smiled at Rose and Thomas—a sad smile, maybe, but big enough to ripple her beautiful wrinkles. "Thank you for asking about the bowl. It is good to remember."

She would not let them help to clear the table, but she seemed to enjoy their company, and they spent another hour on the porch with their neighbor. Mrs. Kiyo asked about Rose's math final. Rose shrugged it off. She'd managed her usual top score in the class, but she didn't like to talk about grades. She let Thomas do most of the talking, thereby keeping the subject mostly on the giant pumpkin plant. But she did tell Mrs. Kiyo about her hopes of studying with Harris Waldenstein. Mrs. Kiyo nodded and said kindly, "I hope it all happens in the best possible way for you."

Eventually she stood and led them back through the house to the front door.

"Thank you, Mrs. Kiyo," said Rose as she slipped on her shoes. "This was really . . . a very special treat for us."

"Super cool," Thomas added. He picked up his shoes, obviously planning on walking across the street in socks. "You should come over and see the pumpkin plant. And come hear Rose practice outside—she'll be out there soon. You can sit on the bench in our back-yard and have a front-row seat."

"I just might do that," said Mrs. Kiyo. "Thank you both for coming. It's been a long time since I made a proper tea. It was wonderful to have you to my porch."

Chapter 15

El Proyecto de la Calabaza Gigante

The next Saturday morning, the doorbell rang. Rose was awake, reading *Charlotte's Web* under the covers. She kept the book under her mattress so it was easily accessible—and easily tucked away quickly if someone came in. A beam of sunshine fell across her bed. The bright warmth felt good on her legs. Maybe things would warm up a little for their pumpkin plant. It had warmed for a few days, but then grown cold again.

Rose heard Gram unlock the front door. Thomas skidded past her doorway and down the hallway in his socks and pajamas. She decided to wait to see who it was before she got up, in case it was a certain tap dancer from across the street.

"Why, Señor Ocampo, good morning!" said Gram, her voice ringing through the house.

"*¡Buenos días, señora!*"

"My, what's all this?" asked Gram.

Rose threw on a clean T-shirt and jeans and headed out to the living room to see.

Gram held a cloth bag full of something. Thomas bounced up and down as he tried to look in.

"From my brother in Saint Paul," explained Señor Ocampo. "His neighbor keeps chickens." He pointed to the bag with a proud smile. "For your compost!"

Thomas let out a whoop. "It's chicken poop!" He took the bag from Gram, which was good because she looked like she might drop it.

"Chicken poop for our compost! It's the final ingredient!" Thomas began to dance around the living room. Had anyone ever been so excited about poop?

"Thomas, take that outside, please," said Gram.

"You aren't mad that we're not buying compost from you anymore?" Rose asked shyly.

Señor Ocampo laughed. "Mad? No, no. My store is good for small projects—how do you say? *¿Modesto?*"

"Modest?" Rose asked.

"*Sí.* For modest projects. When Señora Lukashenko tells me of this project, I know it needs more than bags from my store. Homemade compost is good," continued Señor Ocampo. "We use it in gardens in Mexico. Señora Lukashenko says you are growing a . . . hmm . . . *una calabaza?*"

"Um," said Rose. "*Calabaza?* Is that 'pumpkin' in Spanish?" It certainly didn't sound like pumpkin.

"*¡Sí!*" He spelled the word for Rose. "*¡Una calabaza!*" His *z*'s were the opposite of Mrs. Lukashenko's — soft and whispery.

"Would you like to see?" asked Rose. Señor Ocampo nodded, and she led him out to the backyard. Gram stayed behind, readying their breakfasts.

Thomas was already at the compost bin, mixing the layers with the snow shovel. Steam rose off the pile.

Thomas nodded to the bag of chicken poop resting against the side of the bin. "Dump it in?"

Rose hesitated. "Let's double-check how much should go in. I think chicken manure can cause problems if there is too much. We can research it after breakfast."

Thomas looked disappointed. "Okay. *Right* after breakfast."

They walked to Mr. Pickering's yard. Thomas moved the brick that held down the tent flap and peeked in.

"Thermometer says fifty-six degrees," he said.

Warmer than it was outside the tent. Rose wished she had grabbed a jacket on the way out. A cool breeze lifted her curls. Undoubtedly her hair was all over the place. She hadn't had time to put it up. She tried to smooth it, but the breeze insisted on fluffing it.

Señor Ocampo peered into the tent. "One pumpkin plant?" he said, pulling his head out. "Why so early to plant?"

"It has to get a head start," said Rose.

"It's a *giant* pumpkin," said Thomas.

"Giant?" Señor Ocampo's eyebrows shot up in surprise.

"Super huge!" said Thomas.

Mr. Pickering appeared on his back porch. "*¡Buenos días, mi amigo!* Haven't seen you in a while."

"*¡Buenos días, mi amigo!*"

"Are they telling you about our pumpkin project?"

"*¡Sí!*"

"He brought us chicken poop, Mr. P.! For the compost!"

"Hot diggity!" said Mr. Pickering. "A little chicken poop and Kiyo's leaves and we will have the Elixir of Growth!"

Señor Ocampo smiled politely. Maybe *Elixir of Growth* did not translate. Probably *hot diggity* didn't, either.

"Giant pumpkin . . . like this?" Señor Ocampo said. He held his hands out as if he were grasping a larger-than-average basketball.

"Bigger," said Mr. Pickering.

Thomas walked over and spread Señor Ocampo's arms out straight. "This big!"

"*Calabaza gigante,*" said Señor Ocampo softly. He pronounced the second word *heeGANtey.*

"What did you call it, *señor*?" Mr. Pickering asked.

"*Una calabaza gigante,*" repeated Señor Ocampo, drawing out the whisper that started *gigante.* "Giant pumpkin" sounded even cooler in Spanish.

On his way back across the yard, Señor Ocampo pointed to the compost pile. "You want more things for *el proyecto de la calabaza gigante*?"

"Absolutely," said Mr. Pickering. "Spread the word. We can use *frutas y vegetales y café*, uh . . ."

"Coffee *molido*?"

"*¡Sí!*" confirmed Mr. Pickering with a smile. "Coffee grounds—*café molido.*"

"Coffee *grounds.*" Señor Ocampo's sound in *grounds* was rounder and deeper than Mr. Pickering's.

"*Y huevos* . . ." Mr. Pickering pretended to crack an egg. "*¿Huevos* . . . ?"

"Ah! *¡Sí! Cáscaras de huevos.* Eggshells."

Rose smiled. She loved how they taught each other their languages—translating back and forth, repeating, looping the words in each language. It was like music—similar to the polyphony and symmetry in Bach. One melody, many voices.

Señor Ocampo left, promising more scraps and chicken poop for the compost. *El proyecto de la calabaza gigante* was turning into a neighborhood project. Rose was glad. Their neighborhood had never had a project. And it'd be good to have more people involved. In two weeks, school would be out. The week after that, she would be playing Bach's Cello Suites for Harris Waldenstein. If everything went as well as she hoped, she'd be even busier than she was now, studying with—and maybe, if she was really lucky, *assisting*—Harris after that. Thomas would need all the help he could get for the pumpkin project.

Chapter 16
Worm Delivery

Rose was deep in Bach's second suite when the doorbell rang. It was probably a neighbor. People they'd never even met were contributing to the compost bin now. Thomas said they wanted a peek at the pumpkin plant, which was vining. The vine was close to two feet long. Thomas measured every morning and evening. At first it just climbed up, but then it relaxed a little and came down to touch the ground. They would have to figure out how to anchor it into the composted soil soon.

Rose hoped Thomas was figuring that out—and that someone else was getting the door. She'd come home gritchy and grouchy and had not gone out to the pumpkin. She had to focus; she was thinking too much about the pumpkin and not enough about Bach. She was not in the mood to dig compost or show anyone the pumpkin vine or even think about it. She was thrilled the skies looked like rain again because she also was in no mood to practice outside. She intended to practice indoors, like a normal person—with *focus*—and then she would read *Charlotte's Web* in her room. Those were the evening's goals. She was so sure of them that she didn't even need to write them on sticky notes.

The fingers of her left hand danced through the complicated notes of Suite no. 2's gigue. She forgot all about the doorbell—forgot about everything but the music—as she ripped through the furious gigue. She had to concentrate on this movement. It wasn't skippy and light like Suite no. 1's gigue. No, Suite no. 2's gigue was like a busy, buzzing hive of angry wasps, and since that's how she felt, Rose threw herself into it. The waspish notes zipped up and out of her cello, the spiraling dark cloud inside her swirling and then dispersing with the music.

When she sent the last defiant note into the small living room, she exhaled. Whew! Much better. Bach was a good friend; he gave her the music to release the stuff she didn't always understand. Being limited to only sixty minutes of practice each day was stressful. She was glad to have *Charlotte's Web,* but even that had its limits. She knew Jane must be looking for it. She hadn't asked Rose about it yet, but the knowledge that at any moment she *might* made it hard for Rose to enjoy the book.

The doorbell rang again, surprising Rose for the second time. Mama bustled into the room. She glanced out the window as she went past.

"It's the mailman." Mama heaved the big door open and greeted the mailman with a smile. "Sorry it took us so long to get to the door. We weren't expecting a package today."

"Not a problem," said the mailman. He was new to their block, but Rose had noticed he always smiled as he carried the mail from house to house. She and Thomas called him the Happy Mailman.

"I enjoyed the music while I was standing here," the Happy Mailman said. "That was an amazing interpretation of the second gigue. Sounded like a hornets' nest of energy! What's the recording?"

"That wasn't a recording," said Mama. Rose could hear the pride in Mama's voice, and she was glad the door blocked the mailman's view of her sitting in her practice chair. "That was my daughter practicing."

"Quite accomplished!" said the mailman. "Here's your package. It's marked perishable, so I didn't want to leave it on the steps without you knowing it's there."

"That's funny, I don't recall ordering anything perish—*worms!* Rose, honey, come get this box. Did Thomas order *worms*?"

Rose lowered her cello to the floor and walked to the door. She had ordered the worms, actually, with Mr. Pickering's help and credit card. She was trying to contribute in little ways that didn't require digging or getting dirty.

She tried to stick her arm around the side of the door to receive the package, but Mama opened the door wide, revealing her to the mailman. Rose took the large, flat box in her arms. It was heavier than she'd expected. Not that she knew how much worms weighed. She'd ordered five thousand, which is what Uncle Jim's Worm Farm recommended for an area the size of Mr. Pickering's backyard.

"Say," said the Happy Mailman, "was that you playing the Bach?"

"Yes," said Rose.

"Who do you study with?"

"Frances Holling." She tried to inch behind the door. She didn't want to discuss music with the mailman.

"No kidding! Well, you must be good! Are you in the university's music program?"

Rose was so startled the mailman knew Mrs. Holling that she could only shake her head.

"Rose isn't actually in college yet. She takes some courses there, and lessons, yes, but she's still quite young." Mama smiled. "Do you know Frances Holling?"

"Quite well! Though it's been years and years since I've seen her. I played in a couple of ensemble groups with her—string quartets and the like—back when we were both very young. I played viola."

The Happy Mailman played music with Mrs. Holling? Rose peeked at him from around the door. What clue had she missed?

"Do you still play?" Mama asked politely.

"Some." He held up his left hand. A web of scar tissue wrapped his palm, contorting his fingers slightly. There was a gasp. Rose was not sure if it came from her or Mama.

"Had a bit of a snowblower accident," said the

mailman matter-of-factly. "Stuck my hand in to get a clump of snow out, and it gave way unexpectedly. Stupid, of course."

Rose felt light-headed. She looked down at the box she was holding. The print swam before her eyes.

"Oh, my!" said Mama. "I can't imagine!"

"It's probably better you don't," said the mailman. "Happened almost thirty years ago now. My dad had one of the first snowblowers on our block. It didn't have the safety features they have now, though you should always be careful with those things. Personally, I shovel."

"How old were you?" Mama asked.

"Seventeen. I'd just won a scholarship to study music performance at college. I went through the surgeries and worked hard at the rehab, hoping for the best, but when I got to college, I was not successful. Not because of my hand—though it took me a long time to admit that. There's just a difference between being really good, which I was, and being truly great . . . which I wasn't, even before the accident."

"What—what did you do?" Rose stammered. What she meant was, *How? How could you do anything after that?*

"Well, I transferred—to a college I could afford without a music scholarship—and there I majored in history. But I played in the orchestra through college. I met my wife in that orchestra, in fact. It's funny to think about now. . . . If I hadn't injured myself, I might've taken a different path. Somebody else might be married to my wife!" He laughed. He had a nice laugh.

"Anyway, it's all good—just not what I would've originally chosen. Sometimes life is like that." He hefted his mailbag farther up his shoulder. "Anyway, I've taken up more than enough of you folks' time. You've made my day, Rose. I sure do love the Bach Cello Suites. Say hello to Frances for me. Kirk's my name, by the way. Kirk Stevens."

Mama introduced herself and then Kirk said goodbye. Rose watched as he walked to Mr. Pickering's house. He was smiling, as usual.

Mama shut the front door and turned to look at Rose. Rose set down the box of worms and picked up her cello so she wouldn't have to talk. She needed to think. Was she just really good? Or could she be truly great?

She couldn't wait to meet the maestro—it felt as if her whole life might settle into place when she did.

Chapter 17
Bach for the Pumpkins

Shall I help you move your practice chair outside?" Mama asked the following day when the sun finally came out. "It's a lovely warm afternoon. . . ."

"The pumpkin is still in the tent," Rose grumbled. "It isn't *that* warm."

"Warm enough," said Gram. "Time for you to venture out. Mrs. Holling's orders."

Rose stalled. "I'm worried about the cello."

"Mrs. Holling is not worried about the cello," countered Mama. "She said you might have to tune it more often, but the wood on the cello has seen so many seasonal changes that it should adjust."

Gram and Mama stood together, hands on their hips, smiles on their faces.

"Fine." Rose stood and hoisted her cello. At least she'd be able to say she was accomplishing the wadded-up sticky-note goal in her pocket that read PRACTICE OUTSIDE. "Careful with the chair—the top comes loose from the bottom."

She led the way through the kitchen and out the back door. Mama followed with the unwieldy bottom part of the cellist's chair, and Gram followed her with the top. It felt like they were in a parade.

"Do you need your music?" Gram asked.

"No."

Mama gave her a look that clearly said, *Watch your tone.*

"No, *thank you,*" said Rose. "It's all memorized." Everything but no. 6 had been memorized for months. Apparently, no one had noticed. True, she often used the music when practicing so she didn't get sloppy, but she certainly wasn't going to bring the music outside. The wind might blow it away, and with it all the notations and reminders Mrs. Holling had added over the last year.

Gram and Mama deposited her chair, then went back inside. Before Rose had taken her seat, she heard the kitchen window creak open. Gram would be listening as usual. If she was lucky, no one else would hear. She'd practice for her sixty minutes and then she'd retreat to her bedroom and read *Charlotte's Web*. Which she should have returned by now—it would be Jane's week again starting tomorrow—but she just couldn't stand the thought of being without it. Maybe Jane wouldn't notice; by now the schedule was probably all confused in her head. She still hadn't said anything about it, at least.

"Play us a song, Rose!" Thomas called from next door. "I'm taking the tent off!"

For a week, they'd left the flap open so that the plant could get accustomed to less constant temperatures. Now it would be forced out, too.

Rose started the prelude of Suite no. 4 to give herself and the pumpkin plant courage. It was easy to lose herself in the scales and arpeggios that tangled in and around themselves in Bach's particular and precise magical way. With Bach, everything was so beautifully ordered, as if each note knew what to do and when. She knew what to do, too, when she played Bach.

The long lines ran smoothly, and Rose relaxed in spite of herself. She'd almost forgotten she was outside when Jesse and James arrived. She wanted to close her eyes, but she felt too self-conscious with the boys watching. So she focused on Thomas taking apart the pumpkin's tent instead.

"Hey, what instrument is that?" asked Jesse, or maybe it was James.

"Cello." She attacked the next spiral of arpeggios.

"That's why people call you Cello Girl, I bet! You play cello!"

People called her Cello Girl? What people? Kids at the high school?

"You are the tallest cello girl I've ever seen."

"How many cello girls do you know?" his brother asked.

"Only this one. But she's *got* to be the tallest!"

Rose's cheeks grew warm. She kept playing, but the light allemande movement sounded a little out of control. She tried to slow it down.

"How come you don't play basketball, Cello Girl?"

She ignored the inane question.

"You sure do play cello *a lot*," said one.

"You must really like it," agreed the other.

"I do," Rose said in clipped tones. "And I play so much because I need to be ready for the competition."

Rose concentrated on the music, playing the last of the allemande movement and starting the courante without pause.

"What kind of competition?" asked one of the boys.

"Bach Cello Suites," said Thomas, walking up to greet the Jacobi boys in that weirdly tussling way boys have.

"I've heard of Bach," said the other brother. "Is that what you're playing now — Bach?"

Unavoidably, she was at the end of the courante movement.

"Yes," she said.

"Cool."

Rose started the ominous-sounding sarabande, glad she didn't have to stop to turn pages. Maybe they would lose interest if she played something slower. It didn't sound as flashy, though it was actually more difficult.

"I bet you'll win," said one of the boys.

"She'll win," said Thomas. "She's super good."

"So, *what* do you win?" asked the other twin. Even the sums of the letters in their names were similar: Jesse was fifty-eight and James was forty-eight.

Rose stopped playing so she could finish the conversation and be done with them.

"It's not like winning a prize." She smoothed the curls that had escaped her bun. "If I win, I get to study with Maestro Harris Waldenstein. He's taken a three-year appointment with the Bach Chamber Orchestra in

Saint Paul. He'll be teaching a select number of students while he's here. They call it a fellowship." She liked the sound of the word *fellowship*, even though she wasn't sure what it meant. "If I win, I get one of those fellowships."

"So you'd be a fellow?" Both boys cracked up. "How's that work, since you're a girl?"

Rose decided to ignore the joke. "Maestro Waldenstein is a great Bachian scholar," she said.

"Bachian?" said Thomas. "Is that a real word?"

"Yes." She glared at her brother. "It is." She started the sarabande again and let herself escape into her day-dream about Harris Waldenstein, in which she helped him with his research while he was in town. She'd get new sticky notes and notebooks. . . . The maestro would see how organized she was and he'd beg her to help him with his mess of notes and partially finished books. . . . "I could sure use an assistant," Harris would say. Who knew? Maybe they would write a book together later in life. They'd be a terrific match: Harris (73) + Waldenstein (126) equaled 199, a prime number, and Rose (57) + Brutigan (92) equaled 149—*also a prime number*. It was practically meant to be. *And* the sum of her name linked her to Bach, too. When she added up the digits, she got fourteen: $1 + 4 + 9 = 14$.

"Rose needs to practice, gentlemen," said Mr.

Pickering, who had hobbled over. "Maybe you two could come help Thomas?"

It was a relief when Jesse and James finally followed Thomas over to Mr. Pickering's backyard. One of them walked backward, watching her as she started to play again.

"Maybe we can play together sometime, Cello Girl," he said. "You on the cello and me on the guitar. Jesse can sing, maybe."

"Holy moly! Look at that thing!" said the one who must be Jesse.

The tent was off. Rose tripped over a note—the plant was much larger than yesterday. And it looked like it was creeping toward them. The very end of the vine levitated off the ground, reaching and searching for something to climb up. How could it have grown so much in one day?

As Rose played the last notes of the sarabande, Mrs. Lukashenko lumbered up the driveway with Mrs. Kiyo on her arm.

"That music!" Mrs. Lukashenko said. "So beautiful. May we sit for a listen?"

Rose reached her arms up over her head to stretch out her shoulders. "Thank you. Of course. Please have a seat." What else could she say?

The two women sat on the bench slightly to Rose's left. Rose tried to decide which suite movement to play next—what would Mrs. Kiyo enjoy the most?

Before she could decide, Calamity Jane tap-danced around the corner of the house. "Jesse! James! Mom says to come home right now for supper. She brought home subs."

Jane stopped mid-tap when she saw Rose.

"Is that your cello?" she asked. Rose waited for the accompanying shuffle-tap, but Jane stood absolutely still.

"Yes."

"It sure is big," said Jane.

Rose had played a full-size cello for a couple of years, though Calamity Jane probably hadn't seen it. It wasn't like she usually practiced in the yard.

"It looks old," said Jane. "Why don't you get a new one?"

"The older ones are often better," said Rose. Mrs. Holling said they had settled into themselves—they knew who they were and how they were supposed to sound.

"Can you play something I can dance to?"

"This really isn't tap-dance music," said Rose. The suite movements—the sarabande, bouree, courante, etc.—were all dances, but not tap dances. Ballet, maybe. But not *tap*.

144

"Want to come to my tap class tonight?" Jane asked with a twirl.

"No, thanks." She tried to sound firm, not exasperated.

"You could have sub sandwiches at our house and then I could teach you some steps on my patio," said Jane. "You'd be good at tap, I bet." She tapped in a circle around Rose.

Right. She'd be about as good at tap dancing as Calamity Jane would be on cello.

Mrs. Lukashenko stood and put her hands on Jane's dancing shoulders. "Didn't your mother say it was time for supper? We best get ourselves along. Jesse and James, come now, please! Kiyo—can you get home okay?"

Mrs. Kiyo nodded. "I will just listen a bit and then head home. Thank you."

"Maybe some other time, Rose," said Jane. This is how her ridiculous invitation to tap class always ended. Rose said "No, thanks" and Jane said "Maybe some other time," like she really thought it would happen some other time.

"That plant looks like Rose!" said one of the Jacobi twins as they neared.

"Yeah—tall and skinny and growing so fast you

can almost *see* her stretch!" They laughed at each other's stupid jokes. "I bet Little Squirt wishes he had some of whatever makes that pumpkin vine grow."

Thomas grinned. He liked Jesse and James and he didn't mind that they called him Little Squirt. But it bothered Rose. She tried to think of something to say, some way to defend Thomas, but she came up short. No pun intended.

"Thank you again for lending us a little muscle this afternoon," Mr. Pickering said to Jesse and James, helping to usher them out. "Feel free to come by again; there're a lot more rocks to move around!"

Jesse and James flexed their skinny arms as they started down the driveway, then each of them tweaked Calamity Jane's ponytail. She stopped tapping long enough to growl at them, then ran ahead home.

"I'm bringing my guitar next time I come," called one of the outlaw boys over his shoulder. We'll make beautiful music together!" The boys laughed uproariously all the way down the driveway.

Rose started Suite no. 1's prelude just so she could pretend she wasn't listening. She'd make music with those goofball boys about the same time she learned to tap dance with their sister. Which was never.

Chapter 18
Building

Over the next week — the first week in June — several more neighbors Rose had never seen before made their way to the adjacent backyards filled with cello music and pumpkin vine. Nobody but Jesse and James picked up a shovel or trundled a wheelbarrow, but several more households brought food scraps for the compost. And Mrs. Kiyo became such a regular fixture that Mr. Pickering set up a lawn chair for her right in front of Rose.

Jeff and Simon, who lived behind them and across the alley, were the biggest contributors to the compost pile. They made baby food from organic fruits and vegetables for their fat, jolly baby, Oliver. Every night they brought over a giant bowl of scraps and chatted with Gram about vegetable recipes, diapers, and something called tummy time; it was their "air the baby" time.

Thomas didn't have much interest in Baby Oliver, but Rose thought he was cute. His ears stuck out adorably. And the letters of his name added up to eighty-one, and 8 − 1 = 7! Best of all, *he liked Bach!* He smiled and kicked his legs whenever Rose played.

And Rose played a lot—or at least a lot by Mrs. Holling's restricting standards. But she couldn't just stop in the middle of a movement, even though Mrs. Holling said she could. It made her feel off-balance, and half the time Mrs. Kiyo was listening. Plus, once she started, it was hard to stop, so sometimes she kept going without meaning to.

Thomas had put himself in charge of monitoring her practices, and he wielded his stopwatch like a weapon. "You went over by almost twenty minutes!" he accused on Wednesday. "And yesterday you were at least fifteen minutes over. And I know you pretend-practice on your bedpost at night. I just haven't told Mrs. Holling. Yet."

"I do not!" Rose said defensively. It was true that she was breaking her one-hour practice limit most days, but she hadn't practiced on her bedpost since she'd been harboring *Charlotte's Web*. Bedtime—under the covers with a flashlight—was the only time she could read it without fear of discovery. Besides, the bedpost really wasn't at the right angle to give her the satisfying feeling of playing cello. She'd done that when she was younger, but she was afraid to do it much now. It could ruin her form.

"I have to stay ready," said Rose. She picked up her bow and started Suite no. 5's last movement again at the trickiest spot. The Bach Competition was less than two weeks away. Mrs. Holling kept insisting she was ready, but Rose wasn't so sure. What did it mean to be ready?

By Friday, the additional scraps, Mrs. Kiyo's leaves, and the chicken poop overflowed the compost bin. It got to be too much to turn, and turning it, stirring all the different components, was critical to get actual compost quickly. And they needed it quickly. They were still spreading the bagged compost from Señor Ocampo's store. It was hard to keep up with the plant, and it was getting expensive. Thomas and Mr. Pickering decided another bin would be a good thing; it was hard to imagine they could ever have *too much* compost. They couldn't find the plans for the Best Compost Bin, however, which is what they'd used in building the first bin. Rose had made a copy of them before she returned *Composting 101* to the library, but now they were nowhere to be found.

"They probably got composted," said Thomas. Half the neighborhood was standing around the compost bin. "Pretty much anything that falls in there would be eaten up by the microbes before any of us noticed."

Simon, who had Baby Oliver strapped to his chest in a baby carrier, took a dramatic step back from the compost bin. Calamity Jane leaned over the side. Rose caught herself envisioning Jane falling in headfirst, tap shoes tapping up at the sky.

"It's okay—I don't need the plans," said Thomas. "I'll just use the one we have as a model."

"Need any help?" asked Jeff.

"Might ask you to cut some boards for him," said Mr. Pickering. "The first bin was built with scraps, but all the wood I have left is too long."

"Do you have a table saw?" Jeff asked.

Mr. Pickering nodded. "In the garage. I'm not quite steady enough to use it yet, though — and the kids can't use it at all, of course."

Thomas made a face. Mr. Pickering told grisly stories of table saw injuries and boards being thrown back to dent metal doors twenty feet away. This only seemed to fuel Thomas's interest in the power tool. The rule made by Mama, Gram, and Mr. Pickering was that Thomas was not to enter Mr. Pickering's garage without an adult.

Jeff followed Mr. Pickering into the garage. The saw's scream drowned out Rose's cello music as Jeff cut the boards so Thomas could get started.

Thomas quickly figured out a new Best Compost Bin. He seemed to have a sixth sense about how things went together. By the time the neighbors went home and Rose finished practicing, the project was almost done.

Rose ran through the final line of the fifth suite one more time — it was tricky — and as the last notes faded into the warm late-afternoon air, Thomas hammered the last nail into the slats of the bin.

"Done," he said matter-of-factly.

Rose stopped Thomas's stopwatch. The numbers

56:23 blinked up at her. It was amazing, really, that he could build a compost bin in under an hour. It would have taken her days. And it wouldn't have turned out as well.

"Nice job." She stretched her long legs out in front of her.

Thomas shrugged. "Thanks."

She looked at him. "What, no shout of triumph? No I-just-built-a-compost-bin-in-record-time dance?"

Again, Thomas shrugged. Which was weird.

Mr. Pickering wandered over. "Can I interest you three in some lemonade?" he said. "School's out— seems like we ought to celebrate."

"Sure," said Thomas absently. "Thanks."

Rose studied her brother. Why wasn't he whooping and running around to celebrate the end of the school year? *She* was glad to be done with school, anyway. She'd have more time to practice in this last week before the competition. Surely Mrs. Holling would drop the ridiculous maximum practice times now that school was out and the competition so close.

"Mrs. Kiyo?" asked Mr. Pickering.

"Thank you for the kind offer," said Mrs. Kiyo. "But I think I will return home now." She bowed her thanks to Rose and headed down the driveway.

Mr. Pickering hobbled back to his house to get lemonade.

"Might as well build another bin while I'm at it," Thomas said, nodding toward the new compost bin. "This one will be full in a couple of days if that baby keeps eating like he does."

Rose waited for him to ask her to help. All week he'd been trying to get her to do more for the pumpkin. She thought her suggestion to use chopsticks from Mrs. Kiyo's friend's Japanese restaurant to anchor the growing pumpkin vine was a rather significant contribution. They worked great—placed in an X formation, the wooden chopsticks held the vine firmly to the soil, encouraging it to send down more roots, which absorbed more water and nutrients. Mrs. Kiyo assured them they could use as many chopsticks as they needed. It was a masterful up-cycle. Rose had even helped to put them in, but it didn't keep Thomas from constantly haranguing her to do more.

"I could help," she offered. "I'm basically done with my hour."

"Basically?" Thomas asked. "How much longer do you have?"

"Barely any time: three minutes and thirty-seven seconds."

"You can play a whole movement in that time!" Thomas said. "You shouldn't be cutting corners now, when the competition is only a week away."

"It's nine days away," Rose said. Every day was important. She rubbed her head. Was Thomas actually telling her to practice *more*? And was she actually offering to practice *less*?

"What's going on, Thomas?"

"Nothing," he said.

"Seriously. What?" They could read each other better than anyone else. And he'd been acting strange all day. Something was up.

"It's just . . . what if you don't win?" asked Thomas. "Not that you won't," he added quickly.

"I might not," said Rose. She didn't spend much time thinking about it, but it was a possibility, of course. "If I don't, I'll just keep studying with Mrs. Holling and hope to have another opportunity to work with Harris—I mean, Maestro Waldenstein—in the future. Maybe when I go to college."

"But you can't keep studying with Mrs. Holling," Thomas said. He flinched and looked like he wanted to take it back—like it had hurt him to say the words somehow.

"What are you talking about?" Rose asked. "Even

when I'm studying with Maestro Waldenstein"—she liked using the word *when* as opposed to *if*—"I'll keep taking lessons from Mrs. Holling—maybe not every week, but it's not like she won't be my teacher anymore. We'll just have to be flexible."

"Mrs. Holling is moving," Thomas said. His voice shook. "To London."

Rose laughed.

"It's a three-year appointment," he whispered. He looked like he did right before he started to cry. "I heard Mama talking to Gram last night," he said finally. "I think they've known for a long time. I think Mrs. Holling's move is *why* you're doing this competition."

"You're wrong." Rose shook her head. "You misheard." It was ridiculous. "Don't you think I would know if Mrs. Holling was leaving?"

"You would if she told you," said Thomas.

"And why wouldn't she tell me?" She could hear how shrill her voice sounded. The Bach that usually ran inside her stopped, and her own voice echoed in her head: *Why wouldn't she tell me?*

"I think she didn't want to add pressure to the competition."

Mr. Pickering came out his back door and stood on his stoop. A tray with three glasses of lemonade was balanced precariously on his good arm. Rose could feel him watching them. The high notes—the first of the really difficult ones—from the sixth suite buzzed up inside her. Out of the corner of her eye, she saw Mr. Pickering turn around and go back into his house.

"She's going to teach at a school for musically gifted children," said Thomas.

Rose kept her eyes locked on Thomas's. Besides their curly dark hair, the other physical characteristic they shared was their eyes—big, brown, and beautiful, Mama said. He wouldn't joke about something like this. Why hadn't they told her?

"Mrs. Holling teaches you for free, I guess. And Mama and Gram can't afford another teacher good enough for you. You have to win this fellowship so you have someone to study with until Mrs. Holling gets back."

Chapter 19

Preparing for Competition

Rose played nothing but Suite no. 1 the entire weekend. It was the first suite she'd learned in its entirety, and it was so deep inside her, she hardly had to pay attention while she played. It ordered her thoughts, soothed her nerves, and comforted her heart. She went way over an hour of practice each day, but nobody said anything. Gram asked her at dinner on Saturday if she was feeling okay. Rose looked her right in the eye and assured her she was absolutely fine.

"You don't seem yourself, Rosebud," Mama said as she tucked her in Sunday night. Mama seldom tucked her in anymore. It felt babyish to Rose once she was taller than her mother. Her legs were so long and it was awkward for Mama to sit on the bed. But Mama had firmly scooched her over and perched herself on the edge of the mattress.

"I just have a lot on my mind."

"The competition?" Rose could hear Mama's concern. It was annoying.

Mama waited.

"Does Mrs. Holling teach me for free?"

For a minute, Rose didn't think her mother would answer, but finally she said, "Yes."

"Why?"

"Gram paid for your lessons in the beginning, out of her savings. She wanted to do it and I couldn't scrape together the money. You needed a better teacher than the one we started you with in community ed." Mama smiled and looked out the window. "But eventually that money ran out. We met with Mrs. Holling to tell her you would not be able to continue with her. But Mrs. Holling said she wanted to teach you *gratis*—at no cost to us. Music teachers sometimes do this, apparently, with their very best students. You should feel honored. Mrs. Holling has been very generous."

"Have you been working extra shifts so you can pay for lessons if . . . if lessons need to be paid for?"

Mama studied her for a minute. Rose met her eyes

and did not blink. Mama's eyes dropped first—to her lap, where she picked invisible lint off her pants.

"Rose, you don't need to worry about those things. Mrs. Holling thinks you have a very good chance at winning. Let's cross whatever bridges actually need crossing when we come to them; no need to conjure them up. Your job, honey, is simply to do your best." Mama smiled, but her smile didn't quite look real. "Are you nervous?"

"Not really." There was a sick feeling in her stomach that had not been there before, but she didn't think it was nerves.

"Cool as a cucumber, right? Do you want to practice meeting Maestro Waldenstein again?"

Rose shook her head. They had been over it several times. Mama would stand in a fake regal manner, pretending to be the maestro, and Rose would extend her right hand to shake hands. Though she was a lefty, everyone shook hands with their right hand. She knew to stand tall and confidently, to smile and say, "It's an honor to meet you, Maestro."

She was ready for Mama to leave. She stretched her legs, not-so-accidentally bumping her mother in the process. Mama sighed and stood. She leaned over to kiss Rose's forehead, and then turned out her light.

"No matter what happens, Rose, I am so proud of you. We'll figure out whatever needs figuring out."

Rose lay still in the darkness. She felt her left-hand fingers play through the prelude to Suite no. 1. She'd been playing it since she was a little girl. Funny, she still felt like that little girl. Just larger.

She was tired. She would not read *Charlotte's Web* tonight. Just sleep.

At breakfast, Thomas asked if he could go with Rose to her cello lesson. Mama stared at him over her news-paper. Normally, Thomas hated it when circumstances forced him to go along. And now that school was out, Rose's lessons were in the morning during prime pumpkin work time.

"Rose said Mrs. Holling is going to do a mock-competition—sort of a dress rehearsal for the real competition. I'd like to listen to that. Quietly, of course." He smiled his most winning smile.

Rose stirred her oatmeal. She had not said this to Thomas. She had no idea what Mrs. Holling's plans were for her last lesson before the competition. She was not surprised that Thomas asked to go, however, and she decided not to blow his cover. When she woke that morning, Thomas was sleeping on the floor beside her bed. He'd stuck close all weekend. He read in the living room while she played Suite no. 1 over and over again. He didn't talk to her or bother her. He just sat steadfast on the couch, reading a book about Greek mythology that was almost too large for him to hold properly.

"I suppose that's up to Rose," said Mama.

Rose stopped stirring her cereal. "It's fine."

Thomas's smile was full of gratitude. Rose tried to smile back.

After the breakfast dishes were done, Rose wrestled her hair into the tightest bun she could manage. The pull on her scalp was reassuring. She used Mama's hair spray to keep the wispies under control. When she was done, she felt secure and professional, even if the sides of her head were a little shiny from all the hair spray.

In the parking garage at the university, Rose wiggled into the backpack straps of her canvas cello case. The only downside to using Mrs. Holling's cello was that its hard case was a bright periwinkle blue. It was beautiful, but in a much-too-noticeable way. The canvas backpack was lighter; it was also a nice dull, inconspicuous brown. It provided little protection for the cello, but nothing was going to happen to it just going to lessons and back. She had tucked *Charlotte's Web* in the back pocket with her music. It seemed a good idea to have all of her comfort things with her for her last lesson before the competition.

"I'll carry it for you," said Thomas.

"No, thanks." The straps were adjusted for her height, and they didn't have time to change them. Besides, she felt more grounded when she carried the cello on her back.

"You don't think I'm big enough, do you?" Thomas asked.

"That's not it," said Rose, though in truth she wasn't sure; the cello was nearly as tall as her brother.

They walked down the black-and-white-tiled hallway of the music building to Mrs. Holling's studio. Mama's hard-soled shoes made a *clickety-clackety-clickety-clackety* sound—efficient sixteenth notes marching down the hall. Calamity Jane would love tap-dancing on this floor.

At the far end of the hallway, two people stood in the shadows. The figure on the right looked like Mrs. Holling. The person next to her, who was shorter than her by a few inches, looked like a man in a suit. Maybe Mrs. Holling *had* found someone to sit in on her lesson. Well, maybe that was good. She could get a feel for playing for someone before she sat in front of Harris Waldenstein, the someone who mattered.

Mama's *clickety-clacks* were punctuated occasionally by the stomp of Thomas's tennis shoes. Rose turned around carefully, so as not to get off-balance with the cello on her back. Thomas jumped from black square to black square on the floor tiles. She'd walked down this hall every Monday for five years and it had never occurred to her to jump the black squares. She and her brother were so different.

She turned back around and saw Mrs. Holling coming toward her, the short man hurrying down the hallway behind her. His shoes sounded somehow ominous in concert with Mrs. Holling's. It was like music Johannes Brahms would write: clipped, angry eighth notes set against light dancing triplets.

The man looked up at Rose and then immediately past her. Rose adjusted the cello straps on her shoulders and stood tall.

There was something familiar about him. His hair was meticulously combed. His suit had not one wrinkle. He looked as if he hadn't sat down since putting it on. He looked . . . crisp. Crunchy almost. And unusually short. Why was he so familiar?

"Rose!" said Mrs. Holling. "How fortuitous! You've come just in time! May I introduce you to *Maestro Harris Waldenstein*!"

Chapter 20
The Maestro

Harris Waldenstein! That's why he looked familiar! She knew his face from his book jacket, of course, and for weeks they'd been greeted by his picture on the billboard near the Washington Avenue Bridge that led into the university. He'd been smiling on the billboard. And he was much . . . larger.

"Maestro, this is the student I told you about, Rose Brutigan!" Mrs. Holling's top lip glistened. Was she *nervous*? Rose had never seen Mrs. Holling sweat— not even when she performed.

Rose towered over the maestro. She stepped back so he wouldn't have to look up at her. Not that he was looking at her at all, but she felt very large. Mama elbowed her gently.

Rose stuck out her right hand. She actually had to reach *down* a little bit. "It's an honor to meet you, Maestro Waldenstein," she said.

Her hand remained extended between them. The maestro continued to look past her.

"I do *not* shake hands," he said.

The back of Rose's neck prickled. She willed herself to smile as she withdrew her hand.

At that moment, Thomas leaped again, landing with a *stomp* on the black square behind Rose. Rose whirled around, forgetting about the cello on her back—until she felt a hollow *thunk* through the body of the instrument.

A piercing shriek rang through the hallway.

The maestro!

She had hit Maestro Harris Waldenstein with her cello!

Rose turned slowly. The maestro was down on the floor. She had knocked his crisp wrinkle-freeness to the ground!

"I am so, *so* sorry!" Rose said. *Sorry*—such an inadequate word. She'd *knocked down the maestro with her cello*! She was too tall—too clumsy.

She extended her hand down to the maestro. He didn't take it and he wouldn't look up at her. He stared in fury at her kneecaps.

"Unbelievable!" the maestro exploded. He jerked his shirt cuffs, snapping them—white and bright—out of his suit jacket sleeves again. He got awkwardly to his feet.

"Oh, dear," said Mrs. Holling. "We're not off to a great start, I see." She tried to brush off the maestro's sleeve, but he jerked away. "But, Maestro, I promise you'll forget all about this unfortunate incident when you hear Rose audition for you on Sunday."

"*Th-this* is the student you speak so highly of?" sputtered the maestro. "How can she possibly be as good as you say? She must *dwarf* the cello!" He snapped his shirt cuffs again, as if everything depended on them being properly displayed. "I can tell you right now that she is not what I am looking for in a fellow." His voice was ice—sharp and cold. And although it wasn't loud, the tiled hallway magnified it for all to hear.

Finally, he looked up at her—and when he did, Rose stopped breathing. Nobody had ever looked at her like that—with such anger, such *hate*.

"It's unnatural," the maestro muttered as he snatched up his briefcase. "Girls should not be that tall.

Nobody should be that tall. She is no cellist—she is a . . . an Amazon! And I do not give fellowships to Amazons."

His words bounced off the walls and floor tiles, slapping Rose again and again: *Amazon . . . Tall . . . Unnatural . . . Amazon . . . She must dwarf the cello . . . Girls should not be that tall . . . Nobody should be that tall . . . I do not give fellowships to AMAZONS . . .*

A resounding *stomp* silenced the sharp echoes. Thomas had landed on the black square immediately in front of Maestro Waldenstein.

"The Amazons were a tribe of wild, warlike women," said Thomas, as if it were a greeting. "They rode horses faster and better and fought harder than any men. They didn't have much use for men, really. Except to make more Amazons. If they captured men in battle, they maimed them so they couldn't revolt. That made the men their prisoners—their slaves."

Thomas spoke as if the maestro had asked him for the most pertinent facts on Amazonian history. Everyone was too stunned to move—including the maestro.

"Most people believe the Amazons were very tall and beautiful women. I expect that's why Rose reminds you of them."

167

Rose's heart thumped in her chest. Her eyes burned and her throat tightened.

Thomas took several big steps back, slowly raised an imaginary bow and arrow, and carefully aimed at Maestro Waldenstein's heart. "And did you know an Amazon warrior would cut off her right breast to make shooting with a bow and arrow easier? Rose doesn't have bazooms yet, really," continued Thomas, "but if she did, she'd cut one off *in a second* if it would help her bowing on the cello. That's how much she loves the cello. That's how *good* she is. She doesn't need you, Maestro."

Thomas released the imaginary arrow. The maestro's eyes widened, and he fell back against the wall as if he really had been hit. Mama and Mrs. Holling gasped.

Thomas turned and stepped onto a black square as if he were stepping onto the high board in a diving competition. He crouched and then leapt, landing three full tile patterns away, his feet perfectly centered in a black square. His grin was enormous.

Chapter 21

Two-by-Two

Maestro Waldenstein left looking furious. Or maybe embarrassed. It was hard to tell. Mrs. Holling hugged Rose and promised she'd call later that night. Thomas walked down the hall between Rose and Mama as if it were any other Monday.

The cello was heavy. Rose stopped to adjust it on her back, but it didn't help. She felt fidgety as soon as she got in the van—like she needed to stretch her too-long legs. She shifted the front seat back, remembering too late to double-check that the cello was in the opposite backseat. Fortunately, Thomas was sitting behind her with plenty of legroom, even after she moved back. She rolled down the window. The van was too confining and small for what she was feeling. Mama turned on the radio to a news channel as they left the parking garage.

Rose stared out the window and let the words of other people's snarls, catastrophes, and wars blow over her with the hot summer wind. When they crossed the Washington Avenue Bridge, she turned away from the billboard with Maestro Waldenstein's face on it.

"Hey, look!" said Thomas. "His middle initial is *A*. What does that do to the sum of his name?"

Rose turned quickly to look. Sure enough: Maestro Harris A. Waldenstein. How had she never seen that *A*? He wasn't the interesting prime number of 199 but rather 200. One of the most uninteresting numbers to be found. A double zero. She should have known.

When they arrived home, Rose unloaded her cello from the backseat, and Thomas broke the silence. "You still want to help me build the next compost bin?"

"No, I need to pr—" Rose stopped. Did she need to practice, now that things were . . . like they were?

Mama opened the back door to the house and called over her shoulder, "Go help him, Rose, honey. I need to talk with Gram. Then we'll have lunch."

Rose was so tired. Now that she'd calmed down, she felt like a wrung-out washcloth. Only the faintest phrases of Bach's suites whispered through her. She shrugged out of the cello backpack's straps and carefully leaned the instrument against the back steps.

Thomas was already over by the wood slats Jeff had cut, sorting them into various lengths and widths.

"What do you want me to do?" Rose asked.

Thomas pointed to a jumbled pile of wood on one side of the driveway.

"Go through that pile and pull out four two-by-twos that are about as high as your waist. They'll be the corner posts. I'll make sure we've got the right number of slats for the sides. There's plenty of chicken wire." He looked around at the materials. "We should be able to put it together before lunch with both of us working on it. I'll do the hammering."

He flashed her a smile and started the stopwatch. Rose looked at the pile of wood she'd been assigned to go through.

"What are two-by-twos?" she asked.

Thomas dug in the pile and pulled out a long, thick stick of wood. His hand fit almost all the way around it. He hoisted it up and held it next to himself. It was much taller than he was.

"This is a two-by-two. See? It's square. Two inches by two inches."

"And close to eight feet long," said Rose, looking up.

"Probably exactly eight feet long," said Thomas. "That's the usual length of wood Mr. P. buys. But there should be shorter pieces in this pile. We'll save this one for Jeff to cut in half for another bin."

Rose gingerly picked through the scraps of wood, careful not to smash her fingers. Although maybe it didn't matter. There would be no fellowship, and surely Mrs. Holling's cello would need to be returned before she left for London. That left her without a cello teacher and without a cello. What difference would it make if she had a bruised finger?

She dug in the pile of wood for several minutes before finding two waist-high two-by-twos. But there were no other pieces cut to length.

She looked to see what Thomas was doing. Lying on the driveway were four very neat "sides" for the compost bin. He had lined up the boards leaving a few inches between them, which would allow for the proper ventilation. He was now measuring out the chicken wire that would go over them. Her brother was a compost-bin-building machine.

The antsy, bothered feeling welled up inside her

again. She wanted to do something for Thomas. To thank him—for telling her about Mrs. Holling when no one else would; for sticking by her side all weekend, even while she played the same thing over and over again; and most of all, for the way he'd stood up to Maestro Waldenstein. Even though it was embarrassing, she was grateful.

Her brother had asked her to find four boards, and she'd found only half of that. She looked at the long two-by-two lying on the ground. It wasn't that big—maybe she could break it. As soon as she picked it up, she realized how impossible that would be. It was heavy for a skinny piece of wood. Awkward like her because it was so long. And extremely solid—it did not even bow as she stood holding it in the middle.

"Got the corner posts, Rosie?" Thomas asked.

"I only found two," said Rose.

Thomas walked over to the pile and dug through it, not the least bit careful of his fingers. She cringed watching him.

"Shoot," he said softly. He looked at the length of the long two-by-two Rose held. "It'd be perfect if we could just cut it in half."

"Let's do it, then." The words came out on their own, surprising her.

"Do what?"

"Cut it in half." She nodded at Mr. Pickering's garage.

Thomas stared at her. "You know I'm not allowed to use the table saw."

"Yes, but nobody ever said *I* couldn't." It was as if she were listening to someone else. Her voice didn't even sound like hers.

"Don't you think that was . . . assumed?" said Thomas.

"Fine. Go see if Mr. Pickering is home, then—maybe he parked out front."

Rose sat down next to her cello on the back stoop. She could feel the hair spray failing—curls popping out around her face and at the back of her neck. She tried to calm the fidgety feeling inside with some Bach. She called up the usual—the prelude to Suite no. 1, her good friend in times of trouble. It obediently ran through. But it was too fast and sloppy—it failed to settle her.

Chapter 22
Doing Something

Calamity Jane tap-danced around the corner of the house. Rose startled; she hadn't even heard the warning taps coming up the driveway.

"Hey!" said Jane. She did a shuffle-hop-spin step and flung out her arms as part of her greeting. "Do you know where the *Charlotte's Web* book is?"

"No," said Rose. She glanced at her cello case to be sure the book wasn't peeking out.

"It's weird," said Jane. "I didn't get it the last time it was my week—I got confused on the schedule. But Daddy wants me to be sure to bring it when I visit so he can read it to me, and it's never at the library when I check. I haven't read it since *April*." She made a sad face. "I don't think I've *ever* gone so long without reading it. It should be the shelf week now—me and Mrs. Lukashenko checked the schedule in the back. But it's not on the shelf."

"Maybe someone checked it out," said Rose.

"Nobody but you and me checks it out," said Jane.

"Well, maybe someone *did*."

"Nope, Mrs. Lukashenko says the computer shows that you checked it *in* on May eighth, but nobody has checked it *out* since then." She stopped tapping and looked curiously at Rose. "So you missed one of your weeks, too."

Where was Thomas?

"Did you poke it back when it was on the shelf?" Jane whispered.

"Yes." She did not need this right now.

"Do you think somebody *stole* it?" said Calamity Jane, still whispering.

"Why would anyone steal *Charlotte's Web*?" asked Rose.

"Because it's *autographed*," said Jane. "It's worth a lot of money."

"Mrs. Lukashenko doesn't think that autograph is real," said Rose.

Jane grinned. "Oh, it's real, all right."

"How do you know?"

"Can you keep a secret?" she asked. Before Rose could answer, Jane blurted, "My daddy is E. B. White!"

Rose didn't know what to say. *Charlotte's Web* was an old book. Calamity Jane's daddy was not nearly old enough to have written it. Probably Calamity Jane's *grand*daddy wasn't old enough.

"Why do you think your daddy is E. B. White?" she asked carefully.

"He told me! He signed that book for me on my eighth birthday. 'Calamity Jane!' he said. 'I'm going to sign this book that I wrote for you. Just we will know that secret.'" Jane grinned again. "Of course, now I've told you, but we're friends and I know you won't tell anybody. Daddy said it was our secret."

"But your daddy's last name is Jacobi," said Rose.

"Eddie Burt Jacobi is his real name, but E. B. White is his pen name! You're the only person I've told. Daddy said we can't tell anyone, because he wants to stay anonymous."

Anonymous in jail?

She needed Calamity Jane to go home. "Listen, Calam—Jane. Thomas and I are kind of busy right now. I don't know where *Charlotte's Web* is. It's not my week." That was true, at least. "And I don't want to tap-dance."

"Okay," said Calamity Jane. "But you won't tell anyone about the autograph, will you?"

Who would she tell? She shook her head.

Jane smiled and started tapping backward down the driveway. "This is called a paradiddle. I just learned it!" The step sounded like the word: *paradiddle-paradiddle-paradiddle.*

As Jane disappeared down the driveway, Rose took down her hair and rewrapped her bun. Without a hairbrush, there wasn't much hope for the curls that had sprung out around the bottom, but she felt tidier, at least. She focused her gaze on the pumpkin plant across the yard. It had grown since they left it that morning, she was sure of it. It looked like it was trying to come to her. Reach out to her. It was *so* green. She had not known there were so many shades of green before this pumpkin plant came into their lives.

Thomas slouched back across the yards. "No luck. Should I go see if Jeff is home?"

Baby Oliver was probably taking a nap or something. They didn't need to bother Jeff.

"Let's just finish it up," said Rose. She sounded

confident. But her heart hammered so loudly she couldn't hear the Bach.

"Right," said Thomas. He looked at her like she was crazy. "But we can't use the table saw, and that's what it'll take to cut this thing."

"Probably," said Rose. She tried to sound casual. "But it's just one cut."

"One cut neither of us can make," said Thomas.

"Well, *you* can't." Rose rolled her shoulders back and stood up straight and tall. "You've been told a thousand times not even to go into Mr. Pickering's garage. But like I said, nobody has ever told *me* I can't go near the table saw."

"Yeah, because *why would they?*" said Thomas. "You'd never *do* that! You won't even hold a hammer."

"This is different." She shrugged in what she hoped was a careless and unconcerned way, as if what she was saying made perfect sense. Because it did. Kind of.

"What's going on with you?" said Thomas.

"What do you mean?"

"You never do anything. Why this? Why now?"

"I never *do anything*? What's that supposed to mean?" Her voice was too loud. They both looked up to the kitchen window. No sign of Mama or Gram.

Gram had turned on the air conditioner that morning, which probably drowned out their voices; it was hot and supposed to get hotter. No wonder she felt sweaty.

Thomas started sorting through the wood again. "You just do what other people tell you to do," he explained. "What you're supposed to do. And what you're good at. And now you want to use a table saw? Which I've been told not to do, and which you absolutely should not do, and which you don't even know *how* to do."

His tone wasn't mean, but his words hit hard. A horrible lump rose in Rose's throat, and her head throbbed in the deep place behind her eyes. She looked down at her brother. His face was blurred and multiplied by her tears, a kaleidoscope of Thomases.

Why couldn't she be different? Not so predictable and concerned with being the best. More like Thomas, who dug through woodpiles without worrying about his fingers. She didn't exactly know how to make this change in herself, but maybe she could start by doing something she didn't know how to do, something no one would expect her to do: she'd saw a board in half. It wasn't much, but it was a start.

"It's just one cut, Thomas." She cleared her throat.

"And then we can say we built a compost bin in under . . . what? *Thirty minutes?*"

Thomas's eyes slid to his stopwatch. She had him. They both turned to look at the kitchen window again. Still no sign of Mama or Gram. The windows were closed up against the heat.

"Okay," said Thomas. "One cut."

Music swelled inside her. It wasn't Bach. What was it? Beethoven? Yes, Beethoven's Symphony no. 5. It wasn't the ominous four-note beginning—it was the ending she heard inside her now. She had never played it, but somehow it was in her and it filled her with courage. She picked up her cello from where it leaned against the steps. She couldn't just leave it unattended in the yard—what if Calamity Jane came back? She shrugged it onto her back and felt even better. Beethoven was the perfect music for the moment! A curl fell out of her bun and over her eye. She tucked it firmly behind her ear and led the way to Mr. Pickering's garage.

Chapter 23
One Cut

The side door to Mr. Pickering's garage was unlocked, which was unusual when Mr. Pickering was gone, but lucky for them. Once inside, Rose went to the windows of the big garage door, stood on her tiptoes, and double-checked that the car wasn't parked in the alley where they couldn't see it. Thomas switched on the light inside the door.

"You've been in here before," said Rose, turning around to face him.

"Once."

"With Mr. Pickering?"

"No," admitted Thomas. "By myself. I just wanted to see it."

She followed his eyes to a heavy-looking tool mounted on a square metal table. She walked back to the side door and locked it; she didn't want to be surprised by anyone walking in and finding them there.

Thomas walked around the machine, admiring it, brushing the dust off the top. Any hesitation he'd had was gone. He found the power cord and plugged it in. The table was shiny and cold looking, but Rose didn't see a blade. What cut the wood?

Thomas handed her the giant two-by-two. Rose leaned on the tall piece of wood and hoped her legs would stop shaking. She was grateful for the cello's weight on her back. It steadied her.

Thomas moved a couple of small boxes away from the machine, then turned a crank on the side of the table. A circular brushed-silver blade rose out of the table.

Rose steadied her breathing. She tried to summon the prelude to Bach's first suite again, but it came to her in shards. The blade had vicious-looking teeth— something it would need, of course, to cut through wood.

Thomas examined the front of the table again. He leaned back and pulled a knob, and the gleaming blade was an instant blur. The noise it made was a much louder version of what they had heard coming out of Mr. Pickering's garage in the past. Almost immediately he pushed the knob back in. The sound died, and the blade whirred back into focus.

"Do you think Mama and Gram can hear?" Rose asked.

"Nope. Air conditioner is on, remember? It's just really loud in here. Besides, it should only take a second to make the cut."

She shouldn't do this. This wasn't the way to begin reinventing herself. She should find another way to repay Thomas for his kindness — and prove to him that she wasn't as cautious and predictable as he thought.

Thomas took the tall two-by-two and leaned it against the table saw. "Sure you want to do this?"

The doubt in his voice made her stand up straighter. One cut. That's all it would take. Thomas couldn't do it — that would be disobeying — so she had to. She nodded. Yes, she wanted to do this simple thing. For her brother. For herself.

"That's the knob that starts it up," Thomas said, pointing. "Here, I'll hold your cello while you make the cut."

"It's Mrs. Holling's cello, not mine," she reminded

him—them. "And don't try to wear the case. The straps are adjusted for me—it'll be too big for you."

Thomas rolled his eyes.

"Just stand over there and hold it in front of you." She slid the straps off her back and transferred the cello to Thomas.

"Both hands!"

Thomas obediently used two hands to carry the instrument across the garage.

Rose stepped up to the table saw. She raised the long two-by-two and carefully hoisted it onto the metal table. Her arms shook. She scooted it forward until it was an inch away from the vicious blade, and then adjusted the wood so approximately half of it was on one side of the table and half on the other.

She could do this.

"Aren't there guards or safety somethings?" she asked, not taking her eyes off the ferocious teeth of the blade.

Thomas appeared at her side with the cello.

"I told you to stand over there!"

"Geez—I've got both hands on it. Relax! I'm looking for the safety thingies."

He kept the cello straight and tall with both hands

as he bent and looked under and around the table. Rose tried to take a deep breath; was it possible to hold your breath without meaning to?

"I think there's something on that side that makes sure the wood stays straight." Thomas pointed to the right side of the table. "But you don't need it for this. Besides, it's made for right-handed people, and you're a lefty."

This wouldn't be the first time something was made only for right-handers. And it *was* just one cut. What was there to guard against?

"Put one hand on one side and the other on the other side," instructed Thomas. "You're just going to push the wood through in one smooth movement."

Thomas backed up to the place where Rose had originally put him. He dutifully held the cello with both hands.

There was a small sound from outside the garage — a soft tapping. They both pivoted in their spots to look. Rose was glad she had locked the door; all she needed was Calamity Jane to tap-dance into the garage and rat them out for using the saw.

No other sounds. She checked that the middle of the two-by-two board was lined up with the blade.

One cut.

She pulled the knob. The saw blade whirred and the horrible metallic scream filled the garage again. She fought the urge to cover her ears. They should be wearing ear protection. This was a terrible noise for a musician's ears. But it would be over quickly. And she would have *done* something—something unexpected and courageous. Something for Thomas. Something for herself, too.

She planted her feet wide and strong and placed her hands on the piece of wood as far away from the blade as she could. She pushed the wood up to the whirring blade. She had to hurry; that horrible sound had been going too long already.

For as powerful as the machine sounded, the two-by-two did not zip through as Rose assumed it would. She had to push. The saw's scream changed pitch as it cut into the wood. The power of the machine thrilled through the two-by-two and up her arms, through her torso, and down into her firmly planted feet. She congratulated herself on having planted her feet wide, and she leaned into the resistance. She spotted a small knot in the wood, a discoloration the blade was working through. She pushed harder.

Suddenly, there was no resistance at all. In a split second, the right half of the two-by-two splintered and flew off the table behind Rose. A terrible sound—the sound of shattered cello music—shot through her. Rose turned. Thomas stood holding the cello, a look of horror on his face. The cello's canvas case was crumpled in the middle.

Before Rose could make sense of what she saw, the big garage door rose, the bright sun lightening the darkness of the garage. Mr. Pickering stooped under the door as it rose. Calamity Jane stood, eyes wide, in front of Mr. Pickering's car.

Rose turned back to the saw. As she did, she saw blood spattered across the shiny surface of the table. Her left hand gave a sudden throb.

The only sound was the table saw's scream.

Chapter 24
After

Rose did not look at her left hand as Mama wrapped it in a towel with ice and pushed her into the backseat of the van. Rose felt as if she'd somehow stretched up into the trees and was looking down at what was happening below. She couldn't make out what anyone was saying. The music was too loud.

Where was the music coming from? And *why* was it so loud? She watched from above as everyone scurried around. They seemed so far away, yet the music was close, as if she were wearing headphones. What was it? Beethoven? No. Bach. Suite no. 5 in C Minor. Had it always sounded so sad?

The music crescendoed as Gram wrestled the cello out of Thomas's hands. It was obviously broken. Mrs. Holling's cello. Thomas kept crying, "No! No! No!" He hated it when things were taken away from him. Mr. Pickering held him, his head bent low, thin gray wisps mingling with Thomas's thick brown curls.

Gram buckled Rose in the backseat and then slid herself into the front passenger seat and rolled down the window. Sweat was pouring down her face. Mama was already in the driver's seat, and as soon as Mr. Pickering put Thomas into the backseat beside Rose, Mama started backing the van down the driveway. She and Gram were talking, their voices low and slow. Mr. Pickering was saying something, too. The garbled sounds did not match the movement of their lips, and the music kept getting louder. They needed Bach to order their polyphony, bring their voices into harmony so she could understand what they were trying to decide.

And then, a solo voice rose above the others.

"HOW WILL SHE PLAY HER CELLO?" Jane bellowed.

Everything stopped—the voices, the music, the van. Mama put her head on the steering wheel. Gram grabbed Mama's arm, then rubbed her hunched-over back, whispering something Rose could not hear.

Through the window, she saw that Mr. Pickering held the wailing Calamity Jane just as he had held Thomas, both arms wrapped tightly around her shoulders.

Mama lifted her head, wiped her cheeks, and finished backing out of the driveway. As they made their way down the street, Rose turned to look at Thomas. He sat perfectly straight, looking at Mama's headrest. With eyes so dry they burned, Rose watched giant tears fall down the front of her brother's faded T-shirt, streaking it purply gray.

Rose did not look at her left hand as the emergency room staff examined it. Instead, she watched Thomas. He sat on a chair in the corner of the exam room, straight and silent. So still. People rushed around him. Nobody seemed to notice that his T-shirt was drenched and sticking to his chest.

The music was back, still too loud. She couldn't think which suite it was. It was spinning out of control. Mrs. Holling would want her to stop, think, and breathe, and then begin again and make it right.

A nurse took Rose's uninjured right hand and rubbed something cold and wet over the top of it. Where was her bow? Clearly, she was not playing this Bach that was so out of control; she had no bow.

Rose's teeth chattered. She was suddenly as cold as whatever had been rubbed on her right hand. She watched the nurses try to poke a needle into the vein on the top of her cold, wet hand. They spoke to her, though she couldn't hear what they said.

"Turn down the music," Rose said. But the words didn't seem to come out right, and she'd forgotten to say please. She tried again.

A nurse looked at her and said very clearly, "There is no music, sweetheart."

Rose's right hand shook so badly that the nurses could not get the needle in. She tried to hold it still, tried to cooperate, but she was too far away. She had grown taller again—the emergency room could not contain her, she was so tall. She watched from above as they wrapped her in a blanket. It was soft and warm. They pushed her shoulders gently to get her to lie back on the bed, then gave her a shot in her right arm.

The heavy doors of the emergency room swung open. Mrs. Holling! Rose tried to sit up, but something held her down. She only wanted to ask her teacher to turn down the music. It was not a good recording. She shouldn't be listening to such a poor performance so close to the Bach Competition.

Rose did not look at her left hand as Mrs. Holling did. She watched Mrs. Holling's face. It blurred at the edges, but Rose saw Mrs. Holling press her perfectly lipsticked lips together as if trying not to speak or cry. A doctor moved Mrs. Holling aside and then bent close over Rose's hand.

Rose met Mrs. Holling's eyes over the doctor's head, but before she could ask her teacher about the music, sudden pain stabbed through her left hand. She looked down at her fingers for the first time since watching the two-by-two go through the table saw. She willed her eyes to sharpen the fuzzy edges and her brain to make sense of what she saw.

The fingers that pressed the strings of her cello— the fingers that made the notes that made the music those fingers looked . . . wrong. Part of her middle finger was . . . open. She saw whiteness inside. Something sour came up in the back of her throat. She swallowed it back down. *What had she done?*

The music slowed, and the room's bright light dimmed. People turned to shadows; their voices softened to murmurs. Out of the noise and clamor came something amazing. What was it? She'd heard it so many times before. . . . Ah, Suite no. 1's prelude. Her old friend. Relief and warmth flooded her body. So beautiful. Everything would be okay. They would fix her fingers. She would play again.

As the gorgeous, comforting notes faded to silence, Rose turned to look at Thomas, but darkness covered her eyes.

Chapter 25

The Damage

Rose, honey . . . ?" Mama's voice called from far away.
Rose tried to open her eyes. It was bright. And very
white. She couldn't keep her eyes open.

"That's all right. You rest some more."

She dreamed the pumpkin plant was growing
through the brilliant whiteness of the room. Its green
vine pulsed and brightened, then spiraled to fill the daz-
zling white space. The room smelled like the pumpkin
patch: soil and leaves, worms and sunshine . . .

The next time she tried to open her eyes, they worked
better. Thomas sat on the bed beside her, his eyes wide,
his T-shirt dry.

"Finally!" he said.

She desperately needed something to drink. She'd no more thought this than a straw poked between her lips. The liquid tasted sweet and sour at the same time. She tried to shift so there was more room for Thomas on the bed.

"They gave you a shot to make you sleep." Thomas made a face; he hated shots. "You slept through lunch."

Rose looked around. Mama, Gram, Mrs. Holling, and Mr. Pickering stood at the foot of the bed as if in a family photograph. Mama's eyes were too shiny. Mr. Pickering looked exhausted.

"Me and Mr. P. went to McDonald's. There's actually a McDonald's here in the hospital. Weird, huh? Anyway, that's where we got you this lemonade." He held up a giant cup with a straw sticking out. The red-and-yellow markings on the cup hurt her eyes. She looked up at the ceiling. Too white. She looked at Mr. Pickering's gray hair. Better.

"What did you eat for lunch?" she asked. Her voice was slow and scratchy.

"I didn't feel much like eating," said Thomas. He shrugged. "So we just got lemonade."

A smiley nurse came in.

"She's awake! How are you feeling, sweetie?" Without waiting for a reply, the nurse pushed a button, and the bed began to move. As Rose was moved to an upright position, she saw that her right hand was hooked to tubes.

"Antibiotics, pain meds, fluids," said the nurse. She smiled like this was the greatest thing ever. "We'll take them out now. Just wanted to get you started while you were here. As soon as you see Dr. Clare again, you can head home." She pulled on gloves, then gently peeled off the tape on Rose's right hand and removed the IV. It didn't hurt at all.

"We'll send you home with more meds to take by mouth. Can you swallow pills?"

Rose nodded. Did they think she was a little kid?

Finally, Rose looked at her left hand. It was wrapped in bright-white bandages. Only her thumb and pinky poked out. The rest of her hand looked like a club. She lifted her arm off the bed. Her wrist was wrapped to a thin board, unable to bend.

"It doesn't hurt," she said cautiously. She yawned. Her eyes felt so heavy.

"Good," said the nurse. "That may change, though."

The bandages were unbearably white. There was no blood. That must be good.

"Dr. Clare will be by soon," said the nurse.

Rose didn't open her eyes right away when she woke the second time. She could hear Mama and Gram talking.

"Well, that does give us hope, then, Doctor," whispered Mama. She didn't *sound* hopeful. "Thank you."

"Let's see your girl now," said a voice that sounded familiar. Rose couldn't place it. She tried to open her eyes to see who it was and was surprised when they opened right up.

The smiling nurse was on one side of the bed, and someone tall in blue scrubs and a white lab coat was on the other.

"Hello, Rose." The voice had a beautiful resonance to it. Like the cello. "I'm Dr. Clare. We didn't have a chance to properly meet earlier. I'm a hand surgeon. I was called to your case when you came through our emergency room." She paused and smiled. "May I sit here on the edge of your bed?"

Rose nodded. Dr. Clare even sat tall.

"I'd like to talk with you about your hand injury. Do you think you might like something to drink while we talk?"

Thomas held out the gigantic McDonald's cup. Rose reached with her left hand to take it, and then she realized that wouldn't work. Embarrassed, she switched to her right hand, taking the cup awkwardly. She almost dumped it on Dr. Clare.

Everyone found somewhere else to look. Except Dr. Clare. She bent her head gracefully and searched out Rose's eyes. Rose concentrated on the coolness of the cup in her right hand.

"Your mother tells me you are a strong lefty. Your right hand is going to get a workout these next few weeks."

Rose forced herself to meet Dr. Clare's eyes. They were a warm, comforting light brown. She had a few wrinkles around them—the kind made from laughing. She wasn't wearing any makeup, and her hair was pulled into a ponytail. She seemed to be beaming something at Rose. It felt like the sun on a warm spring day. Rose tried to sit taller.

"Let's talk about what has happened," said Dr. Clare. "Your middle finger is broken and has a torn tendon. I'm suspecting some significant nerve damage as well. In any event, surgery is required."

Dr. Clare turned to Mama and Gram. "It isn't a problem to wait a few days, and my surgery schedule is full until Thursday. I'd like to work with Rose, unless you have someone else in mind?"

Mama's eyes filled with tears. She blinked them back and shook her head. Gram put her hand on Mama's arm. Rose started to shake. Thomas moved closer, his knee steadying her leg.

"Thank you, Doctor," said Gram.

"Your ring finger has sustained some damage as well," continued Dr. Clare, "but I'm hopeful it might experience some healing on its own. I will know more at your pre-op appointment when we take another look."

She handed Mama a business card from the pocket of her white coat. "You'll need to call my office and schedule the pre-op appointment for Wednesday morning. That will give me a better idea of what Thursday's surgery will entail." She turned back to Rose. "We might have to help the skin along in the scarring process—just to make sure it heals as well as it can. I've put in a couple of small, loose stitches to hold things closed for the next few days. I'm hopeful some of the nerves will repair their connections on their own. Younger patients usually come back from accidents like this better than adults. Your body is still growing, which is a good thing."

A good thing for the first time.

"Your pointer finger looks pretty good—just a flesh wound." She said this with a smile, as if she'd made a small joke. Then her expression grew serious again. "Your middle finger is my biggest concern."

Rose's middle finger had been Mrs. Holling's biggest concern when she started studying cello with her. It took Rose a while to learn how to curve it just so, to get the height necessary to produce the best tone and allow for her vibrato to develop.

"We won't know about permanent nerve damage for several weeks."

Permanent nerve damage. The words echoed in Rose's head.

"How are you doing with this information, Rose?" Dr. Clare asked after a moment of silence.

She could not imagine what she was supposed to say.

"What I need you to do between now and surgery is keep that hand 'quiet.' No trying to bend the fingers. Keep it elevated above your heart as much as you can. We want to minimize swelling before surgery. Do you have any questions?"

Rose shook her head. She had questions—she just wasn't sure she wanted to know the answers.

"I hear you're a gifted cellist," said Dr. Clare softly. "You won't be playing cello this summer, I'm afraid. This might be the hardest part of the recovery for you." Dr. Clare's steady brown eyes searched out Rose's again. "Together we'll do our very best to get your fingers back . . . to a new normal. You will have to work hard, but I understand that is how you work. We're all in this together." Dr. Clare gestured to Thomas, Mama, Gram, and Mr. Pickering, then back to Rose. It was then that Rose noticed that Mrs. Holling was no longer there. "We'll work like a fine musical ensemble."

Rose tried to smile—it seemed like the polite thing to do.

Far down the hall, hospital machines beeped. Dr. Clare stood. She had to be more than six feet tall.

Rose wondered if they could put the IV back in her hand and pump in some Bach, because she couldn't summon any music from within. She had been trying the whole time Dr. Clare talked. She couldn't remember how the suites sounded. Couldn't remember the first note of Suite no. 1's prelude.

The music was gone.

Chapter 26
Pre-Op Appointment

When Dr. Clare unwrapped the bandages around her fingers Wednesday morning, Rose did not know what to expect. There hadn't been much pain since the accident, except for some dull throbbing from time to time. There still wasn't any blood, really, and for some reason this bolstered her. She sat up straighter and looked closer at her fingers. Maybe they weren't so awfully hurt. . . .

"Okay, let's take a look here," said Dr. Clare. She moved a small tray of odd-looking instruments closer to her on the table and lowered her glasses onto her nose. She took something that looked like large tweezers off the tray and bent low over Rose's hand, blocking her view of her fingers.

"I need you to tell me when you feel one point or two," said Dr. Clare just as Rose felt two small pokes on her pinky finger.

"Two," said Rose.

"One or two?"

"Two." Her ring finger.

"One or two?"

"One." Her ring finger again.

"One or two?"

"Two." Her pointer finger.

The test, the game — Rose didn't know what to call it — went on for quite some time. Sometimes she felt two points on either side of her finger, sometimes one in the center. And then there came the time she felt nothing.

"One point or two?" said Dr. Clare.

Rose waited to feel the points.

"One or two?" repeated Dr. Clare. "And here? One or two?"

Nothing.

"And one more," said Dr. Clare. Rose felt a touch on the side of her middle finger. She wouldn't have called it a point exactly, but it was something.

"ONE," she said too loudly. "I mean, I think felt . . . something . . . there."

Dr. Clare lifted Rose's hand, turned it very gently, then bent closely over it again. Rose could hear her breathing. And Mama and Thomas, too. Her own breaths were too shallow to hear.

Rose didn't know where to look. She didn't know if Dr. Clare was poking on her fingers and she couldn't feel it, or if she was simply looking rather than touching now. Mama and Thomas were behind her, though she didn't really want to look at them, either. She focused on the painting hanging on the wall above Dr. Clare's head. She could not have said what it was. Abstract. Whatever it was, it was uninteresting in the extreme. She closed her eyes and waited.

"What I like is this," said Dr. Clare finally, sitting back up and perching her glasses on top of her head. "There's not much swelling, which means you followed my directions to keep it quiet, elevated, and immobile for a few days. There's no sign of infection, which is also very nice. Your ring finger has some significant surface damage, but no nerve damage. I will do a bit to help the skin to scar well, but not much else." She smiled at Rose. "This is all excellent."

"What about her middle finger?" Mama asked.

"Well," said Dr. Clare. "What we have there is a partial amputation."

Rose's stomach flip-flopped and she felt herself break into a sweat. Dr. Clare placed a hand gently on her arm.

"Let me explain what that means. Your finger is broken. In addition, your flexor tendon is cut, as is your extensor tendon. Tendons connect muscles to bones and allow you to move your fingers. Your flexor tendon lets you bend your finger in; the extensor tendon lets you open your hand and straighten your fingers. You can do neither with your middle finger right now. You also have a lacerated radial nerve, which is why you don't feel the points on that finger."

Rose felt like she might throw up.

"The good news is that your ulnar nerve is intact, as is the skin on that side of the finger. *And* I can fix the other things. It's a clean bone break, easily set. I use special sutures to repair the tendons, and I use sutures that are as fine as a piece of hair to stitch those nerves back together."

Rose thought of Calamity Jane's perfectly straight blond hair. She assumed the sutures were more like that than like her own hair.

"That's the part I do. And then, when surgery is

done, your body will take over the healing process. Remember, the body *wants* to heal, Rose. It will work hard to get those nerves to reconnect, get those tendons gliding well again."

"How long will it take?" Rose asked, her voice froggy.

"What she means is, when can she start playing the cello again?" Thomas asked.

"We'll have indications along the way as to how things are healing," said Dr. Clare, "but we won't know how your fingers will work for the cello until the end of the summer. At the earliest."

The end of the summer.

"During the next ten weeks, you will have a progressive series of hand therapies to do—exercises to strengthen the muscles, work those tendons, and give the nerves time to heal."

"Can't I do some of that exercising on the cello?" Rose asked. She hated that her voice shook.

"No. I'm afraid not. They are very specific exercises—your middle finger in particular will have to relearn how to move."

Rose looked down at her hand lying on the table. She tried to make a fist—just a gentle one. All of her fingers curved in slightly, except her middle finger.

Her hand blurred in her vision. She could not move her middle finger at all. It was just . . . there. Not curved, not straight. Just there.

"And I'll ask you not to do that," said Dr. Clare. She placed her hand lightly over Rose's. "I'm not going to lie to you, Rose. This is going to be difficult—not the surgery so much as your recovery. I will need you to follow my instructions to the letter, do the exercises exactly as I show you how to do them, and be patient with your own healing. That will give you your best chance at full recovery."

"If I do all that, will I be able to play in September?"

Dr. Clare studied her. "I understand you've been working on Bach's Cello Suites."

Rose nodded. She clenched her teeth and willed herself not to cry.

"You won't be able to start back with those," said Dr. Clare softly. "You will need to ease back into playing. Perhaps I can talk with your teacher—Mrs. Holling was her name, yes?—to figure out a reasonable course of study for you."

Was Mrs. Holling still her teacher? Rose wasn't sure. She hadn't heard from her since she left the emergency room. She'd be leaving for London at some point. But maybe after that . . . ?

"Will I be able to play well in three years?"

"With injuries like these, it can be very hard to predict the future. For now, your job is to focus on the present and do what you need to do to help your fingers to heal. I want to emphasize that your age is nothing but helpful in this healing process. As is your fierceness."

There was nothing in Rose that felt fierce—except that she fiercely wanted out of the too-small office. She blinked back the tears that were always leaking out of her eyes. She hadn't cried at all when the accident happened, but she'd hardly been able to stop since.

"What do we need to do to have her ready for surgery tomorrow morning?" Thomas asked. He sounded so grown up. He was standing behind her now—his hand on her shoulder. Rose was grateful for the weight and the warmth of his hand.

"Really, not a thing," said Dr. Clare cheerfully. She pulled out a new bandage and began rewrapping Rose's hand. "A good night's sleep. Nothing to eat or drink after midnight, please. . . ."

"What if she's thirsty?"

Dr. Clare smiled. "A small amount of water would be okay. You are in good hands, Rose. Your little brother is going to take good care of you, I can tell."

"He's not my little brother." Rose pulled her hand away from Dr. Clare and tucked the end of the bandage in herself. "He's my *twin*."

"Ah," said Dr. Clare after a pause. "Please forgive me for falling into the trap adults always seem to. I remember what it was like to be very tall very early and have all sorts of assumptions made. I apologize that I momentarily forgot that . . . experience."

"Apology accepted," said Thomas. He squeezed Rose's shoulder. Rose wiped away the tears leaking down her face with the back of her inept right hand.

"Okay," said Dr. Clare. She stood—she really was very tall. "I will see you all in the morning, bright and early. I am honored to be a part of your ensemble, Rose."

Chapter 27

Measuring the Vine

R o-ose!"

Thomas's voice drifted in through her open window. Rose ignored it. She liked the sanctuary of her room—the cool blue of the walls, the patchwork quilt Gram had made for her four-poster bed, her overflowing bookshelf. Nobody bothered her in here. There were no concerned looks. Nobody tried to avoid looking at her bandaged left hand or smiled too wide when they helped her do something she couldn't do with her nearly useless right hand. Nobody asked her how she was feeling or too carefully avoided mentioning that the Bach Competition was taking place while she spent the afternoon staring at her blue walls.

She had managed to clean her room with her right hand. Sort of, anyway. It was maybe more accurate to say that she'd turned her room upside down one-handed. *Charlotte's Web* was missing. It wasn't under her mattress, in her sock drawer, or behind her old favorite picture books. She sat on the bed and looked around, hoping the things she needed most—Bach and *Charlotte's Web*—would somehow magically just appear. Especially the Bach. But if not the music, it'd be nice to have *Charlotte's Web*. Where was it?

"Ro-sie!"

Why did he have to call her that while he was outside? All she needed was for the Jacobis to hear him and then *they* would start calling her Rosie, which only Thomas was allowed to do. And sometimes Mr. Pickering. And Mrs. Lukashenko could call her Rosa if she wanted. But nobody else. Her name was *Rose*.

People had left things addressed to *Rose* on their front porch over the last few days: books and chocolates, cards and flowers. Church folks were only too happy to deliver a meal to their household; Gram had fed many of them through their trials. Now it was their turn. Gram probably wouldn't have to cook for weeks.

Only Mr. Pickering actually came in the house to see her. Señor Ocampo left a pot of pansies, which seemed so much sweeter than all the bouquets from the florists. And Jeff and Simon brought a delicious home-made strawberry pie. Rose had eaten half of it herself, the strawberry juice running down her chin—she had a terrible time wielding a fork with her right hand. The Jacobis left an enormous bouquet of colorful balloons while she was in surgery. There was a homemade card tied to them that read, *Made by Jane, who hopes you can play your chello again soon.* Inside was a poem-like verse—lyrics from some musical called *Carousel.* It was about walking through a storm and holding your head up high.

Mama said it was a sweet gesture and had placed the too-cheery balloon bouquet near Rose's cello chair, where they'd stood looming. Every time Rose walked past them, she'd hear Jane wailing, "HOW WILL SHE PLAY HER CELLO?" So she'd popped them all, leaving their shriveled remains attached to tangled ribbons on the floor. Mama or Gram must've cleaned them up, because they weren't there anymore. And someone had put Jane's card on her music stand, which was okay.

The most interesting thing that had appeared on the porch was a brown-paper grocery bag holding some-thing wrapped in newspaper. A small piece of masking tape stuck to the bag read ROSE. When Rose had unwrapped the mystery package with her right hand, she'd nearly dropped it. It was Mrs. Kiyo's *kintsugi* bowl.

Rose had sat with the beautiful bowl safely on her lap, trying to simply breathe, for a long time. She traced the gold scar with her right thumb and looked across the street. There had been no sign of her tiny, ancient neighbor, which was okay because Rose wasn't ready to see her quite yet. And she hadn't been sure what to do with the bowl. She finally decided she needed to keep it somewhere safe, somewhere it wouldn't get broken, so she'd taken it to her room and made a place on her bookshelf for it. She dusted the shelf and made sure no books could slide into the bowl or fall on it. It looked strange and out of place on her bookshelf, but at least it would be safe there. It had given her a focal point as she'd lain on her bed through the weekend.

"Ro-sie! Where are you?"

Rose sighed and tried to summon the energy to go downstairs to find Thomas. She stared at the *kintsugi* bowl. The sun was shining on it, like a spotlight, illuminating the golden repair. The scar was so beautiful—not perfect, not symmetrical, but so lovely and just right. She couldn't imagine the bowl without it.

"Rose," called Mama. "Please go see what your

brother is yelling about in the backyard."

Rose rolled off her bed and shuffled downstairs to the back door. When she opened the door, the brightness of the sun stopped her before she could even go out on the step. She wiped at her eyes awkwardly with her right hand; her right hand was about as handy for everyday tasks as her right foot.

"Oh, Ro-sie!" Thomas sang. She looked over to Mr. Pickering's yard, where she knew he would be. Sure enough, there he was—lying flat on his back in the dirt beside the pumpkin vine. Rose walked across the yards and stood over him. He shielded his eyes from the sun and looked up at her with a grin.

"Is it longer than me? I can't tell from this angle."

Rose stared down at him. His head lay in the not-quite-dried-out mud puddle surrounding the start of the pumpkin vine. He craned his head up, keeping his shoulders pinned to the ground, and looked down toward his toes.

He was measuring the pumpkin with his body? She looked down the length of her brother to where the vine stopped. The end reached off the ground a little, like a very large caterpillar looking for something to crawl up. They'd need another set of chopsticks soon.

"Is it as long as me?" he repeated. "Or longer?"

"Almost as long," she said.

"What do you mean *almost*?" said Thomas. "Almost as long or almost longer? Where does it hit, exactly?" As if his measuring technique had an exactness about it.

"I'd say . . . at your ankles."

"Top or bottom of the ankle?"

She laughed. She couldn't help it. He was so serious! She pretended to look carefully. It was pretty astounding—the vine had grown like crazy over the weekend while she'd been in her room trying not to think about what it could've been like playing for Maestro Waldenstein. It really didn't seem possible that the plant could have grown so much, and yet here it was.

"Top of your ankle."

Thomas sat up quickly and brought his ankle into his lap. He used his thumb and forefinger to measure the height of his ankle from the bottom of his foot.

"Whadya think—is that three inches?"

"Maybe." Did it really matter?

"So," said Thomas. "If I'm four foot six—or at least I was last Saturday . . ." Gram measured Thomas every Saturday on the kitchen door frame. Nothing had changed for months, but he was ever hopeful.

"Do you think I grew this week?" he asked.

She didn't answer. To be polite.

"Okay, so if I'm four foot six and there's three inches of me between the top of my ankle bone and the bottom of my foot, then the pumpkin vine is . . . four feet, three inches long!" He clapped his hands. "Soon it'll be longer than I am tall!"

When Thomas insisted on measuring again after supper, Rose grudgingly agreed to help and was surprised to find that the leaves of the plant were noticeably larger than they had been that morning, their green more vivid. The day had been hot, which must be weather the pumpkin preferred. Rose remembered the dream she'd had in the emergency room, when the plant grew so fast that you could watch it. She'd had the same dream after her surgery, too. Some dreams came true, apparently.

Just as he'd done this morning, Thomas positioned himself in the dirt parallel to the vine and scooched his body as close as he could get to the vine without touching the leaves.

"Some people use a tape measure, you know," Rose

said. She stepped closer to his feet. "Did you flex your feet up like that this morning?"

"Yup."

The vine was most definitely past Thomas's feet now. "Then I'd say the plant has grown about six inches today." That couldn't be right. But before Rose could double-check, Thomas was up dancing around the pumpkin.

"Whoo-hoo! That means it's almost five feet long! I bet it'll be even longer tomorrow!"

How could the vine have grown six inches in an afternoon? That was an inch an hour!

"It's growing just like you! I bet it'll be longer than you in a few days," said Thomas.

And then he'd no doubt want to use *her* as a human measuring stick.

Rose eyed the long vine. "Don't even think about it," she said.

Chapter 28
Ponytail

Rose stood in front of the bathroom mirror and tried again to get a hairbrush through her hair with her clumsy right hand. Her goal was a ponytail. She had not written this goal on a sticky note; her right-handed writing was too large and sprawly for small sticky notes, and anyway, she'd decided she was done with sticky-note goals. She'd ripped up all of her old goals after her surgery. This had not been easy to do with one hand, but she'd worked hard at it. She'd wanted to flush them down the toilet, but she was afraid it would create what Mama called a "plumbing nightmare." In the end, she'd simply thrown them in the trash.

She sighed at her reflection. She and Mama had just fought over her hair. All she wanted was a little help to get it in her usual bun. It wasn't even nine in the morning and already it was hot and sticky. Her hair was large and *everywhere*. Mama said she should just leave her hair down for once, but it was a mess, and that made Rose feel like a mess. Mama couldn't get the ponytail tight enough—it was useless loose!—and she had walked out of the bathroom for the second morning in a row saying she would not be drawn into an argument about hair.

The doorbell rang and Rose dropped her hairbrush for the third time. For a minute she thought she might cry. Over hair. So dumb. She got down on her knees and stretched to retrieve the brush from behind the toilet with her right hand. The effort made her sweat. She sat back on the cool floor tiles, leaned against the bathtub, and closed her eyes.

She heard tapping on the other side of the bathroom door. Before she could get up off the floor, she heard Mama say, "Go on in, Jane. Maybe *you* can help her with her hair."

Jane opened the door without a knock. Rose looked up from where she sat.

"Are you crying?" Jane whispered. She shut the

bathroom door behind her and leaned against it as if to prevent gawkers from entering.

"No," said Rose, and it was true. She was done crying. She felt dried up now.

"Your mom says you need help with your hair. I bet it's hard to do with one hand." Jane did a small shuffle tap on the tiles. It was very loud. "I can help. I'm pretty good with hair."

"My hair isn't like your hair," said Rose. She knew she sounded bitter, but what did Calamity Jane know about hair problems? She had perfectly straight silky hair that went into a ponytail easily. No wispies. Certainly no unruly curls.

"I know." Jane sighed as she looked at her sleek ponytail in the mirror. "I wish mine was curly."

"Curly hair is a pain." Rose struggled up to sit on the edge of the tub. "I can't even get it in a ponytail—it's too thick. And the curls frizz out no matter what I do."

"You should use a pick instead of a brush," said Jane. "My cousin has curly hair and she puts a little hair gel in and then uses a pick to kind of arrange it. That way her curls stay curls instead of just a mess of more and more hair."

"I don't want curls," said Rose.

"Well, you're not going to get rid of them," said

Jane. "Why do you always put your hair in a bun, anyway?"

"Keeps it out of the cello strings," said Rose.

"But you aren't playing cello now," said Jane.

Rose looked down at her left hand. Her bandaged fingers were Velcroed to a piece of finger-shaped white plastic that kept them protected and slightly bent. Dr. Clare was careful not to make any guarantees after her surgery. She said it had gone well but that it would be about ten weeks before Rose could try to play cello again, and there would be a lot of hard work until then.

She did not have a cello, of course. Worse, she hadn't heard any music since she was in the emergency room—the last few strains of Suite no.1's prelude had faded as she went to sleep, and she couldn't get it or any other music back.

"Anyway, I can get it in a ponytail for you." Calamity Jane walked with surprisingly quiet steps across the bathroom tile and climbed into the bathtub behind Rose. "Give me your hairbrush."

Jane brushed firmly, the way Rose liked her hair brushed. The rubber band snapped efficiently as Jane expertly wound it around her thick ponytail. Rose felt better immediately. It was the best ponytail she'd had since the accident. Maybe ever. Jane sure knew how to get it tight.

"Thank you."

"You're welcome." Jane ran her hands down the length of Rose's ponytail, probably trying to de-poof it. It never worked.

"Let me know if you ever want to cut it," said Jane. "I cut my cousin's hair—the cousin with the curls like yours. It's super cute."

"I don't want to cut my hair," said Rose. The very thought of Calamity Jane with scissors got Rose up off the edge of the tub. She held out her right hand to help Jane step out of the tub.

"If we cut it and you got a pick, you'd have cute curls everywhere," Jane pressed.

"I don't want to cut my hair," Rose repeated. "And I don't want curls."

"Okay," said Jane cheerfully. "Maybe some other time. It's super easy—we'd just cut off your ponytail."

"That's not a real haircut."

"Works great," said Jane. "It wouldn't work for my hair, but your hair will just curl up how it wants. Kind of a curly bob. It's *super* cute! My aunt wasn't even mad when I cut my cousin's because it turned out so great!"

"I think I'll just stick with the ponytail, thanks. Assuming I can figure out how to do it with my right hand."

"I could put it in a ponytail every morning if you want," Jane offered. "I mean, I'm just across the street. I'll do mine and then come do yours."

Rose wasn't sure she really wanted to begin every day with Calamity Jane. But she did do a nice ponytail. . . .

"Anyway, I just came by today to see if you know where *Charlotte's Web* might be," said Jane, her forehead furrowed in worry. "It's your week this week."

"You still haven't found it?" Rose asked, awkwardly cleaning hair out of her hairbrush one-handed. She'd been hoping that somehow the book had been found and returned to the library — like maybe Thomas found it lying unhidden in her room and had just forgotten to say something about it.

"No," said Jane, with a nervous shuffle tap. "And I'll need it next week — my week — because my daddy wants to read it to me when we go visit."

Rose busied herself putting away hair things.

"Well, if the library copy doesn't show up before then, you can take mine." She didn't know what else to say.

"Thanks, but I really need the library copy." Jane stopped tapping and looked up at Rose. "Can you think of anyone else who might have it? I've asked Mr. P. and Señor O. They haven't seen it."

"Why would they have?" asked Rose. Seriously? She was talking to the neighbors? Calamity Jane was making this too much of a big deal.

"What if someone found it behind the paperback?" Jane whispered. "And *took* it without checking it out!"

The bathroom suddenly felt very small. Rose stepped toward the door. Jane didn't move.

"You haven't told anyone, have you? About my daddy being E. B. White?"

"No, I haven't," said Rose. "Excuse me, please." She reached around Jane and opened the bathroom door.

Jane tapped her way out of the bathroom behind Rose, but thankfully did not follow Rose to her room. Rose threw herself on her bed. The calm blue walls did nothing to soothe her frazzled nerves. Not even the gold scar glimmering from the *kintsugi* bowl helped.

Chapter 29
Musicals

True to her word, Calamity Jane showed up the next morning to put Rose's hair in a tight ponytail.

"Would you like to come watch musicals with me and Mrs. Lukashenko this afternoon?" she said as she snapped the rubber band in place. "We're starting our summer tradition today with a triple feature."

Three musicals at once?

"What's the triple feature?" Rose asked, stalling for time.

"*Hello, Dolly!*, *The Music Man*, and *My Fair Lady*!" Calamity Jane tightened Rose's ponytail so tight that Rose's eyes watered.

"You're going to watch all three at once?" Rose asked.

"Not all at once, silly. One after the other. We're starting with three of our favorites! Can you come?"

Jane was really inviting her?

"Did you say it was a summer tradition? I don't want to intrude. . . ."

"You won't be intruding. Mrs. Lukashenko says you don't have anything to do because you can't practice and that's pretty much all you do. And she said we need to mend our fences—whatever that means." She did one small, but loud, shuffle tap; the tile had to be tempting. "Musicals bring people together, Mrs. Lukashenko says.

"Anyway, it won't just be me and Mrs. Lukashenko. Mom got the afternoon off and she's making pizza for dinner, and Jesse and James will be there, of course—they're in charge of making the microwave popcorn. We don't have air-conditioning, but we have three fans. Since you haven't been outside yet, you might not know—it's *hot*. But if you sit right in front of the fan, it's not too bad."

"I'll think about it," Rose said. She stood, opened the door, and walked into the hallway.

"Do you have other plans?" Jane asked, following her.

"She does *not* have other plans," said Mama, who was standing in the living room, obviously eavesdropping. "And she'd be happy to go to the triple feature, wouldn't you, Rose? It's lovely of you to invite her, Jane."

"What kind of triple feature?" Thomas asked, skidding into the living room from the kitchen. He had cookie dough on his face. Gram was making chocolate-chip cookies.

"A triple *musicals* feature!" said Jane. "Me and Mrs. Lukashenko do it every year to kick off our summer of musicals! It's great!" She did a small but exuberant tap dance, ending with her hands in the air.

"Cool. Can I come?" asked Thomas.

"*Everyone* can come," said Jane. "Just like Pastor Nancy says at church: All are welcome!"

"Then count me in, too!" said Gram from the kitchen. "It sounds like fun."

"You should ask Mr. P. if he wants to come," suggested Thomas. "And ask him to bring lemonade!"

"Wish I could join you," said Mama, "but I've got to work. Rose and Thomas will be there, though."

"One o'clock," said Jane. "Don't be late! I better go set up some extra chairs if you guys and your gram are coming—and maybe Mr. Pickering, too. It's like a party!" She tapped out her excitement. "Maybe I can borrow some chairs from the library," she said as she tapped across the living room to the front door.

"Do you need help getting the chairs home?" Mama asked. "Rose could go with you. Why don't you take our red wagon?"

Rose rolled her eyes. Whether she wanted to or not, it would seem that she was going to attend the triple musical tradition.

Chapter 30
Six Feet

Pleeeeeease . . ." Thomas was close to whining. "I'm *sure* it's longer than you now. It'll only take a second. Just lie down right there." He tapped the ground next to the pumpkin vine.

"It's only been three days," said Rose. "It couldn't have grown that much." Though, looking at it . . . maybe. The vine was really long. It had to be much longer than her. "I don't want to lie down in the dirt, okay?" There were five thousand worms in that dirt.

Thomas was off like a rocket. He flew across the yards and into their house. Rose stared into the pumpkin plant and lost herself thinking about Eliza Doolittle from *My Fair Lady*.

Hello, Dolly! and *The Music Man* had been wonderful, but *My Fair Lady* was the best. It was Jane's favorite, too—who would've thought they'd have the same favorite musical? Rose loved how Eliza Doolittle changed from a rough and awkward pauper into an elegant lady by force of will—and lots and lots of practice. Interestingly, Professor Henry Higgins hadn't changed at all. Even the con man, Professor Harold Hill, had changed in *The Music Man,* which gave her hope for Eddie Jacobi. But not Henry Higgins. Not one bit. He stayed a jerk right to the very last scene.

"All of life can be found in musicals," Mrs. Lukashenko had said while they ate pizza between shows. "Love and loss, trials and temptations, wild passions, fate, pigheaded men and stubborn women." She sighed dramatically. *"All of life!"*

Rose smiled, remembering Mrs. Lukashenko's delight at having all of them together watching some of her favorite musicals. And it *had* been fun. She was looking forward to next week, when they would watch *South Pacific.*

Thomas returned with a sheet from the linen closet, startling her out of her musical reverie. He triple-folded the sheet and placed it on the ground parallel to the plant's vine. It looked as though he were making a bed, which was funny because he hated making his bed.

"Three layers of sheet—you won't even feel the dirt," he said.

Mama opened the back door.

"Thomas James! What are you doing with my good sheets in the yard?"

"Rose needs them!" he called.

Mama threw up her hands in exasperation.

"Okay. Just this once," said Rose.

It was actually kind of cool lying on the ground, staring up at the sky. Totally different from staring up at the ceiling in her room. The sky was so . . . high. It was also intensely blue today, similar somehow to the vibrant green of the pumpkin plant's leaves.

"Scoot over—till you're almost under the leaves," said Thomas. "You have to lie exactly like the vine."

Rose moved closer to the vine. It was hard to adjust herself while keeping her left hand up in the air and out of the dirt. "Just measure," she said.

"Scoot up just a little—the top of your head has to be even with where the vine starts to grow out of the dirt."

She sighed and scooched again.

"Perfect," said Thomas. He disappeared from her

field of vision. "The last leaf stretches just below the bottom of your foot!"

"How much below?" she asked.

"Just barely below your shoe," Thomas replied.

"Are you sure? It looked longer than that to me."

"Yup, I'm sure. You're still five feet eleven inches, right?" he asked.

She hadn't let Gram measure her all summer, but she couldn't possibly have gotten any taller since the last time she'd been measured. She nodded.

"In that case, this plant is over six feet, easy. Six foot three—or four, maybe!" He stepped over the vine and considered it from the other side. "Maybe more." He did a little jig around the vine and extended his hand to help Rose up.

"Hello? Anyone back here?"

Rose took Thomas's hand and struggled to her feet. All of her progress in getting up and down off the ground gracefully had been thrown off by her bandaged hand.

The Happy Mailman came across the backyards toward them, though it took Rose a second to recognize him out of his uniform. "Kirk," he said with his hand outstretched and his usual smile. "Your friendly neighborhood mailman—well, just your friendly neighbor today." He laughed his nice laugh.

Rose shook his hand and realized too late that her right hand was covered with dirt. Everything was awkward with her right hand—even the few things she'd always done with her right hand, like handshaking. Kirk didn't seem to notice.

"I finally got around to calling Frances Holling to catch up a little, only to find out you'd had an accident."

Rose wondered what Mrs. Holling had said about it. Her teacher had come to the hospital on Thursday just before Rose went in for surgery, but she'd left quickly and Rose had not seen her since. She was probably busy packing for London.

"How's it feel?"

"Fine." Her hand didn't hurt much at all. It was just useless all bandaged up.

"I had extensive nerve damage, too," said Kirk. "The hand therapy is very important—tiny little exercises that make a big difference. You have to practice those exercises as faithfully as you practiced cello. It gives you the best chance at healing. Don't get discouraged."

Rose blinked back tears—she was already discouraged.

"May I ask what you know about your prognosis?"

She appreciated that Kirk used a medical word like

prognosis. He didn't talk to her as if she were a kid. "Dr. Clare said we have to wait a while to see." Rose didn't say *until the end of the summer.* She was still hoping it wouldn't take as long as that.

"The injury we are most worried about is the healing of the nerves," said Thomas. "They've been stitched back together—with sutures that are as fine as a piece of hair! Now we just wait and let her body do the healing."

Kirk nodded. Thomas sounded like a doctor. Mama said he was the one with the most questions when Dr. Clare came to talk with them after the surgery.

Mr. Pickering came out onto his back stoop. "Kirk!" he said. "Good to see you—thanks for stopping by."

"Yes, indeed!" said Kirk. "I thought I'd check in on this pumpkin vine while I'm here—and check in on Rose, too." He smiled kindly at Rose.

"Lemonade, anyone?" asked Mr. Pickering.

"Sure," said Kirk. "Thank you, Otis." He didn't bother with a chair—he just sat down in the dirt beside the vine.

"Tell me about this pumpkin project!" he said. "Are those worms I delivered in here somewhere—I'm not sitting on any of them, am I?" he asked, looking around in pretend panic.

"Probably," said Thomas, grinning. "But they're

deep under the dirt by now—they carry the compost down into the soil. They're way quicker and better at it than humans are."

"Amazing!" said Kirk.

Rose took a seat on the porch step. She looked down at Kirk's hands while he and Thomas talked. They were clasped casually around his knees, his right hand holding on to his left wrist, hiding his injured hand. For some reason, Rose wanted to see that scarred hand again. It had looked so awful when he'd held it up to show Mama in their front doorway. And yet he was still able to play viola. Was that how her hand would look when the bandages came off?

Kirk shifted on the ground, crossing his legs and placing his hands in his lap. His left palm faced Rose. She stared.

The scars ran across Kirk's palm and up his third and fourth fingers. The scar on his middle finger was thicker than the delicate line on the side of his ring finger. It reminded her of Mrs. Kiyo's *kintsugi* bowl somehow. The scarring looked organized, as if someone had helped the healing order itself.

"Rose . . ." Kirk looked up at her. "Frances told me you had a bit of a run-in with Harris Waldenstein."

Rose choked on her lemonade.

"I studied under him at Tanglewood when I was in high school," said Kirk. "He was a young up-and-coming conductor then."

"Really!" said Mr. Pickering.

"It's a small musical world," said Kirk with his friendly smile. "It was the summer after my junior year of high school, the summer before my accident with the snowblower. I was very serious about music then. It was a wonderful summer"—he laughed—"despite Maestro Harris Waldenstein."

"He's supposedly brilliant," said Thomas.

"Oh, he is," said Kirk quickly. "Absolutely brilliant. But just because you're brilliant doesn't mean you're not a jerk."

"Too true," said Mr. Pickering, taking a sip of lemonade.

"We were together at Tanglewood the summer after his surgery," said Kirk. "That was the summer Harris started cello."

"His surgery? The summer he *started* cello?" Rose repeated.

"Yes. Did you not know that Waldenstein was originally a violinist?"

Rose shook her head. How had she once thought she knew most everything about Harris Waldenstein?

"His father was not unlike Mozart's father—he pushed his son to have the musical success he himself had been unable to achieve. Harris practiced too long and hard and started to have problems with tingling and numbness in his hands when he was a teenager. The origin of the problem was found to be a pinched nerve in his vertebrae, if I remember correctly, but everything was complicated by long hours of violin practice. By the time he was twenty-five or so, the vertebrae in his neck had to be surgically fused, which took away most of his mobility from the shoulders up."

"That doesn't work for violin," said Thomas.

"No, it doesn't. So Harris switched to cello, which worked better—though if you watch him play, you'll see how stiff he looks. Brilliant musician . . . he just never loved the cello the way he'd loved the violin."

Rose tried to imagine having to switch to the violin because of her accident. The violin was lovely in its own way, but maybe certain people were made for certain instruments. She was absolutely made for cello.

"Please don't misunderstand me," said Kirk. "I don't tell you this to excuse anything about his behavior. I just thought you should know—it's probably one of the many reasons he is . . . who he is. He knows what it is to lose The Music."

The Music. She heard the capital letters. Yes, that was it. That's what had happened. She had lost The Music.

"Anyway, he transferred his exceptional talents to other areas and became a renowned Bach scholar before he was forty, and he now enjoys conducting and teaching all over the world." Kirk shrugged. "Like I said, life doesn't always work out the way you'd planned it, but that's not always a terrible thing."

"You haven't seen him since that summer?" Rose asked.

"I have not," said Kirk. "But once you meet Harris Waldenstein, you never forget him." He laughed again.

After a moment's pause, Mr. Pickering stood up. "Well, I should probably go get it."

"Do you need any help?" Kirk asked, already starting to stand.

"No, no. I can manage."

"Get what?" asked Thomas.

But as she watched Mr. Pickering hobble through the back door, Rose knew what.

The cello.

Chapter 31

Assessing the Damage

Mr. Pickering carried the cello as if it were a body, as if he'd scooped up a hurt child and was carrying her to her mother. Kirk met him at the top of the stoop and took it. He placed it gingerly on the picnic table.

Kirk looked to Rose. "Is it okay by you if we take a look?"

She tried to nod, but she wasn't sure if she actually did. She'd kind of forgotten about the cello. Well, not forgotten, but every time she remembered the sound it had made when the board hit it, she removed the thought from her brain.

Kirk unzipped the canvas case. It looked as if he were on a crime show, unzipping a body bag. Thomas peered into the bag, which gave Rose the courage to stand. She walked over and stood close to Thomas. He leaned into her a little bit and his curls tickled her arm.

The bridge was broken—cracked, with half of it falling off to one side. That was the first thing she saw. The strings were lying as if they'd been blown around by a fierce wind. Then she saw that the neck, too, was cracked. It looked as if something had tried to tear it from the body of the cello—perhaps the board hit right where the neck and body met. Rose felt light-headed. She leaned into Thomas. As she did so, she noticed a long crack that ran the entire length of the cello's body.

"Can any of that be glued back together?" Thomas asked, his voice weak. "Maybe with superglue or something?"

"Glued? No," said Kirk. "A cello is held together by tension, really, and glue is no match for the tension the strings provide." He felt around the neck breakage. "A new neck will need to be grafted. But the scroll looks good, and so does the pegbox. The neck breakage is what has caused this crack." He traced the crack down the body of the cello. "You're going to need a real artist for this repair."

"But you think it can be repaired?" said Mr. Pickering.

"Oh, I believe so. It looks worse than it is, I think. I'd imagine that a cello this age has had more than one neck already."

"Really?" said Rose. That seemed strange.

"Sure," said Kirk. "They actually wear out—hours of playing each day, every day, for years and years . . . A musician's hands alone will wear it out over time."

"But what about that crack?" said Thomas.

"It happens," said Kirk. "More often than you might think. There are fixes. As it happens, our fair city is home to a wonderful luthier: Will Stringer, of Stringer's House of Music. It's quite close to here, actually. You could bike, even, though I think the cello might appreciate a car ride."

"What's a luthier?" asked Thomas.

"Someone who makes—and repairs—stringed instruments," explained Kirk.

Rose's eyes stung as she looked at the ruined instrument. She was so ashamed that it had been wrecked while in her care. "How . . . how much do you think all of those repairs would cost?"

"I wouldn't have the foggiest idea," said Kirk. "More than a musician can pay, I'm sure. But Frances will have insurance on it, so then it's just a matter of paying the deductible."

"Do you mean special insurance for the instrument itself?" Mr. Pickering asked.

"Yes," said Kirk. "There's usually a deductible of five hundred to a thousand dollars for an instrument like this—and then the rest is paid by insurance. Do you have a hard case for this cello? It's probably best to minimize any further damage."

Thomas took off across the yards and returned, struggling with the bulk of Mrs. Holling's periwinkle cello case.

"Oh, my goodness!" Kirk laughed. "Only Frances could get away with a case like this." He carefully transferred the cello into the hard case. He adjusted the neck and body a few times and then gently closed the lid. Rose could not help but think of the case as a casket. How could something that ruined be fixed?

"You'll want Will—that's Mr. Stringer, himself," said Kirk. "Tell him I sent you. He's an interesting guy—a little odd, but you'll enjoy him, I think. And I mean it when I say he's the best—people all over the country send their instruments to him."

Rose tried to say thank you, but her voice wouldn't quite work.

"Hey," said Kirk, his own voice soft. "Not everything can be fixed, but so many things can—more than you might guess. Go see about the cello—and don't give up hope."

"I'll get my keys," said Mr. Pickering.

Chapter 32

Stringer's House
of Music

Stringer's House of Music turned out to be an actual house in a neighborhood. Had there not been a sign out front, they'd never have thought it was anything but a tall, very odd-looking purple house. With dark-pink shutters around the windows. Magenta—that sounded more dignified than dark pink.

"Do you think those colors are on purpose?" Thomas asked as he and Rose carried the cello—she holding the neck of the cello case under her arm and Thomas struggling with the body—up to the front porch of Stringer's House of Music.

The porch was lovely, and when they stood on it, they could see that each of the banisters was carved in the shape of a stringed instrument. A pair of cellos framed the porch steps, and Rose suddenly felt more hopeful than she had in more than a week. She quickly added the numbers of Will Stringer's name. Will (56) Stringer (110). No real clues there, but maybe Will was short for something, like William (79) or Wilbur (85). Wouldn't *that* be something—if the luthier shared a name with the pig from *Charlotte's Web*! Probably not, but still, she decided to go with her gut—hopeful.

The front door—the same magenta as the shutters, but trimmed in a lively lime green—was open, and they could see into the house. A long hallway led from the front door to a bright room in the back of the house. Mr. Pickering knocked on the brilliant-turquoise screen door.

The outrageous house colors did little to prepare them for Will Stringer's colorful appearance. Nothing he wore matched: red pants, a bright-blue-and-pink-and-green-plaid shirt, neon-purple suspenders, and a sunny-yellow bow tie with music notes all over it.

"Hello, friends! Good day to you! Will Stringer here! How can I be of service to you?" His voice boomed, and his long, twirled handlebar mustache rose and fell with his words. It fell dramatically when he saw the cello case in its unusual horizontal position.

"Oh, dear . . ." He fumbled with the screen door. "Come in, come in—make haste!"

Awkwardly they made their way through the door with the periwinkle cello case.

Mr. Pickering introduced them as they traveled the length of the hallway to the back of the house, following Will Stringer. "Our friend Kirk Stevens sent us."

"Very good, very good. Right this way . . ." said Will as if time were of the essence.

They followed him down the hallway into what had probably been the kitchen, dining room, and living room at one time but was now one large open room. Stringed instruments lined the walls. There were several workbenches and long tables spaced around the room. Each was full of giant clamps holding various parts of instruments. It looked both chaotic and well ordered at the same time. It smelled like wood. And music.

Will Stringer cleared off a space on a workbench. "Let's put her up here." Gently he took the cello case from them and laid it on the workbench. He pulled a lamp on a giant spring down from the ceiling. A warm, bright light bounced off the periwinkle case.

"This case—love it." He smiled, but immediately turned serious again as he flipped the latches on the case and opened it.

"Oh, my . . . Oh, my, my . . ." He covered his face with his hands. He peeked through his fingers and then covered his eyes again. "How did it happen?" he whispered.

Mr. Pickering cleared his throat. "A table-saw accident involving a thrown board."

"AH!" cried Will.

"It was in a canvas sort of case . . ."

"OH!" Will said as if someone had stabbed him. He took his hands down to his heart, and his eyes roamed over the cello pieces in the case. "I can see she has a distinguished history. . . . Tell me what you know of her origins, please."

"Um, I think it's — she's — French," said Rose. She tried to steady her voice, but Will Stringer's reaction worried her. He looked stricken. "A couple hundred years old, I think. I don't know exactly. . . . It's my teacher's, actually. I just know that it's a really nice cello."

"I can see that." He glanced back at her. "I can only assume that you are an excellent cellist."

"Was." It slipped out. She held up her bandaged left hand.

Enormous tears filled Will's eyes. "Same accident?" he whispered.

Rose nodded.

He took a red bandana out of his shirt pocket and blew his nose with a loud honk. Then he closed his eyes and took several huge breaths in and out.

"All right. Let's have a real look now," he said.

And then it was like he dove into the cello case. Rose found herself watching his hands. Will Stringer had a musician's hands: long fingers that moved as if they were dancing. She wondered what instrument he played—probably most of them, but which one was his favorite? He clipped off the strings as if they were extraneous ribbons in his way and lifted the cello's body out of the case. He ran his beautiful fingers over the front, back, and sides. He took the neck, which had broken off completely since they'd looked at it with Kirk, and placed it next to the broken body of the cello. Then he dusted off the fingerboard with a soft cloth taken out of his back pocket. He held the scroll up to the light and smiled—at least that's what Rose thought he did: his incredible mustache moved up and out. Then he put on a headlamp and looked into the f-holes, turning the cello's body this way and that. The sound of something rattling around inside made Rose feel as though something were rattling around inside of her.

"Soundpost is dislodged," he said. "To be expected, of course, with this kind of trauma."

"What's a soundpost?" Thomas asked.

"It's a small dowel—nothing fancy, really—that is placed up here inside the top of the cello's body. It's held in place by friction and tension—just wedged between the front and back on the instrument, if you can believe it. But without it . . . well, there'd be nothing without it, really." His mustache bobbed up and down.

"Like, the cello wouldn't play without it?" said Thomas.

"Well, in theory it could, though it'd be a bad idea, if not impossible, to string the instrument up without it. Probably get a crack down the front similar to the one you've already got." He ran his hand down the long crack in the front of the cello again. "The soundpost is a structural piece, but it's sometimes called the *anima* of an instrument—that's the Italian word for 'soul,' or 'essence.' It is the reason a particular instrument sounds the way it does. It both holds the cello together *and* makes it sing."

He turned and looked up at Rose, his headlamp shining in her face. "I expect your soundpost has been dislodged as well." His voice and his eyes were kind, and Rose appreciated that he *said* it and didn't *ask* it. Instead, he nodded as if everything were confirmed, and then began listing the repairs that would need to be made.

The list was long. Very long. And full of words and processes that made Rose's head spin.

"How much does all that cost?" Thomas asked when Will was finally finished.

"Well, that's really a matter for the insurance company. I'm sure your teacher has the instrument insured," he said to Rose. "Who do you study with?"

"Frances Holling."

"Frances Holling! Of course."

"Do you know her?" Rose asked. It really *was* a small musical world.

"Know of her," said Will. He twirled his mustache absently while he continued to gaze at the cello. "Know enough to know that she wouldn't have an instrument of this caliber without protecting it with an insurance policy. I'm not worried—you can get me that information as you get it. As it happens, I've got some time in these next few weeks and it would be a pleasure, in addition to a challenge, for me to repair this beauty. So I'll get started right away and then we'll be in touch about insurance and other details. How's that sound?"

It sounded wonderful—almost too good to be true. They thanked him and shook his hand—Rose managed a very natural-feeling handshake with her right hand—then Will walked them to the front door. On the front porch, he turned to Rose and stood at attention like a soldier.

"I am Will Stringer, and I *will string 'er*!" he barked. Then he laughed—a rumbly Santa Claus kind of laugh that set his mustache bouncing. "I just love saying that to people!"

Chapter 33
Mrs. Holling Visits

The next morning, as Rose was coming back across the street from Calamity Jane's house after getting her ponytail done, she saw an unfamiliar car pull up in front of her house. Just as she got to the middle of the street, Mrs. Holling stepped out of the car and waved. Rose was so surprised that she tripped on her own feet.

"Where are you coming from?" asked Mrs. Holling.

"Calamity Jane's."

"A friend of yours?"

"She does my ponytail."

Mrs. Holling smiled, but it looked a little strained. "That sounds like a good friend." Rose shrugged.

They climbed the steps to the porch. A plate of scones sat on the porch table along with an insulated pitcher of coffee, two cups, and Mama's pretty blue cream and sugar set. Obviously, Gram had known Mrs. Holling was coming.

Rose peered into the house through the living-room window. Gram and Thomas were nowhere to be seen. She was all alone on the porch with Mrs. Holling.

"Shall we?" Mrs. Holling asked at last.

Rose took a seat at the small table. She figured it was her job to pour the coffee since she was the host—or was she, if she hadn't actually known this little get-together was happening? Of course, she spilled trying to pour with her right hand, but Mrs. Holling graciously helped her wipe it up.

When Rose had served them both—she didn't usually drink coffee, but that's all Gram had provided and it seemed rude to go inside to get juice—an uncomfortable silence fell between them. Mrs. Holling smiled tentatively, then held out her hands for Rose's, just as she often did at the beginning of a cello lesson.

Rose hesitated. She wasn't sure why, exactly. Because her left hand was bandaged? Because so much had happened since she last put her hands into Mrs. Holling's? Because she was too ashamed about the cello?

After an awkward moment, Mrs. Holling folded her hands and placed them in her lap.

"Are you in any pain?" Mrs. Holling asked.

"Sometimes it hurts a little at the end of the day."

Mrs. Holling nodded. "And how are you otherwise?"

Rose shrugged. She didn't mean to be rude, but London and the accident and the cello and Maestro Waldenstein felt like big, enormous *things* sitting between them. And there had never been anything between them.

"The Music is gone." She didn't mean to blurt it out, and at first she regretted it, but when she saw the look on Mrs. Holling's face, she knew her teacher understood.

"Oh, my," Mrs. Holling said. She sat back in her chair as if Rose had shoved her there. "Oh, Rose." After a moment she sat up and tentatively held out her hands again. This time Rose took them, and as soon as she did, she felt a weight lift from her.

"The Music will come back," Mrs. Holling said after a time. Her voice was low and quiet, but sure. She gave Rose's right hand a gentle squeeze, then let go.

Mrs. Holling took a deep breath. "Rose, I came this morning because . . . I owe you an apology. Several apologies, actually." She took another breath. "I'm so angry about what happened with Harris Waldenstein. My hope was that meeting him before the competition would lessen any nervousness you might be feeling. I had no idea he was such . . . such an *ass*."

Rose choked on her scone.

"I did not handle that situation as well as I should have. For one, I should have given that fool a tongue-lashing." She shook her head as if she still couldn't believe she'd missed the opportunity. "And then I sent you out of there without our properly . . . processing it." Mrs. Holling looked positively anguished. "To think of you using a power tool when you must have been so upset—"

"Mrs. Holling," Rose interrupted. She wanted to tell her that the accident wasn't her fault, because it sure sounded as though that's where her teacher was going with this apology, but Mrs. Holling held her hand up and continued.

"Most of all, I'm sorry for not being here these first days after the accident, after your surgery." Her chin quivered. "It breaks my heart to imagine what you must be going through . . . and not knowing what to do to help. I've let my guilt and shame and heartache get in my way. I am so very sorry, Rose. Can you ever forgive me?"

How could she ever *not* forgive Mrs. Holling? Rose threw her arms around her teacher in a clumsy hug, her scone trailing crumbs down Mrs. Holling's back. Mrs. Holling held her tight. Rose felt a sob, but she wasn't sure from which one of them it came.

Thomas burst through the door and onto the porch.

"Hiya, Mrs. H.! Can I join you guys for a scone?" He sat and grabbed the largest scone off of the plate before either of them answered.

Rose and Mrs. Holling quickly wiped their eyes; Thomas seemed not to even notice that he'd interrupted. Or maybe he just pretended not to. Mrs. Holling asked him if he would like some coffee.

"Naw," said Thomas. "Gram says I'd be *too much* if I had coffee."

Mrs. Holling laughed—her usual laugh. Rose splashed some cream into her cup of coffee. Some of it splashed on the tray, too, but she pretended she didn't see. Then she scooped three spoons of sugar into her cup without spilling at all.

"I've been anxious to see you both," said Mrs. Holling. "I want to hear all about the pumpkin project.

In fact, I want to *see* it. Would you show me when we finish these amazing scones?"

As they toured the pumpkin patch, Thomas regaled Mrs. Holling with pumpkin vine facts, while Rose mostly stayed quiet. Mrs. Holling seemed genuinely interested. She asked questions, provided encouraging comments, and laughed at all the funny things Thomas said.

"I think this is the most exciting project!" said Mrs. Holling as they made their way up the back steps to the Brutigans' kitchen; Mrs. Holling insisted on doing the dishes to thank Gram for preparing "such a lovely breakfast." "I had never heard of giant pumpkins until you told me about them, Rose. And then I read an article in the paper about the pumpkin weigh-off in Stillwater. Sounds like some people who grow these giants are quite competitive. Did you know they have judges who inspect the pumpkins to make sure nobody has cheated?"

"How could you cheat?" Rose asked.

"Apparently, some less-than-honest growers inject their pumpkin with fluid to make it heavier." Mrs. Holling shook her head. "Where there's a will, there's a way, I guess."

Chapter 34
The Deductible

Inside, they plugged the sink and filled it with hot water. Thomas squirted in the dish soap that smelled like lavender. "I'll wash," said Mrs. Holling. "Thomas, you rinse. Rose can dry."

As lavender-scented steam rose over the sink, Rose tried to figure out how to bring up the cello insurance issue. She and Thomas had talked about it and they agreed that they'd pay the deductible—though they weren't at all sure *how* they'd pay it—but she had a feeling it would take some convincing to get Mrs. Holling to agree to that.

"Mrs. Holling?"

"Yes, Rose?"

Rose took a breath. "I think maybe now is a good time to talk about your cello."

Mrs. Holling nodded and handed Thomas a plate to rinse. "I think perhaps you are right."

"It's my fault that your cello got wrecked," Thomas said quickly. "Rose thinks it's her fault because she brought it into the garage, but I was the one holding it, and I think maybe I was too close to the saw and—"

"Thomas," interrupted Mrs. Holling. She braced her soapy hands on the edge of the sink. "I cannot tell you how relieved I am that the cello took the force of that flying board and not you."

"But your cello is broken! It's *really* bad."

"My cello is just an instrument," Mrs. Holling said, looking first at Thomas and then at Rose. "A beautiful instrument, yes, but an instrument all the same. The two of you matter more to me than any cello possibly could." She cleared her throat. "And perhaps there are repairs that might be made. I'll have a better sense of that once I see it."

"We took it to Will Stringer at Stringer's House of Music already," said Rose. "Kirk told us about him. Was that okay?"

"It's fine—of course it's fine. That's exactly where I

would've taken it myself. But you didn't need to do that," said Mrs. Holling. "What did Will Stringer say?"

"He's got a whole long list of repairs," said Thomas, "but he says he *will string 'er* again!"

"Well, how wonderful!" said Mrs. Holling. "That is terrific news."

Rose tried to think of a graceful way of bringing up the matter of insurance and the deductible.

But Thomas simply blurted, "Do you have insurance for it? If you do, what's the deductible? 'Cause me and Rose—*Rose and I*—will pay for it."

"I do have an insurance policy for it, yes," said Mrs. Holling. "And I believe the deductible is five hundred dollars. But that's not for the two of you to worry about. What happened to the cello was an accident," she continued. "There is no *fault*. Please don't give it another thought."

Suddenly, Rose was angry. "But there *is* fault, Mrs. Holling. The accident was *my* fault. I used the saw, even though I knew I wasn't supposed to and didn't even know *how* to. And I brought the cello into the garage, and I told Thomas to hold it in front of him—" She swallowed hard. "I don't know if we'll be able to fix my hand, but we can fix *this*. Please. We need to do this."

Mrs. Holling bowed her head. It was hard to tell if

261

she was praying or staring at the floor. Finally, she raised her head and looked at them.

"Five hundred dollars is a lot of money," she said.

"We'll find a way to get it," said Thomas immediately. "We'll do odd jobs around the neighborhood or something. Anyway, that's not for you to worry about," he said, using Mrs. Holling's own words.

Mrs. Holling's steady gaze focused on Rose, then Thomas. Again, she seemed to be thinking things through.

"I will need to pay Will upfront," she began slowly, then held up her hand when both Rose and Thomas opened their mouths to protest. "I can hardly ask him to begin working without payment. But if this is something you two are really determined to do, then I suppose I can agree to be reimbursed for the deductible. We can figure out some sort of payment plan," she continued. "Something that seems reasonable . . . Agreed?"

Rose and Thomas nodded. Mrs. Holling shook their hands very formally—then she opened her arms and pulled them both into a hug. It was a little awkward: Rose was a head taller than Mrs. Holling, and Mrs. Holling was a head taller than Thomas. But they managed.

Mrs. Holling picked up her purse in the living room. "Walk me out to my car, Rose?"

Thomas zipped out the back door to the pumpkin patch, and Rose and Mrs. Holling went out the front door. Rose suddenly felt shy escorting her teacher out.

"Rose," said Mrs. Holling as they approached her car, "there is one more thing I must apologize for. I regret not having talked with you about my London plans from the beginning. I told myself that I was doing it to protect you, but in truth I think I was protecting myself by putting off a very difficult conversation. I need to ask your forgiveness for that, too. I've rather bungled this whole affair. I'm so sorry."

"I forgive you," said Rose. The words sounded so formal, but she sensed that Mrs. Holling needed to hear them.

"Thank you, Rose."

"When do you leave?" Rose asked. The word *leave* came out squeakier than she would've liked.

Mrs. Holling adjusted her purse on her arm. "I'd been planning to go at the end of August. But their term doesn't actually start until the end of September, so I think I could delay that by a few weeks. I could stay to see how those early weeks of cello rehabilitation work, if you want me—"

"*Please*," said Rose. She could not imagine those initial attempts at the cello without Mrs. Holling by her side.

Mrs. Holling smiled with tears in her eyes. "Then I'll make the arrangements today." She opened her car door.

"Mrs. Holling?"

"Yes, Rose?"

"How do you know? I mean . . . you said The Music would come back. How do you know?"

"I lost it once myself." Mrs. Holling shut her eyes tight. "It feels like you're falling, doesn't it? It's as if there's no net to catch you—you just keep falling."

Rose nodded, though Mrs. Holling couldn't see her. Yes, that was exactly what it felt like: free-falling.

"It will come back," Mrs. Holling repeated, opening her eyes. "You'll be so surprised: the losing of it will almost seem like a gift." She hugged Rose hard. "It's just somewhere you can't reach right now. It will find you again. I promise."

Chapter 35
Odd Jobs

After lunch, Thomas made a flyer:

WANTED: Odd Jobs—The Odder The Better!
Two local, responsible, creative,
hardworking kids looking for work.
We'll do most anything!
Especially if it can be done one-handed.
(Only one of us is one-handed.)
Saving for a very good cause!
For more information, inquire at the library.

Gram said they couldn't put their personal information on the flyer. If someone was interested, they could talk to Mrs. Lukashenko, who would weed out any shady would-be employers.

"Do you think we *have* shady would-be employers around here?" Thomas asked.

"One never knows," said Gram.

Gram also said they could only personally inquire to their immediate neighbors, not canvass the city.

"And you need to let *them* set your wage," she said. "No charging twenty-five dollars an hour to pull weeds or wash patio furniture."

Rose tried to think what other odd jobs they might be qualified to do, because pulling weeds and washing patio furniture sounded . . . Well, it'd just be nice to have variety.

"You can start by introducing yourselves to the new neighbors." The long-empty house finally had new owners—they'd moved in quickly and no one had seen them since. "I haven't gotten over there yet, though I will. Maybe they'll need some help with boxes or cleaning or something. Here, take them some of these brownies."

The new neighbors turned out to be very nice—and very appreciative of the brownies. They were a young couple named Stanley and Wanda—they wanted to be called by their first names, which Rose was pretty sure

Gram wouldn't approve of. Wanda was pregnant and on something called bed rest, which meant she spent most of the day in bed or on the couch on her left side. "It's about as boring as it sounds!" she said with a laugh. "I can only see slivers of the neighborhood through my bedroom window. So, it's been very nice meeting you both! Hopefully I'll get to see more of you one of these days. . . . In the meantime, I'd sure like one of those brownies."

Stanley grinned at Rose and Thomas. "As you can see, we haven't progressed quite as far with our unpacking as we'd hoped!" He gestured around the living room, which was empty except for a couch, a coffee table, a TV—and a big pile of boxes in one corner. "But I'd be grateful if you'd be willing to collapse the empty moving boxes in the garage. Is ten dollars enough? It shouldn't take more than twenty minutes or so."

Rose and Thomas happily agreed to the terms, and Stanley led them out to the garage. Thomas did the actual collapsing while Rose stacked the cardboard in the corner with her one working hand. She wasn't sure she was going to be able to do much of the earning; it was amazing how many things required two hands.

But as it turned out, that wasn't much of an issue

anyway—they struck out everywhere else on the block. Señor Ocampo said they weren't old enough for him to pay them to do work at the hardware store. The Jacobis had no money to spare. They didn't even bother asking Mr. Pickering; he probably would've been happy to pay them a little something to help with odd chores, but it didn't seem right to start charging him for being neighborly. Most of the other neighbors either weren't home or didn't answer their door. It was hard not to get discouraged.

Rose made Thomas deliver the flyer to Mrs. Kiyo. She wasn't yet ready to see her; she knew she needed to thank Mrs. Kiyo for loaning her the *kintsugi* bowl, but she worried that once she did, Mrs. Kiyo might ask for it back. And Rose wasn't sure she was ready to part with it yet.

"She's not home," said Thomas when he joined her back on their porch. "Looks like she's been gone awhile, actually. There were a bunch of old newspapers on the stoop. I put them in her recycling bin in the back."

Rose looked at Mrs. Kiyo's house across the street. The potted plants in her Listening Garden were wilted. Fear shot through her. She opened the front door and called to Gram. "Have you seen Mrs. Kiyo lately? It looks like she hasn't left her house in a few days and her plants are all droopy."

"Kiyo is just fine," Gram said. "She's in Japan, actually—it's only the second time she's been back since she left so long ago. A niece came to escort her; it's a long trip for an old woman, though Kiyo's pretty lively."

"How long is she gone?" Rose asked, her pulse slowly settling back to normal.

"Let's see . . . I wrote it down somewhere. . . . Until a few days after the Fourth of July, I believe."

That gave Rose a couple more weeks with the bowl—and more time to figure out how to properly thank her neighbor for such a meaningful gesture.

In the meantime, there was at least one thing she could do.

She filled a pitcher with water and walked across the street. It took three trips—she sloshed out a lot of water going down the steps—but when she was done, the potted plants were well watered.

It wasn't much of a thanks, but it was a start.

Chapter 36
Blossoms

Rose and Thomas were eating breakfast the day Mr. Pickering knocked on the back door with the news.

"We have blossoms!" he announced when Gram opened the door.

"Blossoms?" Thomas jumped up from the table and knocked over the syrup. He righted it before it could puddle everywhere. "Male or female?"

"Male," said Mr. Pickering. "They show up first. It'll probably be another week before the female blossoms appear."

Rose reached for another pancake—with her right hand! Instead of starting with her inept left hand and quickly changing to the right! She congratulated herself on this small milestone. With luck and a little hard work, she'd be able to brush her hair soon and wouldn't need Jane to put it in a ponytail.

"Let's go see," Thomas said, making a dash for the door.

Mama grabbed his shoulder as he tried to duck by. "Finish your breakfast first."

"But we have to cover them right away so the bees don't get in."

"After breakfast," said Mama. "Actually, not after breakfast." She looked at the clock. "You have a dentist appointment at eight thirty and we need to take the bus; I'm too tired to drive."

"Why can't Gram take him?" Rose asked.

"She's at church all morning with the quilters," said Mama. "Which means you'll have to come along, too."

"But I already had my dentist appointment."

"Rose could stay with me, Tess," said Mr. Pickering. "She could help cover the blossoms—she'd be a real help, in fact. I don't relish all that bending and looking under leaves." He rubbed his ribs. "I can only see one, but I'm sure there are more."

Rose wasn't sure *she* relished bending and looking under leaves, but at least it was better than tagging along to the dentist. And maybe there'd be time to read one of her library books and do her hand exercises. Dr. Clare had removed the stitches on the outside of her finger yesterday—there were still stitches in the tendon, though. During hand therapy was the only time her fingers weren't in the slightly bent position. It was the only time she could look at the scars and try to imagine what they'd be like when everything healed.

"Well, if you're really sure, Otis . . ." said Mama.

"I can't believe I have to go to the dentist," grumbled Thomas. "Rose doesn't have any idea what to look for, Mr. P. You'll have to show her the pictures."

Rose rolled her eyes. How hard could it be to spot a pumpkin blossom?

It didn't take long. Mr. Pickering brought out red plastic cups—the kind he served lemonade in—and Rose walked the length of the pumpkin vine, gently lifting the leaves and looking for the golden flowers. They weren't open yet, but Mr. Pickering said they might open later in the morning, so they had to be covered. Once she located a blossom, Rose slipped a cup over the unopened flower. That was it: comb through the leaves, find a flower, slip on a red cup.

Mr. Pickering came out his back door with a pitcher

of his famous lemonade. "Next week we should have some female blossoms," he said. "We'll cover those, too, until they're ready to open. We'll use the pollen from these male flowers to pollinate the female flowers. Then it's pumpkin time!"

"Wouldn't the bees and butterflies do all that?" Rose asked.

"Oh, indeed they would," said Mr. Pickering. "But the seed we planted has quite a pedigree behind it—generations of giant pumpkins have given their genes to the seed we are growing. The growers have used strictly controlled pollination techniques. We want to make sure we continue that, and the only way we can know for sure which pollen is pollinating the plant is to do it ourselves."

It sounded like a lot of work. Rose covered the last male blossom. There had been ten male flowers in all. She sat down on the steps.

"Thanks for helping me," said Mr. Pickering. He sat down slowly in his chair on the stoop and wiped at his forehead with a handkerchief.

"How are you feeling these days, Mr. Pickering?"

"Oh, pretty good. A little tired. Moving around still requires so much effort."

Incremental healing, Dr. Clare would call it. She'd

told Rose to celebrate every tiny milestone because the healing would take place in small, incremental ways.

Rose took the brace off her hand and unwrapped the protective bandages. The week's hand therapy consisted of using her right hand to bend her injured fingers into her palm—making a gentle fist—and then letting her left hand do the work of extending them. She was supposed to do this two to three times a day—it got the tendon "gliding" again, Dr. Clare said. It was a long way from cello playing, but Dr. Clare said it was a step *on the way* to cello playing.

"You and your family are a great help to me," said Mr. Pickering as she rewrapped her hand. "And the excitement of the pumpkin plant—well, there's a reason to get out of bed if ever there was one! I understand for the first time why Edith liked gardening so much."

"Who is Edith?" Rose asked.

"My wife."

Of course. Mr. Pickering's wife had died before she and Thomas were born. Rose couldn't even imagine a Mrs. Pickering.

"You would've loved Edith, Rose." Mr. Pickering stared into the giant leaves of the pumpkin plant. "And she would've loved *you* to pieces."

It was hard to imagine someone you didn't know loving you to pieces. Someone who was dead.

Mr. Pickering chuckled. "Edith played the bassoon. My, how she loved that thing! She was as horrible at the bassoon as you are good at the cello."

"Why did she love it if she was horrible at it?"

"She thought it was amazing to be able to blow into such an unusual-looking instrument and have it make such a funny sound. Of course, a bassoon properly played is beautiful. But, Lordy! Edith was awful!" Mr. Pickering shook his head and laughed out loud. Mr. Pickering did not laugh all that often.

"Jonathan, her brother—the one who left us the pumpkin seed—said she used to go out to play her kazoo in the garden when she was a little girl. I guess the bassoon followed the kazoo—I think they had an aunt who played, and Edith found the instrument languishing in an attic or cellar. She believed, just as your Mrs. Holling does, that plants love music. So she'd go out and honk away at her vegetables and flowers. It sounded like a war of ducks out there in the backyard. It brought her such joy."

"Did she *practice?*"

"Oh, no, no," said Mr. Pickering. "She was

'self-taught' and took great pride in simply playing, not practicing."

"But without practice, she'd *never* be any good."

"Rose, you may have yet to discover the joy of doing something *badly*. I'm here to tell you, it can be a lot of fun. As they say, anything worth doing is worth doing badly."

"That's not the saying," said Rose. "The saying is, anything worth doing is worth doing *well*."

"Hmm," said Mr. Pickering. "There's some truth to that, too, I guess."

Mr. Pickering wasn't making sense. She had always done everything to the best of her ability. Some things she did better than others, of course, but she always *tried* her best. How could doing something badly be fun?

"Now, you," said Mr. Pickering, "you do things the very best you can, am I right?"

Rose watched her neighbor's profile as he stared out over the pumpkin vines.

"And your abilities are prodigious — sizable and wondrous. But the question is, what do you do just for fun, even if you aren't very good at it?"

There was the Fun Question again. Mrs. Holling had asked it, too. Before everything, when Rose still knew what she was doing, even if it wasn't having *fun*. Rose still didn't have much of an answer.

"What do *you* do badly just for fun?" she asked. Maybe she just needed an example.

Mr. Pickering smiled. "Well, I'm working at growing a giant pumpkin. And I'm having a fine time of it, Rose. A fine time."

"But you aren't doing that badly," said Rose. "The plant is growing great."

"Well, yes—though I don't think I can take much credit for that. But the growth of the plant isn't as much the point as the *growing* of it. That's the fun part." He paused. "And while I am having fun, I'm not sure everyone is."

"Thomas is!" said Rose. "The whole summer is different because of this pumpkin project."

"The whole summer is different because of what happened in my garage," said Mr. Pickering, quietly.

"*My* whole summer is different because of that," said Rose.

"Quite so. Thomas's, too."

"Thomas is fine," said Rose. The cello had taken the force of the thrown board—Thomas hadn't even been hurt.

"Thomas is fine on the outside," said Mr. Pickering. "His heart, however, is very worried about you."

Was that true? Did Thomas have a hurting heart? How had she not noticed?

"The question, Rose, is what are you going to do with your different summer? I understand from your gram that hand won't be ready to try the cello before Labor Day."

"I can't do *anything* before then."

"Sure you can," said Mr. Pickering. "You just have to ask yourself, *What can I do badly?*"

Rose opened her mouth to protest, but then closed it again and looked down at her club of a left hand. Anything she did with *it* would be done badly. Undoubtedly there were other things, as well. In any event, Mr. Pickering was right—she needed some new things to focus on.

She just had no idea what. Or how to start.

"Work on the pumpkin with us, Rose." Mr. Pickering's voice was steady, but there was something underneath his words. She could hear it and feel it. It was the closest thing to hearing music she'd managed since the accident.

"Thomas and I really don't know what we're doing," Mr. Pickering continued, his voice soft but clear. "But we would welcome you to have fun doing it with us."

"I can't."

"Why not?"

She'd ruin it for Thomas. "I'd make it—"

"—*wonderful*," said Mr. Pickering. The firmness in his voice made Rose look up at him. "You would make it wonderful, Rose."

Mr. Pickering turned back to the pumpkin vine, and Rose let her gaze follow. The vine had stretched while they'd been sitting there on the stoop, she was sure of it.

"I only have one hand to work with."

"We could sure use a one-handed researcher," said Mr. Pickering. "We have all these books on growing giant pumpkins and gardening. I'm sure they contain important information that would help us out, but Thomas and I get them all mixed up and we can never find what we need when we need it."

"You should use sticky notes," said Rose.

"Well, sure. Sticky what?"

"Sticky notes. Mark the pages you'll need to refer to later." She took a shaky breath. "I don't know how much digging and all that I can do one-handed, but I can do research. I'm good at research. Though I guess I'm supposed to be doing something I'm *not* good at."

Mr. Pickering chuckled. "The point of doing something badly is to free yourself up so that you can have fun. Will you have fun doing research?"

Rose nodded vigorously.

"That settles it, then!" said Mr. Pickering. "Let me go get the books; they're right on the kitchen table. We'll have to get some . . . sticky notes—is that what you called them?"

"I've got plenty of sticky notes," said Rose. The stack had probably grown dusty on her music stand. "I'll get the books—you rest."

In Mr. Pickering's kitchen, Rose found three piles of books.

"Are *all* these books about growing giant pumpkins?" she called out the window. She recognized the ones Gram had ordered, but there were several more than those few.

"Some are just general gardening books—they were Edith's," Mr. Pickering called through the screen. "She liked the research."

Rose stared at the piles. Who knew there was so much information on growing a plant that looked like it could not be held back?

"Where do you want me to start?" she called. She might as well get something done while they waited for the female flowers to show themselves. She'd look up the pollination process first. Then she'd figure out a way to standardize and keep track of all the measurements Thomas took.

She needed to get home and dust off her sticky notes. She had a new goal to write down: ORGANIZE THE PUMPKIN PROJECT. Maybe this one, too: HAVE FUN. And if she was going to do that: *BE* FUN.

"Welcome to the team, Rose," said Mr. Pickering when she carried the books back out to the stoop.

Chapter 37
Pollination

The darkness had only a hint of sunrise when Thomas crept into Rose's room.

"Rose! Wake up!"

"I'm awake." She had woken up thinking of the pumpkin flowers and couldn't get back to sleep.

Thomas had spotted the first female blossom the night before. They'd been sitting on Mr. Pickering's back stoop. Rose had been marking the various estimated-growth charts in the pumpkin books with bright-orange sticky notes. There was enormous variation in the charts. The only thing that was clear was that they would soon have to be very intentional in the decisions they made about the pumpkin plant. Everything seemed to count—especially once there were pumpkins.

"They're here!" Thomas had shouted. He'd lifted the leaves gently, combing through the plant looking for others. "Here's another! And another!"

There were four female flowers in all. Thomas had covered them with red plastic lemonade cups. Rose had found the hand-pollination chapter in *Growing Giant Pumpkins* Volume II and had flagged it with a hot-pink sticky note so they wouldn't have to search for it in the morning if they needed it.

The plan had been set: they would meet Mr. Pickering on his back stoop just before sunrise. He'd assured Gram and Mama that he would be waiting for them. "I'm the one who wakes up the birds," he'd said.

"Rosie!" Her brother was a terrible whisperer. "Come on!"

"Shhhhh! Give me a minute to get dressed."

"I'll go get the picnic basket. Meet you downstairs."

She sat up in bed and stretched her arms over her head. There was a tingle in her middle finger! It was gone as quickly and unexpectedly as it had come. But she'd felt it—she was sure of it. Dr. Clare said "tingles, buzzes, and zings" might happen as the nerves began to heal. It was a good sign, she knew. There—again! A buzzy little zinger! An Incremental Milestone, and an important one. It was a big day—pollination *and* nerve tingles. *And* fireworks that night—it was the Fourth of July. Rose pictured the tingles and zings in her finger like fireworks.

Rose turned to look at the *kintsugi* bowl on her bookshelf. Mrs. Kiyo would be back in three days. Rose was determined to appreciate the bowl as much as possible until then. Like right now, she noticed that even in the half-light of early morning, the gold scar glowed. Her middle finger zinged again. Today would be a good day.

The back door squeaked open. He'd left without her! She threw off her covers and ran down the stairs as quietly as she could.

Thomas stood at the back door, grinning. He held an overflowing picnic basket. "Looks like Gram packed lots more than just muffins!"

It wasn't until they got to Mr. Pickering's yard that Rose realized she was still in her pajamas and her hair was its typical morning explosion. Thomas hadn't gotten dressed, either.

Mr. Pickering sat in his lawn chair, sipping coffee.

"Zowee!" he said when Thomas heaved the breakfast basket onto the stoop. "Your gram has fueled us for days."

They unpacked. Blueberry muffins, hard-boiled eggs, fresh strawberries, yogurt, and Gram's homemade granola.

"She's a good one, your gram," said Mr. Pickering. "She wouldn't let me make a thing except the coffee and hot chocolate. With thankful hearts, I say we feed ourselves well for the strenuous task of pollination. The sun will be up soon, and when it is, the flowers will open."

Mr. Pickering had already uncovered the four new blossoms so they could watch them open while they feasted. Rose had read chapter after chapter about the hand-pollination process, but she still wasn't quite prepared for how miraculous it was to watch the flowers unfurl in the sun, as if they were stretching to greet the day.

Once the female flowers fully opened, Rose uncovered one of the male flowers, snipped it off the vine, and peeled back the floppy petals to expose the stamen. The petals were silky, their color a magnificent golden orange. She held the stamen up close to her eyes and could see each grain of pollen.

She carried the male blossom over to the nearest female flower, which looked to be a good ten feet from the base of the plant—though it was difficult to see where the plant began now. Giant leaves sprawled everywhere. The last two weeks had been astounding in terms of growth. Their pumpkin plant looked a lot like the one in the magazine picture with Jonathan: vine and leaves as far as you could see.

The female flower was fully open. Rose stood before it, frozen to the spot. *It was so beautiful.* You could tell it was a girl flower. It was feminine, somehow. She looked at the male flower in her fingers for comparison. The golden-orange petals had started to wilt from her touch.

The books had instructed them to use the male flowers like a painter's brush to gently paint the stigma down in the blossom. Rose steadied the female blossom with her left hand, her bandaged fingers cradling it carefully. With her right hand, she guided the stamen in as gently as she could and painted the stigma.

"Hey!" Thomas's loud voice shattered the moment. "Look! A pumpkin has already started."

Mr. Pickering and Rose walked over to where Thomas was crouched. He held aside the petals of a female flower so they could see underneath. Sure enough, a thing about the size of a golf ball had sprouted.

"Ah, yes," said Mr. Pickering. "But if the flower is not pollinated, that withers up and dies. Some folks would fry those blossoms up to eat. They are wonderful! But we need them to make a pumpkin.

"Speaking of which," he continued, "we have three more females to fertilize here and probably not much more time before they close up and we've missed our opportunity. Pick a male flower—any of them."

Rose sat on the stoop and let her brother pollinate the remaining flowers. She looked at her bandaged fingers. There was bright golden pollen smeared on the white gauze. She had helped make a pumpkin! She hoped so, anyway. So much could go wrong. There were chapters and chapters in the giant pumpkin books about dealing with all of the problems that could arise. But Rose decided to be hopeful.

When they finished, Thomas and Mr. Pickering sat with Rose on the stoop. Mr. Pickering poured more coffee and hot chocolate. Rose dug in the picnic basket.

"Cream or sugar?" she asked Mr. Pickering.

"Well, I usually drink it black," said Mr. Pickering. "But today's a celebration, so yes. Both!"

Rose poured some of each into the coffee cup he extended. She didn't spill a drop with her right hand.

She sighed with happiness—actual happiness! Even though she was outside in her pajamas, even though her hair was probably as wild as the pumpkin vine, she was happy. Mostly so, anyway. If she could just call up a little Bach. . . .

She sat on the stoop between her brother and her neighbor and watched the female flowers close.

"And now . . ." said Mr. Pickering, "we wait."

Chapter 38

A New Notebook

Within the week, they had four baby pumpkins. The pumpkins' growth made the vine's growth seem like it had just lollygagged around. Every night after supper, Rose took Gram's measuring tape and wrapped it around each of the pumpkins. They grew four to five inches in roundness most every day. Three were already the size of softballs, and one was almost the size of a soccer ball! At first she simply scribbled down the daily measurements on a sticky note and pasted it next to one of the growth charts in *Growing Giant Pumpkins*. After a week and a half's worth of sticky notes, however, it was obvious that the pumpkins needed their own notebook.

She learned from the charts in the books that the pumpkins' weight gain was not as regular or predictable as their circumference. The weight charts were only estimates, and they could be off by hundreds of pounds by the end, apparently. The estimates themselves made for interesting math. She tried to figure it out in her head as she walked to Señor Ocampo's hardware store. It had to be a complex formula. There were so many variables. . . .

"*¡Hola, Rosa!*" said Señor Ocampo when she entered the store. "What do you need today? Something for *el proyecto de la calabaza gigante?*"

"*Sí.* One of my notebooks for *el proyecto de la calabaza gigante,*" said Rose. She tried to imitate the music of Señor Ocampo's speech, but she felt like she was missing consonants. Or maybe vowels. Or maybe her tongue simply tangled the sounds.

"Moved your notebooks. Aisle *número quatro,*" said Señor Ocampo. "Your Spanglish is getting pretty good, Rosa!"

"*¡Gracias, señor!*" Rose had bought her cello lesson notebooks—the ones Mrs. Holling wrote her practice instructions in—from Señor Ocampo for years. He only carried one kind of notebook, but it was exactly the right kind—perfect size, shape, and binding. She flipped through the stack to find an orange one. There weren't any pink ones anymore. For a long time, Señor Ocampo carried pink just for her. She had switched to red when preparing for the Bach Competition. Mama said red was the color of confidence. Rose thought of it as a more mature version of pink.

She didn't know where the red cello notebook was now. She didn't even know where her music was. Not that it mattered; she didn't need either of them now. Maybe she'd need them again. Maybe she'd just start a new notebook and new music if that time came.

How she hated that *if*! The week's hand therapy had her discouraged. Eight to ten times each day she was supposed to make a gentle fist—she didn't need to use her right hand to help it into position anymore, at least—and then hold it, squeezing firmly but not tightly, for a few seconds. It was difficult to do, though—and it was so very obvious how weak her hand had grown. She tried not to think about it and just focus on the exercises, but it was hard.

She pushed her sadness aside in favor of looking for the perfect pumpkin notebook—in a pumpkin-orange color, if at all possible. She hoped their pumpkins would be a nice normal orange. They were gray-green now, but according to the books, many pumpkins changed color as they grew.

She flipped through several notebooks before she found an orange one. It was the perfect shade: deep and dark—a wonderful shade for a pumpkin! She bought it quickly and headed home to get it organized.

As she approached her house, she noticed Mrs. Kiyo sitting in her Listening Garden. Rose felt her stomach clench, but she knew she couldn't put off returning the bowl any longer. She cut through Mr. Pickering's yard and entered her house through the back door. She went to her room and placed the pumpkin notebook on her bed, then carefully retrieved the *kintsugi* bowl from its special place on her bookshelf. She cradled it in her left elbow but kept a firm grip on it with her right hand.

Mrs. Kiyo smiled as Rose approached and she scooted over on the bench. Rose sat down with a too-rushed "How was your trip to Japan?"

Mrs. Kiyo seemed to really think about the question. Finally, she said, "I left so long ago. . . . I have been back only one other time, when my mother died. And that was forty years ago, and only for a few days. It was good to spend time with my niece and her family. But . . . Japan is no longer my home." She swung her legs out, as if she were on a swing, and smiled at her shoes. Her smile seemed thoughtful, neither happy nor sad.

"We missed you."

"Well, how nice!" said Mrs. Kiyo, turning on the bench to face Rose better. "My flowers did not seem to notice my absence."

Rose smiled. "I watered them a few times. I didn't want them to die while you were away."

"I thank you!" said Mrs. Kiyo.

They sat in silence for a time.

"Thank you," Rose said at last. She was surprised at how strong her voice sounded. "Thank you for lending me this bowl while you were gone. It meant a great deal to me."

Mrs. Kiyo held out her hands and Rose handed her the bowl. She watched her neighbor rotate the bowl so the gold scar faced her. She traced it with her thumb, much as Rose did when she held it.

"I did not give it to you as a loan, Rose. I want you to have it."

Rose was stunned. "You can't give it to me, Mrs. Kiyo—it is so much a part of you." The too-familiar lump rose again in her throat. "It should stay in your family. And it's so valuable. . . ."

"I've never thought of this bowl as an asset worth money, Rose. I have treasured it because of its beauty, its history in my family, and its assurance that when something breaks, it can become even more beautiful through being mended. I've needed to remember this wisdom many times in the last seventy years. And now I am very honored to share its beauty and wisdom with *you*. You have given me such a gift in your music, Rose. And you have honored me with your friendship. Let me honor you with this gift."

Mrs. Kiyo stood, and with a deep bow she placed the bowl back into Rose's hands. The brace that protected Rose's fingers curved them just right around the bowl. She held it with both hands, one bandaged, one not, and when the tears started, they were different from her usual tears. Instead of just leaking down her face, they came in a rush. Mrs. Kiyo sat down again beside her, so close that their sides touched, and let her weep.

Only when Rose started to hiccup did Mrs. Kiyo speak. "You need this bowl now, Rose." She reached up with both of her tiny, wrinkled hands and wiped away Rose's tears with her thumbs. "I do not any longer. It is my honor to give it to you. You will honor me by learning from it." She gently brought Rose's face close to her own and kissed the top of Rose's head. "Put it somewhere it can speak to you—where you can hear what it has to teach."

When Rose walked back across the street and through her front door, she placed the *kintsugi* bowl on her cello chair. Through the window, the sun bathed it in golden light. The scar blazed.

Chapter 39

Larry, Curly, and Moe

We should name them," said Thomas. He stood in the middle of the pumpkin patch, teetering on one of the boards that formed a walkway through the vines. They had spent the day before strategically placing long, wide boards from Mr. Pickering's garage through the vines. Calamity Jane and her brothers had helped—which probably made it take longer, but it had been more fun. They had to take measurements of the pumpkins and inspect them for pests and problems each day, and Rose had read that walking in and among the vines—which was tricky anyway—compacted the soil, which wasn't good for the new roots. The boards would distribute their weight better. The risk now was that they would fall off the boards and into the plant.

"I don't know if naming the pumpkins is a good idea," Rose said.

She watched him as she did the week's assigned hand therapy. It was called Block-and-Flicker, and it was the hardest exercise she'd done yet. Dr. Clare had shown her how to do it just the day before. Rose had to hold the lower part of her injured middle finger still with her right hand and then "flicker" the very tip. Fortunately, she only had to do it a couple of times a day. But she would continue to do it, Dr. Clare said, even as she learned other exercises. This one was really important for a chance of full recovery.

"What's wrong with naming them?" said Thomas. "How about Larry, Curly, and Moe, after the Three Stooges?"

"Well," said Rose. She hesitated, wrapping her fingers back into their protective brace. "When we lose one, it will be extra sad because it will have a name." This sounded lame, but she hoped it would gently lead to the next pumpkin care task before them.

"We're not going to lose another one," said Thomas. They had lost the smallest of the four almost right away. The part of the vine it was attached to became hard and woody and the pumpkin stopped growing. The others put on an estimated twenty to thirty, then forty to fifty pounds a day. But the little one had stayed little. In the end, the ants got it.

"The thing is," said Rose, "we *need* to lose another one. We need to lose two, in fact. I read about it last night. The plant can't sustain multiple pumpkins. We have to choose one—and soon."

"No, we don't," said Thomas. He dragged Mr. Pickering's hose along a board, watering the vine as he went. It had been hot for the past three days, and the pumpkin leaves looked exhausted in the late afternoons, which Mr. Pickering said meant the plant was thirsty. It could also mean it was trying to feed too many pumpkins.

"We're dividing precious resources between multiple pumpkins," said Rose. "That means that none of them will do as well as one could do on its own if we focus everything on it."

"Unless there are more than enough resources," said Thomas immediately.

"Yes, but I'm not sure we have more than enough. We made a few mistakes early on." For one, they should've encouraged the vine to grow in what was called Flag Formation, which involved a lot of pruning as the side vines started to grow so that they would all grow in one direction. It was too late now; the vines were tangled over the whole yard. They looked like Rose's right-handed handwriting—all loopy and chaotic and *everywhere*. The whole patch was much less organized than she would have liked. She half expected to come out each morning and find that the vine had grown up and over Mr. Pickering's house during the night. Besides that, chopsticks arranged in X formations stuck up everywhere. Rose was still proud she'd had the idea—the chopsticks really were terrific at anchoring the sprawling vines to the earth—but it looked ridiculous if you didn't know why they were there.

"But they'll all do . . . *okay*, right?" said Thomas. "Even with the mistakes we made?"

"Maybe," said Rose. "But don't you want to do better than just okay?"

"What's the problem?" Mr. Pickering asked from the porch.

"We need to choose one pumpkin," said Rose.

"For what?" asked Mr. Pickering.

"For maximum growth." It sounded dumb out loud.

"Only if that's the goal," said Mr. Pickering. "Is that the goal?"

"No, it's not," said Thomas. He turned to Rose. "This is a project for *fun*, remember? We're not trying to win something. Not everything is a competition."

"Fine," said Rose. She'd thought it would be fun to try to grow the biggest pumpkin they could possibly grow, but maybe Thomas was right. Maybe she shouldn't always be so competitive. She should welcome this opportunity to practice doing things in just a perfectly okay kind of way. Surely that was a stepping-stone to enjoying doing something badly. And if that stepping-stone meant naming the three pumpkins Larry, Curly, and Moe . . . well, whatever.

"Holy moly! Look at it!" Jesse (or James) said. They came around the corner of Mr. Pickering's house with a man Rose had never seen before. Mr. Pickering called Jesse and James the Pumpkin Ambassadors because they always brought someone new to the pumpkin patch with them. Rose kept hoping they would bring someone with an odd job they could be hired to do, but so far it was just pumpkin gawkers. She'd joked once to Thomas that they should charge people to look at the pumpkins, but he'd taken her seriously and argued vigorously for the pumpkins to remain a "free community event." The dismaying fact was that even after Thomas broke down a few more boxes for Stanley and Wanda, and Rose had stayed with Baby Oliver for an hour one night while he slept, they'd earned only thirty dollars so far. That left them with four hundred seventy dollars left to raise.

"Hoooo-weee!" said their visitor. He wore overalls, big red boots, and a hat that looked like it had been trampled by animals. She hoped he wasn't looking for farm help.

"Told you they're humongous!" said one of the twin boys.

For a split second, Rose thought he was commenting on the man's eyebrows. Long hairs reached up and out over his eyes like the pumpkin vines, as if searching for a place to latch on and grow.

"You weren't kidding!" said the man. "You got *three* of 'em growing in this . . . yard?"

"I hate to mow," quipped Mr. Pickering as he limped over to shake hands with the man. "Welcome to our pumpkin patch. I'm Otis Pickering."

The man wiped his hand on his dirty overalls and shook Mr. Pickering's hand.

"Pleased to meet ya, Otis. The name's Letch. Leroy Letch. Friend of mine told me about your pun'kin adventure here. Thought I'd come and see for myself. Ran into these boys down by the liberry—they knew right where to bring me."

Rose was pretty sure Mrs. Lukashenko would've screened Leroy Letch out if he'd come to her inquiring about their flyer. Something seemed . . . shady about him.

"Do you live around here, Mr. Letch?" asked Mr. Pickering.

"Nah. I don't like the city. I live out a ways. Got me some land. I've done some of my own pun'kin growin' in years past, in fact. I'll be back at it next season, for sure. What you reckon your pun'kins weigh at this point?"

"Well, we sure can't lift them anymore!" said Thomas. "Rosie found a chart that estimates their weight from their circumference. We measure them twice a day. We think they've each put on about fifty pounds a day this week." He turned to Rose. "What'd they weigh yesterday?"

"I'd have to go look," said Rose. She didn't, though. She just didn't want to tell Mr. Letch, for some reason.

"Fifty pounds a day is not bad," said Mr. Letch. "Not bad at all! Where'd you get your seeds?"

"Just one seed!" said Thomas.

"You planted one seed and had this kinda luck?" Mr. Letch's crazy eyebrows went up and down in astonishment.

"My brother-in-law grew them in New Zealand," said Mr. Pickering. "He sent me the seed. It's been a great project. We've made some mistakes, but they seem to be growing in spite of us. Who is your friend, Mr. Letch—the one who told you about our pumpkin project?"

"Name's Eddie Jacobi," said Mr. Letch. Jesse and James nearly jumped at this news. "Lives across the street from you, I guess."

"When he's not in jail," mumbled one of the Jacobi twins.

"How do you know our dad?" asked the other twin.

"We used to be . . . business associates," said Mr. Letch. He laughed a downright shady laugh. "He is, as you say, incarcerated right now. But we stay in touch. . . . Your daddy is one of the smartest men I know. I bet you two take after him, don'tcha?" He smiled at the Jacobi boys, who scowled in response.

The way Mr. Letch talked rankled Rose. And it couldn't mean anything good that he was friends with Eddie Jacobi, could it? How did Eddie Jacobi know they were growing pumpkins, anyway? She doubted Jesse and James had told him. Jane, probably.

Mr. Letch turned back to the pumpkin vines. "Whatcha got goin' with these white sticks everywhere?"

"Those are chopsticks," said Thomas. "They work great for anchoring the vine into the soil. They were Rose's idea." Rose's face grew warm. She didn't feel quite so proud of her idea now that she saw it through Mr. Letch's eyes.

"Ya know . . ." said Mr. Letch, his eyes continuing to roam the unruly pumpkin patch, "there is another way to estimate weight—some say it's a little more precise. You take what's called an over-the-top measurement. There's a different table for the weight estimate. Math is different, too—different variables and all that. Some think the over-the-top tables are a titch more accur-ate."

"How do you take an over-the-top measurement?" Rose asked. She couldn't help herself: the guesstimation element of pumpkin growing was frustrating. If they could get a more accurate estimate . . .

"Lemme show you," offered Mr. Letch. "Got a tape measure?"

Thomas found their tape measure among the vines. Rose had taped two of Gram's knitting tape measures together because one wasn't long enough to make it around the biggest pumpkin now.

"First, show me how you measure 'round your pun'kin — do that big one over there," said Mr. Letch.

Thomas skipped out on the boards and demonstrated their usual measuring technique. Mr. Letch offered some correction. Then he had them measure side to side, then stem to bottom. He whipped a well-worn chart out of his pocket, consulted it, and said, "Whooo-wee! You got yourselves a prizewinner, I'd say."

"Really?" said Rose.

"Really!" said Mr. Letch. "I bet that little lady there is right 'bout eight hundred pounds already, and it's only the last week of July!"

Eight hundred pounds! Their circumference measurements had estimated just over six hundred pounds.

"You musta got yourself an awful good seed," said Mr. Letch. "Now, allow me to give you some advice. You're foolish to be growin' three of these. If you want a prizewinner, then you needs to be concentratin' on just *one* pun'kin."

"What kind of prize?" asked Thomas. Rose glared at him. What happened to growing the pumpkins just for fun?

"Why, there's a giant pun'kin competition at the Great Minnesota Get-Together!"

He looked at Rose and Thomas. "Don't tell me you ain't never been to the horticulture building at the Minnesota State Fair!"

Thomas shook his head.

"Well, there's a giant pun'kin competition there every year," said Mr. Letch. "And there's *prize money*!"

"Prize money?" said Rose.

"How much?" asked Thomas.

"I think I heard there's a five-hundred-dollar purse bein' offered this year," said Mr. Letch, waggling his big, hairy eyebrows. "You kids would like five hundred smackaroos, wouldn't you?"

Thomas looked at Rose, the amazement on his face undoubtedly mirroring her own. It was as if it were meant to be — a prize that was exactly the amount they needed for the insurance deductible.

Chapter 40
Ole Bessie

Mr. Letch stayed for a while—long after Jesse and James had been called home, in fact. He had quite a repertoire of giant pumpkin stories. The man who currently held the world record for a giant pumpkin (1,823 pounds—the digits of which added up to *fourteen*!) was a close personal friend, he said.

"We're all of us friends, but deep down, we all want to win." He laughed like he'd made a great joke. "One of these years, someone is going to grow a one-ton pun'kin! Most serious growers think they'll be the one to do it."

A one-ton pumpkin. Two *thousand* pounds!

"Do you think our pumpkin could get to be two thousand pounds?" Thomas asked.

"Well, now, you've got a mighty fine start, but no, I don't think you're going to hit two thousand pounds. Maybe fifteen hundred, though. And I'm *sure* that pun'kin has some marvelous seed possibilities inside her." He looked over the vine again. "Mighty fine seeds, I'd imagine. . . ."

Before he left, Mr. Letch told them what they needed to do to cull the other pumpkins. Rose thought they could simply cut the two pumpkins off the vine and leave the biggest one to grow, but Mr. Letch said they would explode their prize pumpkin if they did that.

"Explode it?" said Thomas.

"All that energy goin' into three pun'kins would suddenly go into the one and *BAM!* No more pun'kin! You gotsta *transition* it."

He told them to cut the stem partway through and to finish the cut the next day. One pumpkin at a time. This way the "energy surge" would be more gradual.

The books hadn't said anything about "energy surges" or exploding pumpkins, but Rose supposed that was because most people culled their pumpkins before they reached several hundred pounds.

"And move them cut-off pun'kins outta there or you'll have pest problems."

"But we can't move them," said Rose. "They're too heavy." That was something else she had read recently—they should've put a board or some Styrofoam or even a pumpkin tarp under each of the pumpkins when they could still move them. The tarps came equipped with handles that allowed several people to work together to lift the pumpkins.

"You know some strong young men, don'tcha?" said Mr. Letch. He jerked his head in the direction of the Jacobi house.

As they walked Mr. Letch back out to his pickup truck in front of the house, Rose added up the letters in his name. Letch added up to forty-eight, which was as insignificant a number as could be found. But the letters in Leroy added up to seventy-five, which was a little more interesting. All told, that made him a 123—one, two, three, which was intriguing. Should she try to be open, despite his friendship with Eddie Jacobi?

"It was really nice of you to help us out," said Thomas as Mr. Letch opened the door of his gigantic truck. "You sure do know a lot about pumpkins."

"Well, I like to help out my fellow growers," said

Mr. Letch. He put a dirty hand on Thomas's head. "You are a welcome addition to our ranks, little man."

No matter what his first name added up to, Rose decided there was something . . . off about Leroy Letch. From the look on Mr. Pickering's face, it seemed he felt the same.

"Now, will I see you at the Great Minnesota Get-Together in a few weeks?" Mr. Letch asked.

"I thought you weren't growing a pumpkin this year," said Mr. Pickering. His tone was not unfriendly — but it wasn't exactly *friendly*, either.

"Nope, not this year," said Mr. Letch as he climbed in his truck. "Takin' a year off to amend my soil, as they say. But I never miss the fair. I hope to see y'all there!"

He started to pull away, then slammed on the brakes. "One more thing!" he called, leaning out the driver's side window. "You should probably put a sheet or towel over your pun'kin. They can get sunburned. Y'all take care, now!"

They watched Mr. Letch's truck drive away. "Good thing he isn't competing," said Thomas. "If he grows pumpkins half as well as he grows eyebrows, he'd be the world record holder in no time!"

* * *

Thomas's attitude about the pumpkin project changed immediately. He just assumed they would enter the pumpkin in the state fair's giant pumpkin competition, even though Gram and Mama had only said, "We'll see. It costs a lot to attend a state fair, you know." Not only that, but he also assumed that they'd win. Thomas talked as though the deductible was all but paid off.

"We need to name her," said Thomas.

"Name who?"

"The pumpkin. The One. What should we name her?"

Rose looked out at the pumpkin destined to survive. It was big. It was round. It was turning a lovely shade of orange, which thrilled her. Thomas had done the cutting of the pumpkin stems under Mr. Pickering's watchful eye—nobody wanted Rose's right hand wielding Gram's big kitchen knife. He'd hesitated before sawing the knife into the vine, but then he did it and it was done—one cut, halfway through the stem. It would be off the vine the next day. Then they could do the same to the second pumpkin.

"How about Ole Bessie?" said Thomas.

"Sounds like a cow."

"Sounds like a pumpkin to me," said Thomas.

"Fine. Check with Mr. P. and make sure he likes it."

311

Thomas ran off to find Mr. Pickering in the garage. Maybe they *would* win. It would be good for Thomas to win at something. But what if they didn't? What if they took the pumpkin to the state fair and didn't win the prize money? Of course, what else were they going to do with a giant pumpkin? It wasn't like Bessie would make it through a Minnesota winter.

Chapter 41
Bridge and Soundpost

Rose stood transfixed on Will Stringer's porch.

She hadn't intended to come to his house, but she'd needed a break from Thomas. He was crazy competitive and intense about the pumpkin, and it just wore her out. So she'd gone for walk and had ended up at Stringer's House of Music.

Through the open magenta door, she could hear music coming from the back of the house. It was like nothing she'd ever heard before. It was violin, but it wasn't classical—not at all. She didn't know what it was, but there was an unusual energy and swing to it.

She had tried listening to music since the accident, but everything had sounded tinny and far away, as though the musicians were playing from inside a school locker somewhere. She knew this had nothing to do with the recordings themselves and everything to do with having lost The Music.

But this music . . . *this* music she could hear. Really hear. She leaned her head against the screen door's frame, listening hard.

"Rose?"

Her head snapped back. "Oh! Um . . . hi, Mr. Stringer."

"Call me Will, please," he insisted, his prodigious mustache bouncing. He opened the screen door wide. "Come to check on the cello, have you?"

"I guess. I mean, yes." Rose's cheeks grew hot. She didn't want to admit that she wasn't really sure *why* she had come.

"I should tell you, she's in pieces," said Will as she followed him down the hallway to the workshop at the back of the house. "I don't want that to upset you. It's all part of the repair process."

Rose nodded. "I understand."

Will smiled again. "Come in, then."

The music was louder in the workshop. It filled

Rose's head and knocked at her heart. Will Stringer gestured to a large table of cello parts, but Rose only glanced at it.

"What is this music?" she blurted.

"Ah! You like it?" The twisted ends of Will's mustache separated in a wide smile. "Stéphane Grappelli—French jazz violinist."

Rose heard the words as if they were part of a math equation: *French + jazz + violin.* She couldn't make them add up.

"Say—if you like this, then you'd really like . . ." He moved to a stereo system and rummaged around a bit. The music stopped and then the French jazz violin sound came through the speakers again, a different song. Will turned it up, and suddenly there was cello under the violin! Cello played in ways Rose would never have imagined.

Will's mustache rose up again in a smile. "Yo-Yo Ma with Grappelli."

Rose was stunned. Yo-Yo Ma played like this? With a French jazz violinist! And now she could hear piano and bass, too. She was practically light-headed.

Will laughed. "Ma is quite versatile. As is Grappelli, of course." He moved back to the corner with the music system and flipped through a couple of drawers. "Both of them have done quite a lot to extend and bend our usual notion of musical genres. Care to borrow a few CDs?"

Rose almost lunged at the small stack Will Stringer held.

"I've got more on vinyl—of Grappelli, anyway—but I'm guessing you don't have the means with which to play records. Or do you? I hear record players have come back into fashion."

Rose shook her head.

"Didn't think so. Well, you're welcome to come listen to them here whenever you like." A new track began—still of Ma and Grappelli. But this one sounded familiar, somehow.

"What is this song?"

"'Anything Goes' by Cole Porter."

"From the musical?" They'd just watched *Anything Goes*. It hadn't been her favorite musical, though she'd liked the music well enough. All the words rhymed—sometimes in pretty silly ways.

"One and the same!" said Will cheerfully. "This whole album is Porter tunes."

Rose sat down hard on a stool next to the table Will had gestured at. Her mind was blown. And it felt like her heart—her soul—had been blown *open*. She could breathe, think, *feel*.

Will watched Rose for a minute. "Have you been listening to music since your accident?"

"Not really. It doesn't sound . . . right."

Will nodded. "Sometimes something wholly different wakes up the system again. Looks like we found something that might work for you."

"It's not Bach," she said.

He laughed. "Nope. Definitely not Bach. But it's good music."

"Yes." She could hardly follow the conversation— she felt like a dry sponge that had just had a fire hose turned on it.

"Listen, Rose, you're welcome to keep me company here as long as you like—I might just move you over to this chair so I can keep working on your cello. But you sit there and soak up these tunes, and feel free to borrow whatever music you need."

She sat for most of the afternoon. Will Stringer showed her where he was in the repair process. The entire cello had been taken apart—the front and back, the sides, everything. It was interesting enough not to be upsetting. The big pieces had so many clamps—precisely placed—with felt and plastic protecting the cello's finish. He explained how the crack would be fixed and the neck regrafted. He showed her evidence of previous repairs, guessing at previous injuries. He could tell that there had been an earlier, yet poorly repaired, soundpost crack.

"Does that make it harder to replace this time?" Rose asked. She picked up a small dowel of wood lying on the worktable and absently turned it end over end.

"No, not at all," said Will. "I'm just showing you so that you know the cello has survived another . . . event. It's a pretty resilient instrument, I'd say. Exceedingly well made—a thing of extraordinary beauty, scars and all." He nodded at her hands. "You're fiddling with the new soundpost right there."

"*This* is a soundpost?" She dropped it like it was hot. It looked like a leftover scrap—a little thicker than a pencil, four or five inches long.

He nodded. "Carved it from a scrap left over from making the top of that violin over there. Some of the best spruce I've ever worked with—couldn't ask for a straighter grain."

"This little piece of wood is the cello's soul?" Rose asked, picking it up again.

"Sure is. It's not cut to fit yet, of course—it's one of the last things I'll do in the restoration. But I'm hopeful. Here's the bridge."

He handed her an unfinished bridge-shaped piece of wood. Rose cupped her hands around it. The edges were rough and splintery.

"That has to be further carved to fit this instrument—but not until it's all back together. The bridge and the soundpost need to work together— that's what gives a cello its sound, its soul. Bridge and soundpost. If you can get that right, you're pretty much good to go."

When Rose walked home that afternoon, she felt lighter than she had since the accident—really, since Thomas had told her that Mrs. Holling was moving to London. She clutched the CDs that Will had let her borrow. She couldn't wait to get home and listen to them. Maybe she'd stay up all night listening to them, one right after another.

Chapter 42
Charlotte's Web

As Rose climbed up the front porch steps, she waved at Jane, who was covering her driveway with chalk art. Maybe she'd go over and help after a while. She certainly wasn't artistic—especially with her right hand—and chalk was so . . . messy—but maybe it could count as doing something badly. In any event, she could spend some time with Jane.

She didn't even think of Jane as Calamity Jane anymore (mostly, anyway). She was just Jane. They were . . . well, friends. Maybe it was the magic of musicals; they shared something now.

Mr. Pickering leaned out his front door and called across the yards.

"Rose! Just who I was looking for. Found some things you might be interested in. You, too, Jane!"

Jane skipped across the street.

"I'll bring 'em over in a minute," Mr. Pickering called.

Rose set the borrowed CDs on the porch table and sat down in the swing. She stared at the stack. She was anxious to listen to them, but it could wait. Jane bounded up the steps.

"Hey!" said Jane.

"Hi," said Rose.

"Are you going to listen to *all* this music?" Jane asked, shuffling through the CDs with chalky fingers.

"At some point," said Rose. "I thought I'd help you with whatever you're doing over there. If you want help, that is."

"That would be awesome!" Jane's smile was wide. "Do you have any chalk? I'm trying to cover the *whole driveway* in chalk doodles, but it's a lot harder than I thought! We could do my driveway and then yours!"

That would be *a lot* of chalk drawing. But Rose decided she could do it for a while anyway.

"We can look," she said. She left the CDs on the porch and opened the front screen door, holding it wide for Jane.

The doorbell rang as they rifled through craft things in the kitchen.

"Coming," Rose called, hurrying to hold the screen door open for Mr. Pickering. He carried a small stack of books and papers and had only his bad arm to balance with.

"Glad I caught you both," he said. "These were in your cello case, Rose."

Before Rose could process what she was seeing, Jane reached out and snatched something from the top of the pile.

"Here it is!" she shrieked. She clutched the library copy of *Charlotte's Web.*

Mr. Pickering smiled sadly up at Rose. "I didn't want you to lose your sheet music, Rose. And I know how important *Charlotte's Web* is to both of you. Sorry I didn't think to empty the case out before now."

Jane looked up at Rose. "You had *Charlotte's Web?* You said you returned it and didn't know where it was!"

Rose couldn't think of what to say. She moved down two steps so she wasn't looming over her neighbors. She had returned the book, of course, on May eighth. But it didn't seem . . . relevant to say so.

"I've been looking and looking for it!" said Jane. Her voice shook. "*And you said you didn't know where it was!* All this time you had it!"

Gram came downstairs.

"Good afternoon, Otis," she said. "What seems to be the trouble, girls?"

"She had *Charlotte's Web*!" said Jane, her voice louder. "She said she didn't know where it was, but it was in her cello case the whole time."

"Rose?" Gram's eyebrows were up in a question.

"I didn't *know* I had it," said Rose. And technically, Mr. Pickering had had it for much of the time—though that was another detail that didn't seem . . . pertinent at the moment. "I forgot I took it to my last lesson. A lot has happened since then." She knew Gram wouldn't like her tone, but she couldn't help it: her whole life had been turned upside down, and Jane was flipping out over a *book*?

"But it's been missing for a long time!" Jane wailed. "Mrs. Lukashenko hasn't seen it since *May*, which means you *stole* it and you've been hiding it!"

"Rose, honey, is that true?" asked Gram.

Rose looked across the room at the *kintsugi* bowl on her cello chair. She had tucked the chair into the corner so that the bowl would be further protected—from Thomas, mostly, running through the living room. The gold scar shone brightly at her.

"Rose?" repeated Gram.

Rose shrugged. "I wasn't hiding it. I forgot where it was."

"But you *stole* it!" said Jane, louder still.

"I didn't steal it," said Rose. "I just didn't check it out."

This seemed different from stealing to her—if only slightly—but she could see it didn't make a difference to Jane.

"Why didn't you check it out?" Mr. Pickering asked.

"Because it wasn't my week to have it and I knew I wouldn't be *allowed* to check it out," said Rose, her voice almost as loud as Jane's. "Because of the stupid agreement we've had for *three years* because she is so *weird* about the book. And I *needed* it."

"*I* NEEDED IT!" screamed Jane. "AND YOU HAD IT AND *YOU LIED TO ME.*"

Jane burst into tears.

Gram reached out to her, but Jane pulled away.

"I thought you were my friend." She hurled the words up at Rose through her tears. "I never would've told you about my daddy if I'd known you aren't really my friend!"

"What's all this got to do with your daddy?" Gram asked, sounding more confused than ever.

Jane clamped her lips together tight and glared at Rose. But Rose no longer cared; Jane already hated her, so she might as well put it all out there. "Jane thinks her daddy wrote *Charlotte's Web*."

"Oh, goodness, Rose," said Gram. "She does not. That's just silly."

Rose didn't say anything. Gram's eyes widened in dismay.

Everyone turned to look at Calamity Jane.

"He *did* write it." Jane looked around the circle. "He wrote it for *me*."

"Oh, Jane," said Gram.

"Your daddy isn't E. B. White, okay?" said Rose.

"He *is*!"

"*Charlotte's Web* was written before your daddy was even born," said Rose. She knew she was being mean, but Jane was being ridiculous. "E. B. White was a famous writer, not a guy who's in and out of jail all the time. I don't know why your daddy told you that he wrote it, but he lied."

"*Rose!*" Gram scolded.

Jane pushed around Rose and ran to the bathroom and slammed the door.

Jane was locked in the Brutigans' bathroom for the rest of the afternoon and into the evening. She'd tried to flush *Charlotte's Web* down the toilet, page by page, which caused a "plumbing nightmare" of epic proportions, but she still wouldn't let anyone in, not even when water ran out under the door into the hallway. Gram called Mrs. Lukashenko, who came immediately. She sat on a towel in the hallway outside the bathroom and sang sad songs from musicals. She sang the one from *Carousel* about walking through a storm with your head held high. It made Rose's throat ache, it was so beautiful. But Jane still didn't come out, so eventually Mrs. Lukashenko called Mrs. Jacobi at work.

"Oh, baby . . ." Mrs. Jacobi had said through the bathroom door. She'd closed her eyes and leaned her forehead against the door. Rose was pretty sure she was praying. "Your daddy is many things," Mrs. Jacobi said finally. "However, an award-winning author is not one of them. He doesn't know how to love, Janey, or how to *be* loved — he thinks he needs to impress people for them to love him." She'd pressed her lips together as if she'd wanted to elaborate but thought better of it.

Gram, however, *did* elaborate on exactly what kind of man E. B. Jacobi was. She did not even attempt to explain his actions in the kindest of ways. "Scoundrel," "fool," "con man," and "poor excuse for a father" were words she muttered as she chopped vegetables for dinner that night.

Rose listened while carefully tearing lettuce for salad into bite-size pieces — pieces smaller than the ones Jane had torn the pages of *Charlotte's Web* into. Rose had cleaned up the mess in the bathroom — it seemed like the least she could do. The book was destroyed — a wet disgusting pulp. Even the cover was ruined.

As was her friendship with Jane.

Chapter 43
Waiting for Rain

It's been seventeen days since we had any rain," Rose announced. She was keeping track of temperatures and rainfall now, too. Everything affected the pumpkin. And Thomas wanted to know *all* the stats.

Thomas walked slowly with the hose, treading the wood planks that roughly followed the main pumpkin vine. The hose trickled water along the way; the vine absorbed it better if the water came gradually. They watered up and down the whole main vine in this slow, dripping fashion three times a day. Tedious, but good for Bessie.

"Try to keep the water off the leaves," said Rose.

"Why?" asked Thomas. "It's not like the rain stays off the leaves."

"I know, but let's control what we can."

Thomas adjusted where the water was dripping so it went mostly between the leaves and directly down to the dirt surrounding the vine.

"It's supposed to rain this afternoon," he said. He'd been a fanatic about the weather ever since they became serious about entering the pumpkin at the state fair.

"It was supposed to rain every day this week."

It just never quite had. It was hazy and hot all day long. It was like the sky *wanted* to rain but for some reason just couldn't. Bessie's leaves sagged, weighed down by the heavy, sticky air. Rose felt saggy and weighed down by everything that had happened with Jane.

But the pumpkin was still growing. Rose scanned the pumpkin notebook. Her right-handed handwriting continued to improve. As long as she wrote big, she did all right. Bessie gained an estimated thirty to forty pounds a day, despite the heat and lack of rain. Having all the plant's energy go into just Bessie really helped. But her weight gain was trending down a little, and Rose didn't know if slower growth indicated a problem or just that Bessie was about done growing.

They still estimated using both the circumference measurement and the new over-the-top measurement that Mr. Letch had given them. Thomas didn't think they should follow the circumference table at all anymore, but it was the more conservative estimate, and Rose didn't want them to get too excited about the larger number provided by the over-the-top tables.

"Your turn," said Thomas. He hated the tediousness of the watering. Rose put the pumpkin notebook down and waited at the end of the board outside the vines for Thomas to meet her with the hose. Very carefully, they changed places. Thomas helped guide the hose down the boardwalk so it didn't wreck Bessie's leaves.

Rose took the brace off her fingers — the bandages were gone, though she still had to be careful to keep the fingers clean. She'd already done the day's hand therapy, but there wasn't much to do standing and dripping water down the length of a giant pumpkin vine, so she isolated the middle joint of her middle finger while holding the hose and flickered her fingertip. It was easier now. She could tell things were healing. The scar down the side of her finger looked less raw and more a part of her now.

Dr. Clare said the internal stitches would "spit"

soon. They were designed to hold the tendon inside her finger together until it could hold itself together again. When their work was done, the stitches somehow knew to spit themselves to the surface and make their way out of her skin. Dr. Clare said the opening would be very small, probably along the scar. She said Rose maybe wouldn't even know the "spitting" happened. There were so many things about the healing process she would have never expected.

Rose moved down the board another few inches. She could barely see the damp tracks from Thomas's watering a few moments before. They could water all day, and it wouldn't be enough. They really needed rain. She looked up at the sky. Heavy clouds. Again. If they would just open up . . .

She readjusted her grip on the hose, isolated the middle joint of her injured finger again, and flickered the top joint another ten times as she watched the heavy clouds above her. She'd amaze Dr. Clare with how strong she was getting at her next checkup. A little extra exercise would probably go a long way—kind of like an extra twenty to thirty minutes of practice each day.

At first she thought it was water on her middle finger—and she was glad to feel it, since it meant sensations were returning—but when she looked down, there was blood all over her hand. She dropped the hose.

"Hey!" said Thomas. "Don't drop it on the vine!"

"Go get Mama," said Rose. "My finger just split open."

Chapter 44

Too Much of a
Good Thing

There *is* such a thing as too much of a good thing," said Dr. Clare. She restitched Rose's middle finger after a thorough cleaning and smeared a thick coating of antibacterial ointment down the length of the stitches. She handed the rest of the ointment tube to Mama.

"My guess is the internal stitches spit, and since you were exercising it so much, that tiny hole I told you wouldn't be a problem split the whole scar open." She sighed and wrapped clean white bandages around Rose's fingers again. "You remind me of *me* when I was your age, Rose. Don't be so eager to speed things along. Some things have to happen in their own time and can't be rushed. When I say do the exercises once or twice a day, that's perfectly sufficient. More can be a problem, as we see here."

"How long will these stitches be in?" Rose asked. She wouldn't cry. It didn't hurt; she just felt so stupid. She watched Dr. Clare wrap her hand in a clean bandage and secure her fingers back in the protective plastic brace.

"A week to ten days, I'm guessing. The tendon is healing nicely. We just need to get the finger itself to stick back together." She turned to Mama. "First sign of any inflammation, call me and we'll get some oral antibiotics going, too. She didn't have any infection the first go-around." She looked back at Rose. "Let's hope you're twice lucky."

Lucky? It was hard to think of anything that had happened this summer as luck.

"No exercises this week. Keep the brace on and the bandages clean. I want to see you the middle of next week. I'm hopeful that we can restart the hand therapy then."

"Do I have to go back to the beginning?" Rose asked. The thought of using her right hand to bend her left fingers made her want to scream.

"No, just a couple of weeks. This is a setback, not a catastrophe. I remain hopeful that you'll be taking that cello for a spin as soon as *it* is whole again." Will Stringer estimated it would take him until about Labor Day to make the repairs, and Dr. Clare found great significance in the cello repairs and Rose's healing being on the same schedule.

"Let's stay positive," said Dr. Clare. "And not overdo things. Keep the stitches goopy with ointment and keep your finger protected at all times." She reached for gloves from the box on the wall. "When you're working in the pumpkin patch, you need to have a glove on. It'll be sweaty, but that's better than dirty." She handed Rose a wad of gloves. "How is the pumpkin, by the way?"

Thomas took over the talking. Rose looked out Dr. Clare's office window. The sky was dark. Long bolts of lightning flashed in the distance. Maybe the rain would finally come.

By the time they walked out of Dr. Clare's office, sheets of rain were falling. As glad as Rose was to see the rain, she was also nervous. It was *a lot* of rain at once. Sure enough, when they arrived home, the pumpkin patch was a mud puddle. The towels they'd put over Bessie to protect her from sunburn had blown off. Rose hastily pulled one of the gloves Dr. Clare had given her over her left hand and stepped on the board that ran along the main vine. It made a *squish* noise and slid to the side in the mud. Carefully she stepped one foot in front of the other, stopping to regain her balance each time the board slipped or tipped in the mud. Bessie's leaves looked bedraggled, but Bessie herself was beautiful: shiny wet with rain, large, and orange.

Rose picked up the heavy, wet towels that had blown off Bessie and wiped at the mud splatters on the pumpkin's underside with her right hand. Bessie's underside looked okay, too. She wasn't sure what she was looking for, but the nervous feeling in her stomach had not gone away. One-handed, she slapped the soaking-wet towels back on top of Bessie and teetered across the board to Thomas. The rain was letting up, but the sky was still dark and threatening.

Just as she stepped off the board and onto Mr. Pickering's back step, Rose felt something sharp hit her shoulder. Then the top of her head. She looked accusingly at Thomas, but he was scurrying on the ground. Rose felt three more sharp stings all at once across her back. Then one on her nose. Thomas stood and held a tiny ball of ice up to Rose.

Hail.

"Rose! Thomas!" Mama yelled from their back stoop. "Come inside!"

Hail was very bad for pumpkins. Rose did not need a book to tell her that. "We need to protect Bessie!" she shouted at Thomas through the rain.

Mr. Pickering opened his back door, a worried look on his face.

"Mr. P.!" Thomas called. "Do you have a big piece of plywood in your garage?"

"Yes, but you should come in out of the storm," Mr. Pickering called back.

"Just as soon as we take care of Bessie!" Thomas sprinted across the yard, so Rose followed.

In the garage, the sound of the hail on the tin roof was deafening. Out on the driveway, pea-size chunks of ice scattered. Thomas yanked at a big piece of plywood against the garage wall. The table saw was in the way. Thomas hesitated for just a second, then pulled the heavy machine aside.

"Go get Mr. Pickering!" he yelled over the noise of the hail on the roof. The board was almost as long as Thomas was tall and not quite as wide; there was no way he could lift it on his own.

A flash of lightning lit up the garage as a clap of

thunder shook the walls. The sound and light broke Rose's gaze on the saw.

"I can do it!" She had to say it twice so Thomas could hear her.

His eyes moved to her bandaged hand. "I don't know," he said. "Maybe we shoul—"

Thunder boomed again—the storm had to be right on top of them. "I'll be careful," Rose yelled. "We've got to hurry!"

They eased the board out from behind the table saw, flipped it horizontally, and hurried out of the deafening din of the garage and into the roar of the storm. The hail—marble-size now—crunched under their feet.

"Slow down!" Rose yelled. She could hardly see Thomas through the rain. And she was afraid she would fall on the icy marbles. The wind blew hard and tried to make the piece of plywood into a sail. Rose held on as tightly as she could with her right hand. The board tipped again; it was too hard to hold it with one hand and move at the same time.

And then, suddenly, it was lighter. Steadier.

"Hey, Little Squirt!" said a familiar voice across the board.

"Cello Girl, scooch over," said an identical voice on her right. "Jane—right here, by Rose."

Rose did not let go, and neither did Thomas. But they shifted around so Jane, Jesse, and James could help. With five of them carrying the board, they moved much faster across the yard to the pumpkin vines. Rose fell once but somehow kept her left hand out of the mud, and Jane kept their side of the board up. Finally, they brought the soggy piece of plywood up and over Bessie. It sagged in the middle, collecting a puddle of water and hail, and it barely covered Bessie's orange flesh. But it was better than nothing.

The rain eased slightly, but the hail grew to Ping-Pong-ball size. The muscles in Rose's arms burned. Wet plywood was heavy, even when the weight was shared. Her left hand wasn't providing much support. It was a very good thing Jane was on her side.

Almost as quickly as it started, the storm stopped. First the hail—like the sky had dropped all it had and was suddenly empty—and then the rain slowed to a gentle mist. Rose looked around the pumpkin. Jesse and James smiled. They lifted their side of the board higher, and their faces disappeared beneath it.

"She looks okay!"

"Really?" said Rose. Thomas and Jane both poked their heads under the board.

"Yup," said Thomas. "A couple of dents, maybe, but—"

"Her skin isn't broken!" said Jane.

Rose bent to look under the board.

Big, bright, shiny, and orange. Bessie was fine.

Carefully, and much slower than they had moved into position, the fivesome moved out of the pumpkin patch. They leaned the soggy plywood against Mr. Pickering's step and turned to survey the patch.

Bessie's leaves were tattered. Some looked as if they'd been put through a shredder. Many had been stomped down in the mud as they'd moved into position with the board. But some just looked half drowned, and Rose hoped they might rally with a little sunshine. There was still a good week before the state fair, and that could mean a couple hundred more pounds of growth.

Jesse and James were still smiling, seeming very proud to have helped—and they *had* helped. She and Thomas would not have been able to do it themselves.

"Thank you," said Rose. "Thanks to all of you."

"No problem, Cello Girl!" one of the boys said.

"That's what friends are for, right?" said the other.

Rose could feel Jane watching her. Until very

recently, the Jacobis had been only neighbors—and sometimes annoyances—but she supposed maybe they were getting to be . . . friends. She and Jane had been, anyway, until the *Charlotte's Web* debacle. But Jane had come with her brothers to help protect Bessie. So maybe there was hope.

"Right," Rose said, trying not to look directly at Jane. "That's what friends are for. Thanks."

"Yes, thank you," said Mr. Pickering, tipping a pretend hat to the Jacobi kids. "Some mighty fine neighbors we have."

Mrs. Lukashenko came around the house with Mrs. Kiyo on her arm.

"Is Bessie okay?" Mrs. Kiyo asked.

"Yup," said Thomas. "She's good."

"Jesse and James and Jane helped us protect her," Rose said. "We couldn't have done it without them."

Mrs. Lukashenko smiled. "And here I thought they were just running out to sing and dance in the rain." Mrs. Lukashenko started to hum the title song from *Singin' in the Rain.*

"*Ooooh!* Look at those puddles!" exclaimed Jane, and she was off to the driveway.

It was a song about happiness, Rose decided, as she listened to Mrs. Lukashenko sing and watched Jane dance. She wondered if the "genre-bending" Yo-Yo Ma had ever played *Singin' in the Rain.* Maybe she'd try to pick it out when she got back on the cello.

Jane tried to organize a dance line with three uncooperative boys. Mrs. Kiyo laughed so hard, she had to sit down on the steps. All of Jane's usual tap steps were accentuated by flying water. The boys started doing high kicks, and Thomas lost his shoe up on the garage roof when it flew off. Through it all, Mrs. Lukashenko sang.

"Go join them, Rose," called Gram from their back stoop. "I knew that drainage problem would be good for something someday."

Rose pretended not to hear. She sat down next to Mrs. Kiyo on Mr. Pickering's steps and wound her mess of wet hair into a loose bun on top of her head. She missed Jane's ponytails.

"I'm sure Jane would be happy to teach you some steps," said Mr. Pickering. "If you're not quite ready to do this badly." He winked at her.

"No," said Rose. "I just like to watch Jane dance." She said it too loudly and it sounded fake, but she meant it. It was fun to watch Jane.

Mrs. Lukashenko finished the song and came to sit

by Rose and Mrs. Kiyo on Mr. Pickering's stoop while the other kids continued splash-dancing.

"You are maybe discouraged, Rose?" Mrs. Lukashenko said. "There is a song just for this kind of moment, you know. You learn something from Little Orphan Annie now. . . ."

She sang a song about sunshine and the promise of tomorrow. And Rose did feel better. A little, anyway. She couldn't shake the feeling that their troubles were not over with Bessie, though.

When the "dancing" was finished, Mrs. Lukashenko said, "Well, Jacobi kids, we best go get you cleaned up before your mother is home." She helped Mrs. Kiyo off the step, and the two women and two goofball boys started down the driveway. Jane lingered, gently tapping in the puddle.

Mr. Pickering went inside his house and Gram went inside theirs.

Jane came and sat down beside Rose on the steps. Rose was so grateful.

"I miss having you do my ponytail," she said after a few minutes of uncomfortable silence.

"I didn't think you'd want to see me after . . ." said Jane. The word *after* hung between them.

They watched a rabbit hop through the bedraggled pumpkin vines.

Rose took a deep breath. "Listen, Jane . . . I'm really sorry about *Charlotte's Web*. And I'm sorry I told everyone about your daddy."

Jane didn't say anything for a minute, and Rose worried she'd made things worse by mentioning it.

"I'm glad you told me, I guess," said Jane with a heavy sigh. "You probably thought I was a real idiot, believing my daddy wrote *Charlotte's Web*."

Rose decided the kindest thing was not to say anything.

"Mom says he's a liar and a cheat," continued Jane. "My daddy, I mean. Mrs. Lukashenko says he's a con man."

Rose nodded. What could she say?

"But he's my daddy." Jane shrugged as if it could not be helped—which Rose supposed it couldn't.

The rabbit had disappeared and the two of them sat in silence staring into the vines. "How come *you* like *Charlotte's Web* so much?" Jane asked.

Rose looked down at her rebandaged hand. She really hoped she hadn't set herself back for weeks. She was just starting to look ahead to September when she'd be able to try cello. Not knowing what to expect — or realistically hope for — was hard.

"It's kind of like Bach's music for me, I guess. Each word is exactly right and in just the right place. There's nothing extra and nothing missing. It's just . . . exactly right." And then she told Jane about losing The Music.

Jane nodded sadly, though she probably didn't really understand what Rose meant. Or maybe she did — she'd suffered a lot of loss, too, after all.

Jane shifted herself on the step to gently lean against Rose. "I'm sorry I flushed your favorite copy just when you needed it most."

Chapter 45
Pumpkin Prescription

The sun did come out in the morning, just as the song promised. Rose could see from the kitchen window that Bessie's leaves had perked up. They were mud spattered but sprightly. The tattered ones were still tattered, of course. All in all, though, the pumpkin patch looked much better than it had the night before.

Gram made them eat breakfast before they went out to check the damage. Rose gulped down a cranberry corn muffin and was out walking the plank to the pumpkin before she realized she wasn't wearing any shoes. As she turned to go put some on, she saw it. A split.

The information she'd read came roaring back to her: Too much water all at once could make the stem—or worse, the pumpkin itself—split in its attempt to absorb it all. Shoes forgotten, Rose continued down the board to Bessie.

The split was about an inch wide in the stem, spreading just a bit into Bessie's orange shell. It wasn't deep, thank goodness—a flesh wound, really. They could fix this. She knew how.

"Thomas!" she called over the yards.

He appeared on their back step almost instantly. "What's up?"

"Bessie has a split in her stem."

"Aw, man!" he said, his eyes wide and worried. "Seriously?"

"It's okay; I think we've caught it in time. Can you run down to Señor Ocampo's and get some fungicide? It's called Captan, I think."

She sounded confident, even to herself, but she was nervous. The books assured her that splits were a common problem; given the opportunity, the greedy pumpkin would suck up water faster than it could grow. That's when splits happened. Sort of like her finger: too much, even of a good thing, was just too much. Left untreated, the split could continue to radiate out from the stem, eventually turning into a deep, open wound in the pumpkin itself. This could expose the seed cavity to the air and everything the air carried in it: germs, or, in the case of the pumpkin, fungus. They needed to form a paste of fungicide and fill the split. It was similar to keeping her own stitches covered in ointment.

Thomas was back with the Captan in record time. He stood beside her in Mr. Pickering's kitchen, breathing hard, while Rose made a thick slurry of the fungicidal powder and water. Then Mr. Pickering found a paintbrush in a drawer, and the three of them trooped outside.

Rose painted the fungicidal paste into the stem's split, then painted it into the crack in Bessie's skin as well. She thought about the amazing *kintsugi* artists and their gold. This wasn't as pretty, but hopefully it would do the trick.

"There!" she said, satisfied.

"Looks like a mighty fine repair job to me!" said Mr. Pickering.

Rose teetered around Thomas on the plank and walked out of the patch and toward her own back door. "I'm going to go find some shoes," she called over her shoulder.

As she turned her head back around, she nearly ran

into Mr. Letch. His cantilevered eyebrows shot up in surprise.

"Hello, Rosie!"

She looked him right in the eye. "My name is *Rose*." Then she walked past him and into the house.

Once her shoes were on, Rose considered waiting inside until Mr. Letch left, but she didn't want Thomas to be alone with him. Thomas was too gullible . . . too desperate to win. Wilbur had asked Charlotte once what *gullible* meant. Charlotte said it meant "easy to fool." Rose didn't know what Mr. Letch would be trying to fool them about, but she didn't trust him. Was it just because he was friends with Eddie Jacobi? That seemed a little unfair. . . . But Mama always said to follow your gut, and her gut told her that something was shady about Mr. Letch.

"I come to check on y'all and your prizewinning pun'kin! I woulda been here sooner if I hadn't had trees go down in the storm at my place. Had to deal with *that* mess before the wife would let me go anywhere. Got my boys workin' on it now. But I thought of y'all during that storm. We had hail out by us. You must've, too. Looks like your leaves took a beatin' something fierce."

"Nothing we couldn't handle," said Mr. Pickering. "We get by with a little help from our friends."

"Don't we all!" Mr. Letch said, and laughed. "Don't we all! That's why I'm so pleased to have made your acquaintance. So pleased we're getting to be friendly-like. We can help each other, I think. For instance, I wanted to come and make sure you had the state fair information y'all will be needin'."

Mr. Letch pulled a pack of papers out of the chest pocket of his overalls and held it out to Thomas. "Pun'kin needs to be there early on the first day of the fair. Judging happens at noon that day, before all the other speck-taters get their paws all over the pun'kins. I'd advise you to load her up the night before, because it takes some doin'. Then you can get an early start in the morning. Y'all been to the Great Minnesota Get-Together?"

Thomas shook his head. It was expensive for a family of four to go. It was also filled with things Gram and Mama liked to avoid: fried foods, crazy rides, and carnival games.

"It's a real fun time!" said Mr. Letch. "You, young man, will love it. There's a Ferris wheel and the Big Yellow Slide. . . ." Thomas grinned. "There's cotton candy and corn on the cob and all kindsa things on a stick to eat. And then you gotch your butter heads and milk shakes in the dairy barn. . . . Mmmm-*MMM!*"

Thomas took the papers, eyes shining. "Mr. Letch, what do you think our chances of winning are?"

"Hold on, now, Thomas," Mr. Pickering said. "I don't believe your mama or gram have for sure decided we're going."

Thomas's shoulders sagged. "Can't you talk to them, Mr. P.? Tell them we *have* to go!"

"For what it's worth," inserted Mr. Letch, "I'd say you have an *excellent* chance of winning. What's the pun'kin measurin' these days?"

"Estimates say she might be over one thousand pounds," said Thomas proudly.

"But the gains have been slower this past week," said Rose, "and I don't know if this split will cause a setback or not."

"Slower gains are to be expected," said Mr. Letch. "It's late August. She'll keep gaining while she's on the vine—some leave 'em on until the end of September, if they're not entering 'em in the state fair. But the growth does slow, that's for sure. As for the split, it doesn't look so bad. I think she's gonna heal up just fine. You put the good stuff on her, and that was just the right thing to do."

Sometimes Mr. Letch dropped the unidentifiable accent. He'd stop rocking back and forth on his heels with his thumbs in his overalls pocket. Like he forgot. Professor Henry Higgins would be intrigued, Rose thought.

"Now, ya'll know how to move your pun'kin? It's gonna be hard, considerin' how you got these vines growin' every which way." He looked around the tattered pumpkin patch. He always looked surprised when he saw Bessie's vines. "But I think you can do it. It's all a matter of physics. You gotch yourself a truck?" he asked Mr. Pickering.

"A friend does, yes," said Mr. Pickering.

"Señor Ocampo?" Thomas asked.

"Yes. I'm sure he'll help us. *If* we decide to take Bessie."

Mr. Letch hooted. "Bessie, huh? Don't that beat all." He pulled out another sheet of paper from a different overalls pocket and handed it to Thomas. "Everything you need to know—including the plans for a tried-and-tested tripod to lift her up in the bed of the truck—is right there on that paper. Keep her on the vine until you're ready to move her."

"Thank you, Mr. Letch," said Mr. Pickering, shepherding him toward the street. "You've given us quite a lot to think about."

Chapter 46

A Terrific Demonstration of the Wonder of Physics

Mr. Pickering insisted they sit down and talk about what he called the State Fair Option. Mama made lasagna and Gram made an extra-big batch of her garlic bread. Señor Ocampo brought a salad made from his sister's garden, and Mr. Pickering brought lemonade. They set a table in the backyard near the pumpkin vine.

As soon as they sat down to eat, Thomas reminded them that they had a very good chance of winning.

"According to Mr. Letch," said Rose. "What if he's wrong?" Or was trying to fool them for some reason?

Thomas ignored this and argued that the state fair would be both fun and educational, which made Mama laugh.

"And it gives us the best chance of being able to pay the deductible," said Thomas. "We gave our word." His argument finished, he stuffed his mouth with Gram's garlic bread.

"Rose asked a good question. What if Bessie *doesn't* win?" said Mr. Pickering.

Thomas considered this. "Well, then we'll just have a fun, *educational* time at the fair," he said, smiling his winning smile at Gram and Mama. "And we can bring Bessie back home and have a party for the neighborhood."

"How expensive is it to go?" Rose asked. This was always the excuse Gram and Mama made for not going to the state fair.

"We'll figure that part out," said Mama. "Don't worry about that. Your job is Bessie."

"All right, then," said Mr. Pickering. "It's settled. I guess we're heading to the Great Minnesota Get-Together."

They spent the week in preparation. Señor Ocampo, Will Stringer, and Mr. Pickering tasked themselves with building the tripod-and-pulley system necessary for lifting Bessie into the truck. Will was fascinated by the pumpkin and was more than happy to help think through the physics of a tripod-and-pulley system. They used Mr. Letch's plans as a starting point and built the tripod from three sixteen-foot-long four-by-fours. To that they rigged a pulley system. It was simple construction, but huge. Rose felt petite standing next to it.

Mrs. Lukashenko researched pumpkin tarps at the library and Gram ordered the biggest one she found. It came from Germany, and they had to pay more in shipping than the tarp itself cost to get it in time. Kirk delivered it on the very afternoon they needed to load Bessie. Rose opened the box and unfolded the tarp. It was red and seemed very sturdy, with its handles reinforced into the rip-proof canvas fabric. But it didn't seem big enough. What if they somehow got Bessie on it, but the handles were so far under her that they couldn't use them to pick her up?

Señor Ocampo pulled his truck up through the Brutigans' backyard to get it as close to the pumpkin as possible. It still looked like a long way to carry a pumpkin the size of Ole Bessie.

Jesse and James wandered over with Jane and Mrs. Lukashenko. The twins were sure they'd be able to lift Bessie onto the tarp by themselves. Rose laughed.

"Let them try, Rosie," said Mr. Pickering. "They'll just keep thinking they can until they try."

It was hilarious to watch. Their wiry arms strained with the effort, but Bessie didn't budge.

"Sheesh — how much does this pumpkin weigh?" grunted Jesse.

"Estimates were twelve hundred eighty pounds yesterday," Thomas crowed. "Could be more today."

Could also be less. Bessie's growth had continued to slow all week. Mr. Letch had said this was to be expected, but Rose couldn't help but worry that something was wrong. What if a fungus had found its way inside the stem despite their precautions? What if Bessie's insides were turning to mush?

"That's about twelve hundred pounds more than my wimpy brothers can move, I guess," said Jane.

Señor Ocampo looked around at their little neighborhood group. "It is probably more than all of us can move," he said. "We need more help."

"How about Jeff and Simon?" Rose asked.

"Excellent idea!" said Mr. Pickering. Thomas ran off to get them and was back quickly. Jeff carried Baby Oliver on his shoulders, and Simon arrived flexing his muscles, which got Jesse and James doing the same.

"All right," said Jeff, holding out Oliver. "Who wants the baby?"

Rose volunteered. It's not like she would be much

help lifting one-handed, anyway. She was surprised how much heavier Baby Oliver was than the last time she'd held him, only a month ago.

"Stick your hip out, honey," said Gram. "He'll sit right up there."

Rose felt a little silly sticking her hip out to one side, but once she shifted him there, Oliver wasn't nearly as heavy. He pulled at the curls that had escaped her ponytail and gurgled at her while they watched his dads, Señor Ocampo, and Jesse and James push the pumpkin up a few inches on one side.

"Holy moly!" gasped Jesse.

"¡Arriba! ¡Arriba!" grunted Señor Ocampo.

Simon and Jeff struggled to get traction in the drying mud.

"A little more, guys," said Mr. Pickering, who was overseeing the whole procedure. "Perfect!"

They got the pumpkin rocked up almost on its side, and then they all leaned against it to hold it up.

"¡Rápido!" said Señor Ocampo. "Quickly, please!"

Thomas and Jane scurried around the legs of the men, dragging the red pumpkin tarp under Bessie. Once they got it about halfway under her, the group gently rocked Bessie down. They repeated the procedure on the other side, then took a break and had some lemonade. With Baby Oliver, Rose walked around Bessie, checking for cracks, oozings, and other problems. She didn't find any, which was a relief. Bessie's insides must be okay. And she was obviously heavy. Maybe Mr. Letch was right. Maybe they *would* win.

"Okay, there's sixteen handles on this tarp," said Thomas. "That's eight people using two hands." He tapped the side of his head. "Rose isn't the only math whiz in the family!"

"Actually," said Simon, "this handle is too far under the pumpkin to grab."

"Okay, fifteen handholds," said Thomas. "We need a one-handed volunteer!" His face lit up. "Rose! You're it!"

Rose handed Baby Oliver to Mama and took her place near the one available handhold. Its mate was indeed too far under the pumpkin to hold. *All* of the handles were nearly under Bessie.

"This tarp looks too small," said Jane.

"It was the biggest one," said Mrs. Lukashenko. "Guaranteed to lift twelve hundred pounds."

"Bessie might weigh more than that," said Thomas.

"Well," said Mr. Pickering, "we're going to hope for the best. We don't really have another option."

Rose looked at the path between the pumpkin and the tripod. Jesse and James had cut some of the vine away—there was a sea of giant green leaves on either side of the path. It was probably thirty long feet to the tripod at the back of Señor Ocampo's truck.

"Okay, now," said Mr. Pickering. "Nobody is to get hurt doing this heavy lifting. We're going to go slowly and carefully. We will rest more than we think we need to. We will not lift higher than we absolutely have to."

"What is this *we*?" teased Señor Ocampo. "I do not understand!"

"Hey, I'm supervising!" said Mr. Pickering.

"Let's do this thing!" crowed James. He and Jesse chest-bumped. Thomas joined in and Jesse chest-bumped him so hard that Thomas fell into the pumpkin vines. One foot peeked out above the giant leaves, making it look as if he were being eaten by the plant.

"We have a task to accomplish, gentlemen," said Gram.

"Sorry, Little Squirt," said Jesse. He extended his hand and pulled Thomas out of the vines.

"No problem!" said Thomas.

They all bent again and took their handles. It was awkward. They were too close together. Rose was glad to use only one hand to lift. She could sort of face out, which felt more dignified somehow. Everyone else had their backside out in the yard.

"*¡Uno, dos . . . tres! ¡Arriba!*" shouted Señor Ocampo.

Rose's arm felt as if it were being pulled out of her shoulder socket. And they only had Bessie a few inches off the ground. They lurched forward together.

"*¡Abajo!*" gasped Señor Ocampo.

"Gently!" called Gram.

"A-what-ho?" said Jesse when they let go of their handles and stretched their fingers out.

"*Abajo*—down," said Mr. Pickering. "*Arriba*—up. *Abajo*—down."

"We didn't make it very far," said Jane. Bessie was out of the indentation in which she had sat. But that was it. They'd moved her maybe two feet.

"Next lift easier," said Señor Ocampo cheerfully.

"Assume the position!" said Jeff.

They all grabbed their handles and Señor Ocampo counted off.

"*¡Uno, dos . . . tres!*"

"*¡Arriba!*" grunted Jesse and James together. They lifted their side so much higher than everyone else that Bessie was in danger of rolling off the other side.

"*¡Abajo! ¡ABAJO!*" shouted Mr. Pickering.

Bessie went down. Not very gently. Rose closed her

eyes. Visions of pumpkin guts oozing all over the yard flashed across her closed lids.

"Whoa!" said Jeff. "You young guys are going to have to take into account that we older folks can't lift that high and fast."

"And it is important that the pumpkin go back down on the ground as gently as you can manage," Mr. Pickering reminded them.

"Sorry," said Jesse.

"I think it was the magic word *arriba*!" said James, rolling the r's in a way that made Señor Ocampo smile.

"Let's all try it," said Thomas.

"Gentlemen and gentlewomen, assume the position," said Simon.

"*¡Uno, dos, tres!*"

"*¡ARRIBA!*" they all shouted, and heaved at the handles. It helped! They lifted Bessie higher than they had before and walked with her farther than Rose would have guessed they could.

"*¡Abajo!*" huffed Simon. They set Bessie down — very gently this time.

"Well done!" said Gram. Baby Oliver clapped.

Rose circled Bessie again, checking her for splits and the tarp for rips. Everything held. So far.

It took only three more *arriba-abajo* combinations to get the pumpkin across the yard to the waiting tripod. On the last one, Rose's handle ripped. Because she was using just one handle, she'd been pulling *out* more than *up*.

"No big deal," said James, smiling at her. "We're done with it now, anyway."

"That's right," said Jesse. "No big deal. We made it, didn't we?"

She could tell them apart now. James had a dimple when he smiled. Jesse had a birthmark on his neck. They both still needed to shave their upper lips.

It took another couple of mini-lifts and some shifting before Bessie was strapped into the tripod. Ten minutes later, she was hoisted onto the pallet in Señor Ocampo's truck, ready to be carried to the Great Minnesota Get-Together.

"A terrific demonstration of the wonder of physics," said Gram, admiring the tripod-and-pulley system.

Chapter 47

An Overdue Cut

While Mr. Pickering went to squeeze another round of lemonade and Mama retrieved the pumpkin cupcakes Gram had made, Rose filled a plastic bag with water to tie around Bessie's stem. Mr. Letch told them the pumpkin would start to dehydrate as soon as the vine was cut.

"If you give that stem access to water, she'll lose less weight while you move her," he'd told them on his last visit. Rose had asked if that wasn't somehow cheating, but Mr. Letch had laughed. "Cheating? No! Just good common sense."

Rose climbed into the bed of the truck, carrying the plastic bag of water. She was proud not to have spilled any—but as she tried to fasten it around Bessie's stem, she spilled a lot. Jeff threw her Oliver's burp rag. She wiped off the water she'd spilled, shining Bessie up a little while she was at it. The pumpkin was the most beautiful shade of orange. Rose felt so proud of the color, even though she knew it was all in the genetics. Pumpkins could be as different as she and Thomas were.

The scar from the split was visible, but it had healed and Mr. Letch was positive it would not disqualify them, so Rose tried not to be nervous about it. Mr. Letch's confidence that they could win first prize had made her hopes run wild the last few days. They had done another round of knocking on neighborhood doors and asking if anyone would hire them for odd jobs, to no avail. More and more it seemed that the pumpkin prize purse was their only hope. She just hoped they weren't being gullible.

Rose climbed around in the truck bed, wiping down the pumpkin. The only way to move around Bessie was to sit on the side and swing her legs carefully over the top of the pumpkin. For once she was glad to have long legs.

She could feel that her hair was curled up all over the place, but she was too tired to care. The ponytail itself was still nice and tight—Jane was really very good at ponytails—but rogue curls fuzzed around her hairline. The thought of washing her hair made her tired. She'd gotten pretty good at one-handed hair washing, but it took a lot longer. At the moment, she felt as if she could sleep leaning up against Bessie in the truck bed. Moving a half-ton pumpkin took a lot out of a person.

"Here, Rose," said Gram, handing her some lemonade. "You stay put and have a little lemonade. I'll go get you a cupcake."

"Thanks, Gram," said Rose. She hesitated for just a second and then called, "Can you bring me scissors, too? Please."

"Sure," said Gram.

Jane struggled to boost herself up onto the tailgate next to Rose. She looked tired, too. Her tap-dancing feet swung silently. When Gram brought the scissors, Rose handed them to Jane.

"Cut my ponytail off?" she said once Gram was out of earshot.

"Really?" said Jane, her eyes wide.

"Quick—before I change my mind. It's going to be hot at the fair—I don't want to deal with hair."

"Okay . . ." said Jane. She stood behind Rose, lifted

her heavy ponytail, and cut. Nobody on the driveway noticed. It felt as if someone were sawing through her hair, but Rose sat up straight and tried to be brave. Jane made a couple of extra snips, and then she pulled the rubber band out. Rose's hair fell forward—her whole head fell forward, in fact, without the anchor of the heavy ponytail. She shook her head, and curls fell around the sides of her face. She tucked one side casually behind her ear and felt the back. It was very short in back. She felt a little dizzy, but what was done, was done.

"Whoa!" said Thomas. *"You cut your hair!"*

"Actually, Jane did," said Rose. "Because I asked her to," she added quickly.

"It looks lovely, Rose," said Mr. Pickering.

"Muy bonita," echoed Señor Ocampo.

"Looks like you're all prettied up for the fair, sweetheart!" said Mama. "A much cooler choice of hairstyle, too." She wasn't mad. Neither was Gram. She just said, "Oh—those curls!"

Jane handed Rose her ponytail. It was thick and almost matted it was so curly. It was about the thickness of Bessie's main vine. Rose hopped down off the back of the truck. Jesse came over and pulled a curl on the side of her face.

"Boing!" he said as the curl sprang up. "Looks good, Cello Girl."

"Thanks," said Rose.

The neighbors headed home, and Rose went in to shower and wash her new hair. It took no time at all — even one-handed. She stood in her pajamas in front of the bathroom mirror, brushing her teeth. The messy curls looked fun. *She* looked fun! And she felt fun, too. She rinsed her mouth and then fluffed her curls with her fingers.

She should've cut it weeks ago.

Chapter 48

The Great Minnesota Get-Together

In the morning, Rose couldn't remember going to sleep the night before—she must have passed out as soon as her short curls hit the pillow. But she remembered her dreams. Dreams of a giant blue ribbon on Bessie.

She felt the heat of the sun as she walked through the living room; it would, indeed, be hot at the fair. She loved the morning light in late August, loved when the sun came through the front windows and fell across her cello chair. She'd loved practicing in that light. Now the sunlight illuminated the golden repair on the side of the *kintsugi* bowl. She'd have to find another place for it when she started practicing again, but for now, she liked being able to see it as she walked through the living room. Sometimes she sat and held it, when no one else was around.

She walked over to her music stand and picked up the Bach suites. Dust motes flew through the sunbeam when she opened the music. She stared at the notes of Suite no. 1's prelude, trying to make them sing through her.

Nothing. She was beginning to doubt that The Music would come back. She loved listening to Stéphane Grappelli and Yo-Yo Ma—and to the other jazz string artists Will Stringer had recommended—but after her initial excitement about the jazz sounds and rhythms, she realized that music didn't sing through her like the Bach. She loved it, but in a different way. It wasn't a substitute—more like an addition. And although she was grateful to have discovered it, she still yearned for *Bach*.

"Rose!" said Mama from the kitchen. "Come see what your gram is up to." Mama stood near the back kitchen window. "She's been out there for twenty minutes." Mama stifled a laugh. "She read that a diluted vinegar wash would shine Bessie's skin *and* remove potential harmful bacteria."

Rose watched Gram wash Bessie's sides with the

same cleaning solution she used to wash her wood floors.

"It's just like *Charlotte's Web*," said Rose. "Mrs. Zuckerman gets up early on fair day and washes Wilbur in a buttermilk bath before they take him to the fair."

"Well, it's good she didn't use buttermilk, because I needed that for the pancakes," said Mama. "Go wake your brother up. We've got to get a move on."

"I'm up!" Thomas announced, bounding into the kitchen. "And I'm hungry!"

Gram came in the back door and slid off her red rubber boots. She looked triumphant.

"Bessie is *stunning* in the morning sun! Wouldn't it be nice if they did the judging outside in the sunshine?"

"It's not a beauty contest, Gram," said Thomas. "It's a *weight* contest."

"Mr. Letch says there's more control in the horticulture building," said Rose. "They've got ropes to keep the crowds back from the vegetables. People always want to touch them." She shuddered, thinking of hundreds of germy hands on Bessie, poking and prodding and possibly damaging her skin.

Mama put three large blueberry pancakes on Rose's plate. They heard singing and heavy steps on the front porch. Mrs. Lukashenko was singing about a beautiful morning and everything going their way.

"Eat up," said Mama. "Mrs. Lukashenko is here with hits from *Oklahoma!* The Jacobis will be here soon."

Señor Ocampo and Mr. Pickering drove Bessie slowly on the back roads to the fair, while Mama and Gram, Rose and Thomas, the Jacobi kids, and Mrs. Lukashenko rode the bus. Mrs. Kiyo waited with them at the bus stop, but she declined to go to the fair.

"No, no, no!" she said. "I will wait for the stories when you come home. And I'll hope to see a blue ribbon, too!"

The smells hit them as they crossed the pedestrian bridge that took them over Como Avenue and into the fair: French fries. Cotton candy. Dust and animals. Something very rich and chocolaty. Hot dogs. Bacon cream puffs? There were signs everywhere offering every imaginable food—all on a stick!

"Do we get to eat this stuff?" asked Thomas as they passed a corn dog stand.

"Of course," said Mama. "We're pooling our money for food and rides. But at the state fair, money goes fast. We will have to make choices."

"But first!" said Mrs. Lukashenko. "We go to see the pumpikins!"

Rose smiled. She loved the extra syllable Mrs. Lukashenko put in *pumpkin*.

They found the horticulture building by following a boy carrying an enormous zucchini.

"Holy moly!" said James.

"That's as big as my leg!" said Jesse.

As soon as they walked in the building, they saw a big sign reading GIANT PUMPKIN COMPETITION THIS WAY! The crowds were already thick, even though it was only eight in the morning. They were swept along in a river of people.

Displays of heirloom fruits and vegetables lined the hallways. There were slices of beehives between glass, real bees working hard on the honey. A woman yelled through a megaphone about a demonstration in flower arranging that was about to start. A man wearing a headset microphone tried to talk over her about a contraption that could "slice, dice, mix, and stir, pulverizing the cell walls of your produce to release their life energy into your salsa!" It cost $19.95 and included a free storage container. Gram looked dubious.

"All you really need is a good sharp knife," she said. No one would ever call Gram gullible.

They slowed to look at the seed art. There were astounding pictures and murals made entirely from plant seeds! The seeds were very small, and the pictures were incredibly detailed. Rose had never seen anything like it.

"We're almost to the pumpkin room!" said Mama, hustling them along. Reluctantly, Rose pulled her gaze from the seed art and allowed herself to be swept along in the current of the crowd.

Chapter 49
To the Midway

There she is!" said Jane as soon as they walked in. Bessie was on a platform, elevated from the rest. Rose couldn't imagine how they got her up there. They must have had another tripod to hoist her so high. Below Bessie, on a smaller wooden structure, there were several large—but definitely not larg*er*—pumpkins.

"She's the biggest one, for sure!" said Thomas.

"Nobody else's pumpkin is even close!" said Jane.

Rose looked at their supposed competition. They were big pumpkins, all right, but they were nowhere near giant. They looked to be about where Bessie was a month ago—a few hundred pounds, tops.

"I bet I could lift some of these pumpkins," said Jesse.

"We're going to win for sure!" said Thomas.

Rose should've been excited, too. But it was strange how all of the other pumpkins were so much smaller than Bessie. They hadn't even known what they were doing until these last few weeks. Where were all the people working to grow the first one-ton pumpkin?

They found Mr. Pickering and Señor Ocampo looking at the giant tomatoes, which were on the other side of the giant pumpkin platform. The tomatoes were bigger than softballs and strangely shaped, as if they had relaxed or melted slightly. Nothing was perfectly round when it was gigantic.

"How did they get Bessie up on the platform?" Rose asked Mr. Pickering.

"Mr. Letch told us to load her on a wooden pallet, remember? Well, when we got here and backed the truck into that door right there, a forklift appeared and picked Bessie up as if she were as light as a feather."

"They *carried* some of the other pumpkins in," said Señor Ocampo. "And they put each one on . . . *la báscula*. . . . How do you say?"

"Scale," said Mr. Pickering. "They weighed them before they put them on display."

"And . . . ?" said Gram.

"How much did that Bessie pumpikin weigh?" pressed Mrs. Lukashenko.

Rose looked at Thomas—he was bouncing lightly on his toes, which was sort of how she felt inside.

"One thousand three hundred sixty-five pounds!" said Mr. Pickering. "We might have the competition sewn up, my friends." Their whole group cheered.

Jesse and James could not get enough of the giant vegetables. They were dangerously close to picking up the tomatoes when Mrs. Lukashenko swatted them with her purse.

"No touching! We don't want any touching on our Bessie, do we? Hands in your pockets!" The boys obediently shoved their hands in their pockets. "Those ve-ge-ta-bles do not need your germs."

"Can I have some money?" Jane asked. "I want to go on the rides!"

"Jane, dear!" said Gram. "You are not going out and about in the fair by yourself. We are going to stick together."

Sticking together probably meant they'd have to go through the arts and crafts building, which was all Mama, Gram, and Mrs. Lukashenko could talk about on the bus ride to the fair.

"Tell you what," said Mr. Pickering. "How about Señor Ocampo and I take the kids to the midway while you ladies go look around?"

"But we can't just leave you with all the kids," said Mama.

"Sure you can," said Mr. Pickering. "We'll meet you at the Big Yellow Slide in a couple hours and find ourselves some lunch on a stick before the pumpkin judging at noon."

The adults argued in a friendly way for a few minutes, pushing money back and forth and asking "Are you sure?" kinds of questions, but then everyone agreed to the plan. They had to stand and listen to Mama, Gram, and Mrs. Lukashenko give instructions before they were allowed to go, however.

"You must stay together," said Mrs. Lukashenko to the Jacobis. "You give Mr. Pickering and Señor Ocampo *no* trouble."

"And that goes for you two as well," said Gram. "Stay together."

"If you need to use the bathroom," said Mama, "you must take someone with you."

"No carnival games!"

"What's so bad about carnival games, anyway?" asked Thomas.

"They're rigged to make sure you lose," said Gram. "And even if you *do* win, the prize you get isn't worth the money you paid to play. You might as well throw your money directly in the trash!"

"And hold on if you ride those terrible swings that go 'round and 'round up in the air!" Mrs. Lukashenko shuddered.

"They'll be fine," said Mr. Pickering, herding the kids toward the midway.

"Don't eat a lot of junk that will make you sick to your stomachs!"

"Try not to get dirty, Thomas!"

"Watch out for pickpockets!"

"They will be fine!" said Señor Ocampo, laughing.

They said good-bye to Mama, Gram, and Mrs. Lukashenko, and then they were out in the sunshine and back into the smells of the fair, headed in the direction of the Ferris wheel.

They stopped at the dairy barn for a milk shake. Rose and Jane decided to share a strawberry one. While they waited in line, they watched the first of the fair's butter heads being carved, curlicues of butter falling to the floor. It didn't look like much besides a gigantic block of butter, but supposedly it would become the head of

Princess Kay of the Milky Way, the state's dairy princess, by the end of the day.

They walked through the animal barns. The mama pigs were more enormous than Rose ever thought possible. Some of them were bigger than Bessie, even! They didn't look as if they could stand on their own legs.

"They're bigger than Uncle, I bet," Rose whispered to Jane. Jane smiled up at her. Uncle was the pig who won the first-prize ribbon in *Charlotte's Web*. Not Wilbur, though Wilbur won a special prize.

When they got to the midway, Mr. Pickering and Señor Ocampo found a bench to sit on, and they handed Rose money to buy tickets for rides for everyone.

"If you need more, come back to this bench and we'll negotiate," said Mr. Pickering. He looked each one of them in the eye. "You must stick together. All five of you need to come back to this bench together in exactly one hour."

A whole hour on the midway by themselves? They bought tickets at a ticket stall and looked around for the first thing to do.

"Step right up! Step right up! You! Young man!" someone called in a loud, rough voice.

Chapter 50
The Carnival Game

Young *men,* I should say! Seein' double, I am!" A carnival barker looked from Jesse to James and then shook his head as if to clear his vision.

"Step right up, both of you! Two tickets gets you a roll of the dice! A prize is guaranteed!"

A small crowd gathered. Both Jesse and James began to swagger, as full of themselves as when they sang Tom Petty outside the library.

"Sure, I'll give it a try," said Jesse.

The game was a tic-tac-toe sort of board with squares numbered two through twelve. The first square had a star and not a number. Each square had a "prize"—junk that looked like it had been purchased at the end of a garage sale, a quarter for a bucket of odds and ends. There were smudgy erasers in the shape of a cat, cheap plastic jewelry, little-kid stickers, and a rubber duck that looked as if it had mold inside. The number two box didn't even have anything in it.

"I'm going to win Rose that music bookmark in number twelve," said Jesse. "How many tickets?"

"Just two," said the man. "It's your lucky day!"

The music bookmark was nice: a shiny gold treble clef that slipped onto your book's page like a paper clip. Rose had noticed it right away. Still, the money from Mr. Pickering had bought them only forty tickets. They shouldn't waste two on the bookmark—assuming they could even win, which Gram had seemed pretty confident was an impossibility.

"Don't," she said. "Let's go on a ride instead."

"Not until I win something," said Jesse.

"How come the number two square doesn't have a prize in it?" asked Jane as Jesse handed over two tickets.

"Why, that's where I put your tickets," said the man with a smile that flashed a gold tooth. "If this big guy rolls a two, you win your tickets back! Not hard to roll a two—such an itty-bitty number." He handed two blue plastic dice to Jesse.

"But it *is* hard to roll a two," said Rose.

Jesse shook the dice in his hand, waiting for her to explain.

"The probability that you will roll a two—or a twelve, if that's what you're hoping for—is not very good at all, actually. Only one in thirty-six. Which is less than a three percent chance."

Everyone stared at her, including the carnival game worker.

"How do you *know* that?" said James.

"It's just probability," said Rose.

"Just as much chance of rolling a one or a six as any other number!" said the man. "Roll 'em, son!"

Rose reached out and stopped Jesse's arm from throwing the dice. "He's right. When you roll a single die, you have a one in six chance of rolling any one number. But you have to roll *two* ones or *two* sixes. The odds of doing that are much worse. It's much more likely—six times more likely, actually—that you will roll a seven than it is that you'll roll a two or a twelve. To get a seven, you can roll a one and six, a two and five, or a three and four. But you only have one combination each to get a two or a twelve."

"Eeewwww," said Jane, looking at the seventh square. "A yucky duck!"

"Man, I hate probability problems," said Jesse.

"Well, you have a probability problem here," said Rose. She loved probability problems. "And we don't have many tickets."

The carnival barker glared at her, but then wiped off his glare with a gold-toothed smile.

"Smart lady!" he said to the growing crowd. "How about if I sweeten the pot? I'm gonna let you put two tickets on any square you like—Ms. Probability here can feel free to advise—and if you win that square, I'll give your two tickets back to you and two more, besides!"

"Sounds like a deal to me," said Jesse. "Rose, which one should we put our tickets on?"

"Well, you're most likely to roll a seven. But you still have only a one in six chance of that happening."

The carnival barker rolled his eyes back in his head and pretended to snore.

"So I guess you have to decide if you want to waste two of our tickets," Rose said. "Because your chance of doing that is more than eighty percent."

Everyone in the crowd looked at her as if she were from outer space. This really was not a difficult math problem—nothing like the equation for guesstimating a pumpkin's weight. If more people remembered their elementary probability problems, carnival barkers would probably be without a job.

"Okay, kids," said the man, his voice hard. "If you all aren't going to play, why don't you move on and give someone else a chance?"

"I'll play, I'll play!" said Jesse. He put his tickets on square number seven and moved the moldy duck to square number two. He shook the bright-blue dice in his hands and threw them.

"A seven!" barked the man. He smiled. "I guess the odds are working in your favor, after all!" He handed Jesse four tickets.

"Try your luck again?" said the man. "You put those four down, and I'll double them again if you win."

Jane tugged on her brother's arm. "Come on, Jesse. Let's go on some rides now!"

"In a minute," said Jesse. He put the four tickets down in number seven's box and rolled the blue dice again.

"Seven again!" The crowd around them clapped. "This boy is l-u-c-k-y!"

Jesse hadn't just rolled a seven again—he'd rolled a three-four combination again. Rose puzzled over the odds of rolling that specific combination twice in a row.

It was a more complicated probability equation to work without pencil and paper or a calculator, but she knew the chances weren't good. Not good at all.

"Tell you what," said the man. "Third time is the charm, I bet! Why don't you put *all* your tickets down—any square—and I'll double *all* of them if you win."

"Do it!" Thomas said. "If we win again, we'd have ninety-two tickets!"

"I think you mean ninety-*six* tickets," said the man. "You started with forty, right? And so far you've won eight. Forty-eight times two is ninety-*six*."

"We've only won *six* tickets, though, not eight," said Thomas. "Those first two tickets we bet with were part of our forty already."

"Smart boy," the man said. "And you just saved me four tickets—assuming you win again, of course! Whadya say," he said, turning back to Jesse. "Third time's the charm?"

"I don't know," Jesse said, full of doubt now that all their tickets were on the line. But Rose had done the math.

"We're in!" she said, pushing their pile of tickets onto the board—and onto the number seven square again.

"Rosie!" said Thomas, shocked.

"Look who's come around!" The man grinned broadly, his gold tooth flashing. "And because I like you kids so much, I'm going to give you my Extra-Special Lucky Dice to play with!"

He handed Jesse a pair of red dice that sparkled when they caught the light. They looked like rubies. Jesse took them gently in his hand, as if they'd cast a spell over him.

Rose's stomach flip-flopped. "No, thanks," she said firmly. "We'd rather use the blue." Her whole plan required them to use those blue dice.

"Hey, now," argued the man. "Are *you* playing, or is it this handsome young man here who's throwing the dice? Surely he can have the same good luck with new dice!"

Jesse shook the ruby-red Extra-Special Lucky Dice in one hand. He leaned toward Rose. "What should I do?" he said softly. He smelled like boy.

Rose looked at the carnival barker with narrowed eyes. "Use the red dice," she whispered. "But . . . put the tickets on twelve." It was just a hunch. She hoped she was right.

Jesse moved the gold treble clef bookmark from the

number twelve square to the number seven square and put their tickets on twelve.

"Whoa, now!" said the man. "Sure you want to do that?" He laughed a nasty laugh. "Chances of rolling a twelve are slim indeed! What are the odds did you say, missy?"

"One in thirty-six," said Rose. She was sure now.

Jesse prepared to toss the red dice.

"I think you better use the blue dice, after all," said the carnival barker. But it was too late. Jesse had already thrown down the sparkling red dice.

"TWO SIXES!" screamed Jane. "We won!" The crowd hooted and clapped.

James and Thomas chest-bumped. Jane collected their forty-six tickets off the game board. Rose held out her hand to the man, who was glowering.

"Forty-six more tickets, please."

Chapter 51
Lunch

So, what just happened?" asked James as they continued walking through the midway. "Were *both* sets of dice rigged?"

Rose nodded. "I was fairly certain the blue ones were rigged to roll only sevens, but I thought his so-called lucky red dice were regular dice—until he panicked when we moved our tickets to the number twelve square."

"But how'd you know to do that?" asked Jesse, his voice full of admiration. "What made you think they were rigged to roll a twelve?"

Rose shrugged. "I had a hunch." A gut feeling. Mama was right—trusting that feeling was a good idea. "The best prize was on the twelve, so I figured he'd need someone to win that prize from time to time in order to stay in business."

"How'd he rig the dice, anyway?" asked Thomas. "They looked like regular old dice to me."

"I saw a movie once," said James, "where they altered the dice by putting them in the microwave. Plastic dice will get soft and then the weight will sink to the bottom. Maybe that's what he did."

"Isn't that cheating?" said Jane.

"Yes, it is," said Rose.

"You saved us, Rose!" said Thomas. "We must've looked pretty stupid."

"Not stupid. Gullible," said Rose.

"That man was a liar and a cheat," said Jane.

"I'm sure they're not all like that," said Rose. She hoped not anyway. "But maybe we can be done with the games now."

"Finally!" shouted Jane. "Rides!"

"Right on time!" said Mr. Pickering when they ran back to the bench forty minutes later. "Have fun?"

Jesse and James told them about the two different roller coasters they'd ridden, and Thomas and Jane told them about the Octopus, the bumper cars, and the carousel.

"What ride did you like, Rosie?" asked Mr. Pickering.

"The Ferris wheel." Jesse and James had fought over which one would get to ride with her, and while they argued, she'd climbed into a chair by herself, leaving them squabbling below. It had been wonderful up above the fairgrounds alone. She could see the horticulture building, the grandstand, the bungee jump. . . . The people below were tiny and far away.

"We'd best make our way to the yellow slide," said Mr. Pickering. Señor Ocampo led the way. It felt like they were in a parade marching through the crowds out of the midway and on to the pumpkin competition. Mr. Pickering even raised his cane up and flourished it as though he were Professor Harold Hill in *The Music Man*.

The relief on the faces of Mama, Gram, and Mrs. Lukashenko was evident. Mrs. Lukashenko actually counted them, as if they were little ducks returning from an adventure.

"We rode the swings, Mrs. Lukashenko," said Thomas in a teasing voice.

"*Those swings!*" She closed her eyes in horror. "Did you hold on?"

"I did," said Thomas. "But Rose waved her hands in the air the whole time."

Mrs. Lukashenko pretended to faint. Actually, Rose had held on the tightest of anyone. The swings looked like such a gentle ride, but she had to agree with Mrs. Lukashenko—it was awful.

"Did you play any carnival games?" asked Gram.

"Nah," said Jane. "We're not *that* gullible."

Jesse and James smiled. Thomas raised his eyebrows at Rose. She shrugged.

They had French fries and foot-long hot dogs for lunch. Gram had picked up a new yardstick in the home-improvement building, and she measured the hot dogs.

"Twelve inches exactly!" she said.

"Measure me!" said Thomas.

Rose took Gram's yardstick and had him stand up against the wall of a food stall that fried candy bars and put them on a stick. She measured very carefully, twice.

"Well?" said Thomas.

"Four feet . . . *seven and a HALF* inches tall," said Rose with a smile.

"*I've grown?*" said Thomas. "Are you sure?"

"You know how precise I am."

Thomas leapt in the air and ran to tell the others.

Señor Ocampo bought fresh-squeezed lemonade

(which wasn't as good as Mr. Pickering's) for everyone. "We need to get back to Bessie," he reminded them.

"We'll get our dessert-on-a-stick after the awards," said Mama.

Gram handed out wet wipes from her purse, which was embarrassing, but also nice for getting the stickiness off. Rose was starting to feel sticky everywhere, and she was struggling to keep her left hand clean. She was back to wearing the brace without the bandages now, but she almost wished she'd wrapped up her fingers for the day; the Great Minnesota Get-Together was a grimy place. She fluffed her curls with her right hand, very glad she'd cut her hair.

They walked back to the horticulture building, too stuffed and hot to be tempted by anything else—on a stick or otherwise.

"Are you nervous?" Jane asked as they made their way through the building.

"Why would I be nervous?" But maybe she was. She knew Bessie was the biggest of the pumpkins at the fair—by far—and so she felt confident that they would win. But she didn't feel the calm that usually went along with confidence.

If she had to put a name to it, she'd say that what she was feeling was *uneasy*.

Chapter 52

The Awards

Rose saw the blue ribbon as they rounded the corner into the room of giant vegetables. The deep blue looked fantastic on Bessie's orange skin. She didn't say anything because she wanted Thomas, who was worming his way through the crowd, to see the ribbon for himself.

It was five minutes to noon and the room was crowded. Who knew so many people enjoyed giant pumpkins? A small stage had been put together near the giant zucchinis. Someone was testing a microphone, and it popped noisily over the conversations swirling around them.

"We won!" Thomas shouted, darting back through the crowd to find Rose. Jesse and James high-fived him. They high-fived Rose, too. Mama and Gram and Mrs. Lukashenko hugged each other and then Señor Ocampo and Mr. Pickering.

"We couldn't have done it without you, you know," said Mr. Pickering when Rose hugged him.

"Hey!" said a voice behind them. "You the growers of the winner?" Rose turned to see a friendly-looking young man.

"Indeed we are!" said Mr. Pickering. He reached out a hand and introduced himself. "And these are my next-door neighbors, Rose and Thomas Brutigan, the primary growers of our prizewinning pumpkin."

"She's a beauty!" said the man, who introduced himself as Alex Kenning. "And *one thousand three hundred sixty-five pounds*! You're almost a thousand pounds bigger than my buddy's pumpkin that came in second place. I was a distant third." He had a grin like Thomas's.

"We couldn't have done it without these guys — and a few others, besides!" said Mr. Pickering. He introduced Señor Ocampo, Mrs. Lukashenko, Mama, Gram, and the Jacobi kids. "It's been sort of a neighborhood project," added Mr. Pickering.

"Often is!" Alex laughed.

Another man came up and slapped Alex on the back.

"Congrats, my friend!" the man said. "Third place—safely played!"

"Yeah, you too," Alex said. "Bob, this is Otis, Rose, and Thomas, the first-prize growers."

"Nice to meet you. I guess I was your closest competition."

"Some of the glory but none of the pain!" said Alex.

"Say, we've been wondering," said Bob, "how big is your Big One?"

"Bessie *is* our Big One!" said Thomas.

The grin fell off of Alex's face. "This pumpkin is your biggest one?"

"We only have one," said Thomas.

"And you brought it *here*?" said Bob.

Rose suddenly felt cold. "Where else would we bring it?" she asked.

"Anywhere but here," said Alex.

"LADIES AND GENTLEMEN!"

The sound system crackled and popped.

"OOOOOHHH-WEEE! SORRY ABOUT THAT!" said the voice again, no softer at all. The man's voice was familiar.

"JUST GETTING THINGS SET UP HERE. . . ."

There was horrible shrieking feedback from the microphone. The crowd covered their ears, which made it difficult for Rose to look over the heads and see who was booming into the microphone.

"ALL RIGHT! IS THIS ANY BETTER? I'M NOT HURTING ANY EARS *NOW*, AM I?"

She had definitely heard that voice before. Rose carefully sidestepped to look between Jesse and James. The speaker was turned to the amplifier, so she could only see the side of his face. He was wearing a striped suit, his hair was slicked back, and he wore dark sunglasses, even though they were inside. He looked like an old-timey gangster.

"LADIES AND GENTLEMEN! BOYS AND GIRLS! IT'S TIME FOR OUR GIANT PUMPKIN AWARDS!"

His voice buzzed in the center of Rose's brain. Suddenly, the man shifted position so he was facing her. Giant cantilevered eyebrows rose out and over the sunglasses.

"Is that . . . Mr. Letch?" she said. Her stomach hiccupped. Mr. Letch had dropped his pumpkin-farmer bumpkin act—no accent, no overalls, no trampled hat.

He was all spiffed-up now. He looked like a completely diffcrent person. Except for the eyebrows.

Bob and Alex turned around quickly and stared at Rose.

"You know Leroy Letch?" said Bob.

Rose nodded.

"He helped us these last few weeks with Bessie," said Thomas.

"WE'RE GOING TO START WITH THIRD PRIZE. . . ."

"What do you mean, he *helped* you?" said Alex.

"He showed us how to do over-the-top measurements," said Rose. "And he told us we needed to cull down to one pumpkin, and . . . he encouraged us, I guess, to enter this competition."

"Ycah, I bet he did," said Alex. He exchanged a knowing look with Bob.

"THIRD PLACE, AT TWO HUNDRED NINETY-SEVEN POUNDS—COULDN'T BREAK THAT THREE-HUNDRED-POUND MARK, I GUESS!—ALEX KENNING! ALEX, MY FRIEND . . . COME ON UP!"

The crowd clapped and whooped as Alex headed to the stage to claim his prize.

"Did Leroy tell you how the state fair competition works?" asked Bob over the cheers for Alex.

"A CERTIFICATE AND A SHINY YELLOW RIBBON!" barked Mr. Letch. He handed Alex what looked like a simple piece of paper and a limp, faded ribbon. He stuck his hand out to shake Alex's hand, but Alex stepped away without shaking it.

"Let me guess," said Bob, "this is your first time growing a giant pumpkin?"

Rose nodded.

"AND OUR SECOND-PLACE WINNER . . . AT THREE HUNDRED NINETY-FOUR POUNDS— NOT QUITE BREAKING THE *FOUR-HUNDRED-POUND* MARK . . ." Mr. Letch chuckled like this was a good joke. "BOB OLSON! COME ON UP HERE, BOB!"

"Be careful," said Bob. He was already being pulled through the crowd and up to the stage. "If I were you—"

"BOB OLSON! DON'T MAKE US WAIT ALL DAY."

The crowd started to chant: "Bob! Bob! Bob!"

Bob climbed the steps and took his piece of paper and a crumpled red ribbon from Mr. Letch—he also did not shake hands—then took his place next to Alex.

"AND NOW . . . I'VE SNAGGED ONE OF THE DRUMMERS FROM THE MARCHING BAND SO THAT WE CAN HAVE A NICE DRUMROLL! BECAUSE THIS IS THE MOMENT YOU'VE BEEN WAITING FOR! A MINNESOTA STATE FAIR *RECORD*!"

Rose covered her ears. He was so loud, she couldn't think. The drum started to roll.

"OUR FIRST-PRIZE WINNERS, WITH A PUMPKIN NAMED OLE BESSIE . . ." The crowd chuckled with him. "WHO WEIGHS *ONE THOUSAND* . . . THREE HUNDRED . . . SIXTY-FIVE POUNDS!" The crowd went wild. "WILL BESSIE'S GROWERS PLEASE COME UP? ROSE AND THOMAS BRUTIGAN!"

Chapter 53

To Win or Not to Win

The crowd parted so they could make their way up. People whistled and clapped and hooted. Rose followed Thomas without even meaning to, and they were on the stage before she could think what else to do.

"Hiya, Mr. Letch!" said Thomas into the microphone Mr. Letch was holding. "I didn't know you were in charge of things here at the fair."

Mr. Letch yanked the microphone over Thomas's head. "LET'S GET YOU AND YOUR BIG SISTER A GREAT BIG PRIZE, NOW." His enormous eyebrows clinched down on his sunglasses.

The crowd's applause started up again. Rose looked for Jane and Jesse and James, but she couldn't find them in the crowd. She looked for Mr. Pickering, for Mama and Gram, but all the faces swirled together. She didn't know what was happening, but she knew something was wrong. And then she heard a voice: "He takes the pumpkin."

At first she thought the voice came from inside her, like The Music, but then she realized it was Alex, who was standing behind her. Mr. Letch was posing Thomas as though he were an easel. He made Thomas spread his feet apart and then hold his hands down by his hips with his fingers curved. The crowd laughed. Thomas tried to play along, but he looked confused.

Alex whisper-shouted in her ear, "The prize giver gets to take home the biggest pumpkin, according to the competition rules."

Mr. Letch would keep Bessie? What did he even want with her? Rose's head swam.

"AND NOW, A GIGANTIC CHECK FOR A GIGANTIC PUMPKIN!" Mr. Letch placed a huge cardboard check on Thomas, the bottom held by his bent fingers, the top resting against his head. Only his legs stuck out. The crowd hooted and clapped.

Mr. Letch pulled a check from the breast pocket of his suit coat and held it out to Rose, waving it in the air. "THIS HERE'S THE REAL THING!" He waggled his horrible eyebrows. "FIVE HUNDRED SMACKEROOS!"

Somehow the check was in her hand. She didn't remember taking it, though. Five hundred dollars, sloppily written, swam before her eyes. She looked at Thomas, who'd set the huge cardboard check on a giant zucchini. What was happening?

A clear, strong voice rang out over the crowd: "Mr. Letch, you're a liar and a cheat! And you can't have Ole Bessie!"

Rose turned to look. Jane was standing at the foot of the stage's steps—hands planted firmly on her hips. Bob and Mr. Pickering stood on either side of her.

Mr. Letch laughed his terrible laugh. "WELL, YOUNG LADY, THAT'S THE RULES OF THIS CONTEST! ROSE AND HER LITTLE BROTHER GET FIVE HUNDRED DOLLARS, AND THE PRIZE GIVER—THAT'S ME!—GETS THE PUMPKIN! QUITE A DEAL, I'D SAY!"

"Did the kids know that ahead of time?" someone from the crowd called up to Mr. Letch.

Others in the crowd murmured.

"OF COURSE THEY DID!" boomed Mr. Letch. Rose saw sweat beading up over his eyebrows. "EVERYBODY KNOWS THAT'S HOW THIS

COMPETITION WORKS! BESIDES, IT'S ON THE ENTRY FORM! I WON THAT BIG PUMPKIN FAIR AND SQUARE!"

Rose met Mr. Pickering's eyes. Her neighbor looked sick with remorse; if that information *was* on the entry form, she knew that he'd missed it.

"I don't understand," Rose said to Alex, who was still by her side. "What does he even want with Bessie?"

"He doesn't want the pumpkin," Alex said. "He wants the seeds."

Seeds? That's what this was about? He wanted Bessie's seeds?

Rose looked down at the check in her hand. She looked at Thomas.

"TELL YOU WHAT," said Mr. Letch, his voice smoothing out. "To make sure there are no hard feelings—and since the two of you worked so hard on growing this pumpkin—how about I DOUBLE THE PRIZE PURSE? FIVE HUNDRED DOLLARS *FOR EACH OF YOU!*"

One thousand dollars! Two things zipped through Rose's mind:

1. This was twice what they needed to pay the deductible on the cello insurance policy.
2. Mr. Letch really wanted Bessie.

"I'LL WRITE YOU THE SECOND CHECK RIGHT NOW!" Mr. Letch reached into his suit coat pocket again and brought out a checkbook. "ANYBODY GOT A PEN?" he yelled out into the crowd. "GOTTA GET THESE KIDS THEIR MONEY!"

Rose locked eyes with Thomas. The rest of the room melted away, and it was just the two of them. They had to decide: Did they take the money and let this shady con man grow a whole field of pumpkins related to their Bessie? Or did they refuse the prize money and take Bessie back home with them? If they did that, how would they ever get the five hundred dollars they needed?

And then suddenly, there was Bach! The prelude to Suite no. 1 coursed through her as if it had always been there—as if the volume had just been turned down for a while, or maybe everything else had been turned up.

The relief that flooded through Rose almost buckled her knees. As the beloved prelude from Suite no. 1 pranced its way through her—dancing around her heart, swirling through her body—Rose nearly laughed. Mrs. Holling was right: it almost seemed like a gift to have lost The Music so that she could experience its return.

Rose immediately knew what to do. She looked to Thomas, who nodded once and smiled.

"Another check won't be necessary," said Rose. Confidence flooded through her as the last line crescendoed to measure forty-two's final chord. Somehow — she didn't know how, but somehow — they would figure out another way to get five hundred dollars.

"You can't have our Bessie, Mr. Letch." She ripped his check in half and handed him the pieces. "She's ours and we're taking her back home with us."

Chapter 54

The Pumpkin Party

They invited the whole neighborhood to the pumpkin party on Labor Day. Others, too. They invited everyone who'd been involved in the summer's pumpkin project, in fact, which was most everyone they knew. Except Mr. Letch—they did not invite him.

Gram had given Bessie two more vinegar-and-water baths during the week. A soft spot had developed on Bessie's backside, but she still looked great. Big and round(ish) and a gorgeous pumpkin-orange color.

A few minutes after Señor Ocampo parked his truck outside their house and uncovered the pumpkin, their front yard started to fill with neighbors and friends.

Jesse and James arrived first, which made Rose nervous. What if they ate all of Gram's treats before everyone else came? But then Mrs. Kiyo was second, and that made Rose feel better. And Señora Ocampo came, bringing her parents, who were visiting from Mexico. They spoke no English at all, but their joy and wonder over Bessie needed no translation.

Even Mrs. Jacobi managed to get the afternoon and evening off from her second job. She came across the street with a very tall woman who turned out to be Jane's tap teacher, Miss Sarah.

"Jane has been telling me about this project all summer, and she invited me to the party. Like Jane does." Miss Sarah laughed. "I hope it's okay that I came."

"Of—of course. We're happy to have you," Rose stammered. She stared at Miss Sarah—she couldn't help it. Jane's tap teacher was tall! She thought all dancers were little, like Jane.

"Also," said Miss Sarah, "I brought you something. And again, I hope I haven't . . . overstepped in doing so. Jane says she thinks you might like to come to our tap class sometime. It can be hard to know what's true and what's just Jane's wishful thinking . . ." She smiled. "But in case it *is* true, I took the liberty of bringing you these." Miss Sarah held up a paper bag. "Size ten tap shoes. Is that close?"

Rose nodded. Miss Sarah held out the bag.

"You're welcome to come to a class anytime."

Rose took the bag of shoes. "Thank you. I just . . . I think I'd be really bad at it," she said at last. "My legs and feet just don't work like that."

Miss Sarah smiled. "Long legs help in tap."

"Really?" said Rose.

"Well, they don't hurt!" Miss Sarah laughed. "Come try! You seem like a young woman with dance steps inside you that ought to be let out."

Rose wasn't so sure about that, but she still had not yet succeeded in having fun doing something badly. Maybe she'd write a new sticky-note goal for herself: GIVE TAP A TRY.

Will Stringer came very festively dressed in at least ten different colors. Rose wanted to ask him if Mrs. Holling's cello was finished—it was Labor Day, after all—but she lost her nerve. Besides, Mrs. Holling would be taking it to London. Rose had no idea what cello she'd be playing when her fingers were ready.

Will climbed up in the truck and ran his beautiful fingers over Bessie just as he had done with the cello. "It's so beautiful, Rose!" he said. He blew his nose in his bright-red handkerchief. "So very beautiful!"

Kirk came—in regular clothes, not his mail uniform.

"It really does feel like a holiday!" he said, looking around.

Dr. Clare showed up a few minutes later. She whooped when she saw Bessie.

"Oh, my gosh, Rose! I had no idea! I mean, you said *giant,* but I just didn't realize!" She kept walking from one side of the pickup truck to the other.

"You can climb up in there, if you want," said Rose.

"I'm not sure I can do that gracefully," said Dr. Clare.

"I'll show you how," said Rose. She boosted herself up on the tailgate and then stood. Dr. Clare followed, and Rose stuck out her right hand to help her doctor up. She showed Dr. Clare how to sit on the side of the truck and swing her long legs over Bessie so she could get to the other side. Dr. Clare laughed when she did it. "It's like turning a cartwheel," she said. "Haven't done that since I was a little girl."

Mrs. Holling came, of course. She and Kirk and Will chatted over Gram's pumpkin cookies and Mr. Pickering's lemonade. Stanley *and* Wanda came. Wanda was enormously pregnant.

"It's been a long summer of bed rest," she said as Stanley introduced her around to all the neighbors. "I just got the okay to be up and about again—this baby can come any day now."

"Looks like the baby could come any minute," Thomas whispered to Rose. "She's about as big as Ole Bessie. Maybe she's having twins! We'd have three pairs on the street!"

Jeff and Simon and Baby Oliver came. They exclaimed over Wanda's pregnant belly and the two couples discussed diaper services and day-care options.

"Holy guacamole!" said Stanley when he saw Bessie. "How much does that pumpkin weigh?"

"One thousand three hundred sixty-five pounds!" said Thomas.

"The compost from this block's vegetables grew this pumpkin," said Mr. Pickering.

"Gracious of you to include us," said Jeff, "but I don't think we can take any credit. You guys won first place all on your own."

"Five hundred dollars, right?" said Wanda. "I saw the article in the *Star Tribune*. What will you use the money for?"

Rose looked to Thomas. They had not talked about how to handle this. The reporter must've left before

Rose ripped up the check, because the entire article was filled with quotes from Mr. Letch about the camaraderie of pumpkin growers.

"We didn't take the prize money," said Thomas.

"Didn't take it?" said Stanley. "How come?"

"There were . . . some strings attached," said Rose.

"Like what?" asked Wanda, lowering herself into a chair Señor Ocampo brought over for her.

"Well . . ." said Rose. She was not sure how to tell the story.

"The person who pays the prize money," said Mr. Pickering, "keeps the pumpkin. It was on the entry form, but I didn't read the paperwork closely enough."

"Ah," said Stanley. "Keeps the pumpkin and therefore gets the seeds."

Mr. Pickering nodded.

"Wow," said Wanda. "And I bet the seeds are worth a lot of money, aren't they?"

Mr. Pickering nodded again.

Rose and Thomas exchanged a look.

Bessie's seeds were worth money?

Chapter 55
Seed Harvest

Rose had assumed that Mr. Letch wanted the seeds to *plant*. She imagined him having a large field somewhere where he intended to grow hundreds of pumpkins and then pick the biggest one for the next year's weigh-offs. They'd learned that some of the prize purses at other weigh-offs were thousands of dollars—that's why most people never brought their biggest pumpkin to the Great Minnesota Get-Together.

"How much are Bessie's seeds worth?" she asked Mr. Pickering.

"Well, now . . ." said Mr. Pickering. "I'm not sure just yet. I'm making some inquiries. And we don't know how many we have, of course, until we cut into her."

"Cut into her!" said Rose.

"Only when you're ready," said Mr. Pickering gently. "But remember, she's been off the vine for almost two weeks at this point. She might not last much longer. She's already got that soft spot there in back. . . . Her seeds are all we'll have. And they won't be worth saving if we don't get them out before she starts to rot."

"I saw giant-vegetable seeds for sale one time at a county fair," said Simon. "Some of them were going for a lot of money."

"Like how much?" asked Thomas.

"A hundred dollars, some of them."

"One hundred dollars for a pack of seeds!" Thomas burst out laughing.

"No," said Mr. Pickering. "One hundred dollars for *a* seed."

One hundred dollars a seed. Rose was flabbergasted. Was there a black market for giant pumpkin seeds? Were Eddie Jacobi and Leroy Letch part of some pumpkin seed mafia?

Jeff looked at Simon. "Growing a giant pumpkin sure would be fun. . . ." he said.

"Oliver will be a toddler next summer," said Simon. "We are not going to have time to grow giant pumpkins!"

413

"We would help you," said Thomas. "We could grow two in the neighborhood. Or maybe more, even!"

Mr. Pickering laughed. "Now, Thomas . . ."

"It's too late, Otis," said Jeff, digging for his wallet. "I'm sold! We'd like to buy a seed, please."

Jeff took a one-hundred-dollar bill out of his wallet and held it out to Rose. Rose stared at it. Nobody had ever handed her that much money, let alone in one bill. She'd never even *seen* a hundred-dollar bill before. She didn't know what to do or say.

Jeff chuckled and gently pressed the bill into her hand. Just then, a car pulled up—a fancy one. Rose might not have noticed if Jesse and James hadn't whistled as it drove up. The windows were tinted, so they couldn't see the driver.

The door opened and one foot stepped out, clad in a shiny black cowboy boot. Too shiny—like it had never been worn, let alone worn in dirt and dust. Was it Eddie Jacobi out of jail on good behavior? That was all they needed.

"Maestro Waldenstein!" Thomas called. "You made it!"

Mr. Pickering's steadying hand was on Rose's back, which was good, because she felt a little dizzy.

Thomas ran to greet their uncomfortable-looking

guest. The maestro adjusted the waist of his jeans, retucking his button-down shirt, which did not look like it went with jeans. But he looked pretty unaccustomed to wearing jeans, so maybe he didn't have anything else to wear with them.

"Hello, Thomas. Thank you for inviting me to this . . . pumpkin party."

Maestro Waldenstein looked down at his shiny boots and then up at Rose. "Hello, Rose. I'm glad to see you."

Instinctively, Rose put her left hand behind her back. It was the first day she wasn't wearing the protective brace, and it felt suddenly . . . vulnerable.

Mr. Pickering walked over and introduced himself, then introduced the maestro around. Rose was surprised to see how politely—if stiffly—Maestro Waldenstein greeted everyone. Where had this graciousness been when she and Thomas had first met him?

"Come on, Maestro," Thomas said when the introductions were over with. "Come see our Bessie!" He grabbed Harris Waldenstein by the arm and turned him around to Señor Ocampo's truck.

The maestro gasped. "I had no idea," he said finally.

"One thousand three hundred sixty-five pounds!" crowed Thomas. "We won first place at the fair. And then we didn't. I mean, we did, but we decided we didn't want to. We just wanted to bring her home. And have this party!"

"I am honored to have been invited," said Maestro Waldenstein. And he actually sounded honored.

Mrs. Holling walked over and greeted the maestro politely. "It was good of you to come, Harris," she said. "I wonder if I might steal you away for a moment; there's something I'd like to speak with you about."

When Mrs. Holling and the maestro were out of earshot, Rose turned to Thomas.

"Why on earth did you invite Harris Waldenstein to our pumpkin party?" she asked, trying to keep her voice calm.

"He called the other day when you were at the library. We invited everyone else who has been a part of this summer, so I thought he could come, too," said Thomas.

"He hasn't been a part of our summer!" said Rose.

"Sure he has," said Thomas. "He kicked the whole thing off. Besides, he said he needs to talk with you."

At six o'clock, they decided to cut into the pumpkin. The soft spot on the back of Bessie had grown, sitting in the warm sun. If they were going to salvage the seeds, they needed to do it now.

They started with Mrs. Kiyo's largest kitchen knife. It stuck fast in Bessie. They tried a couple more kitchen knives from up and down the street. All got stuck.

"The pumpkin looks like a knife block," said Will Stringer, his handlebar mustache twitching with suppressed laughter.

Finally Señor Ocampo went to the hardware store and brought back a chain saw. Gram protested. Mr. Pickering explained that nothing else was going to make it through the pumpkin's thick shell.

Señor Ocampo also brought chaps, a helmet, a face shield, and thick work gloves. He insisted that everyone stand at least ten feet from Bessie while he made the hole. When he revved up the chain saw, Rose covered her ears; the chain saw had a different pitch to its scream than the table saw, but it was just as loud. Even with her ears covered, she could hear the pitch change when the saw made it through Bessie's thick shell—it almost sounded like it slipped. She wondered if the table saw had changed in pitch like that when the board had slipped. She couldn't remember.

When Señor Ocampo was done, he set the chain saw down and had Jeff and Simon hop into the truck and help him lift the top off Bessie. They heaved the top over the side of the pickup, where it thudded to the ground.

The men hopped down, and Rose followed Mr. Pickering and Thomas to the back of the truck. Thomas effortlessly jumped up on the tailgate, and Rose boosted herself up almost as effortlessly. They peered into the top of Bessie.

The inside was not filled with the goop and slimy strings Halloween pumpkins usually had. It was dry, like a cave. Bessie was a beautiful golden color inside — a deeper orange version of the blossoms from which she came. Large seeds hung from dry, pulpy strings. Thomas reached in and pulled one out. It was the largest seed Rose had ever seen — at least three times bigger than a normal pumpkin seed. He rubbed the stringy stuff off of it and held it up to the crowd gathered around the truck. Everyone cheered.

Mr. Pickering called up to them, "Seeds okay?"

"Looks like it to me," said Thomas.

"Rosie, how many do you think there are?"

Rose peered back into the pumpkin and made a quick guesstimate. "Maybe sixty or seventy?"

"Excellent!" said Mr. Pickering. He leaned against the tailgate and spoke more quietly. "I don't know that we're going to get a hundred dollars a seed this year — apparently it was a good year for giant pumpkins, which means there'll be lots of seeds for sale. But we should be able to make a very nice sum: a thousand dollars, at least—probably more."

Rose nodded. They would be able to get the five hundred dollars to Mrs. Holling, after all—with money left over besides, even after Mr. Pickering recouped his expenses. "We don't have to sell them all, though, do we?" she asked.

"Not if you don't want to," Mr. Pickering said. "These seeds are yours and Thomas's to do with as you see fit."

"For sure we'll keep one to grow next year, right?" said Thomas. Rose nodded, but Mr. Pickering did not answer.

Rose pulled her gaze away from Bessie and turned around to look down at her neighbor. He wiped his eyes with his handkerchief, then put it back in his pocket and smiled up at them in the truck bed.

"Of course we will," he said. "If that's what you two would like to do, I'd be proud to join you."

"And it'd be nice to give some away, too," said Rose, looking at Bessie. "To some other kids, maybe? Someone who . . . needs one?"

She thought back to Thomas saying that she *needed* the pumpkin plant, way back when it was just starting to grow. She'd thought it was silly then. But maybe he was right—maybe she *had* needed it.

Chapter 56
A Word

Thomas did the actual harvesting of the seeds, his back end sticking out of Bessie as he pulled seeds from her insides. Rose was happy to sit on the tailgate and pick the dry pulp-like strings off the seeds. She wasn't sure what else had to be done with them, but she could research that later.

There were seventy-seven seeds in all—as wonderful a number as could be imagined. Thomas hopped down from the truck bed and ran the bowl inside to Mr. Pickering's kitchen, passing Maestro Waldenstein on the way.

The maestro walked slowly—almost reluctantly, it seemed to Rose—up to the truck, looking awkward and ridiculous in his pressed shirt, jeans, and cowboy boots. Why was he wearing cowboy boots, anyway? Did he think there would be horseback riding at the pumpkin party?

And then it dawned on her: he was wearing them to make himself *taller*! She almost felt sorry for him; he must be very sensitive about his height.

"Hello, Rose," the maestro said as he drew near.

Rose smiled politely, swallowing the giggle that threatened. From up in the bed of the pickup truck, she noticed that the maestro had a bald spot starting on the top of his head. She wondered if he knew.

"Are you . . . enjoying the pumpkin party?" he asked awkwardly. He seemed to have trouble looking up at her—probably because of his fused neck. She sat down on the tailgate, swinging her legs off the end.

"I am." She knew she should ask him if he was enjoying himself, but she didn't think either of them was interested in small talk. "Thomas told me you called earlier; what did you want to talk to me about?"

Maestro Waldenstein nodded stiffly. "The head of the music department at the university showed me a video of a lesson you had with Frances Holling last fall—she was being evaluated as an instructor, I believe, for the London position."

Rose vaguely remembered when a video crew had been at her lesson. Mrs. Holling had said to ignore them, so she did.

"Your playing is quite extraordinary, Rose. Especially given your age, which I now know is much younger than I guessed when . . . when we first met."

Why was it that people assumed you were older if you were taller, and younger if shorter? She and Thomas—and she and the maestro, for that matter—were the perfect contradiction to those assumptions.

"I . . . regret the first impression I made, Rose."

It wasn't exactly an apology. But then, you weren't likely to get an apology from the Henry Higgins / Harris Waldenstein type. They really were only concerned about themselves, and they rarely changed. But this was obviously a peace offering, which was more than she'd expected from him.

"Thank you, Maestro," she said, feeling quite grown up and gracious. The Henry Higginses of the world might be set in their ways, but the Eliza Doolittles of the world were capable of growing and changing, and Rose now considered herself the Eliza Doolittle type. The letters in *Eliza* added up to fifty-three, a respectable prime. Surely that wasn't coincidence.

There was a long, awkward silence. Rose tried to just sit with it, gently swinging her legs, waiting for the maestro to make his next move.

"I am very sorry about your accident," he said at last. He sounded like he had practiced saying it. "I understand you will be undergoing extensive rehabilitation this fall."

Rose nodded. The maestro looked hard at her, as if he were trying to decide something. Rose held his gaze.

Kirk walked up to join them.

"Did you ask her yet, Harris?" he asked cheerfully.

Maestro Waldenstein looked at his shiny boots.

"Ask me what?" Rose said.

The maestro sighed. "I wondered if you would consider playing—when your fingers are up for it—in a quartet with us."

A quartet? *With the maestro?*

Kirk grinned. "It will be a private group—just a little something to unwind with." He looked at the maestro. "Some might say 'for fun.'"

The maestro made a face. "We shall see. In any event, nothing too intense. I'm going to . . . I'm . . . I will play first violin."

There was a long pause. Rose wasn't sure she was

supposed to know his history of switching from violin to cello. But she *did* know it, so eventually she asked, "Have you been playing violin again?"

"Not much," he said. He looked up at her. "You'll soon learn how difficult it is to relearn how to play something that once seemed like an extension of you."

"The second violinist would be Will Stringer," Kirk said. "He's normally on viola, but he's interested in getting better on the violin. And that means that yours truly will be the violist."

"The quartet was their idea," the maestro said. "We all have reasons for benefiting from such a group, I guess you could say."

"And we've spoken with Frances Holling about it," said Kirk. "She is not opposed. We've discussed some . . . ground rules." His eyes flicked to Maestro Waldenstein. "She thinks it could be good for you, Rose—*if* you are interested—it is your choice."

"I don't have an instrument," Rose reminded them. "And I haven't done a lot of ensemble playing."

"If you had won the fellowship, I would have had you doing more of that once you were done with the Bach solo suites," said Maestro Waldenstein. "So the timing is right, I think. And I am certain we can find you a cello to play."

"What music will you be playing?" she asked.

"Probably some Bach. Some Mozart, maybe," said Maestro Waldenstein. He shrugged. "We'll just have to see how it goes."

"Will Stringer has great recordings of some jazz musicians who are string players," said Rose. "Stéphane Grappelli, Esperanza Spalding—even Yo-Yo Ma sometimes plays jazz. Do you think we could look into some of that music?"

Maestro Waldenstein looked startled. But Kirk answered, "I'm sure we can; it's just the four of us, so we should be able to play whatever we want."

Rose hopped off the tailgate of the truck and stood straight and tall in front of Harris Waldenstein. His cowboy boots didn't do much to close the distance between their heights. She waited for him to look up and meet her eyes. When he did, she smiled.

"Thank you, Maestro. I will consider the offer."

Chapter 57
A Seed

As they cleaned up the yard and said good night to their guests, Thomas sidled up to Rose and flashed a one-hundred-dollar bill. Rose grabbed for her pocket, thinking she had dropped the money from Jeff, but it was still there.

"Where'd you get that?" she asked.

"Maestro Waldenstein."

"You're kidding."

"I didn't *try* to sell it to him, if that's what you're thinking," said Thomas. "He said he might plant one of Bessie's seeds while he's staying here in Minneapolis. Then he asked how much a seed cost, and I told him you'd just sold one for a hundred dollars. So that's what he paid." He shook his head. "I can't believe people just walk around with one-hundred-dollar bills in their wallets!"

"*I* can't believe the maestro thinks he's going to grow a giant pumpkin!" Rose started to laugh. Maestro Waldenstein digging in the dirt, learning about worms, anchoring vines, pollinating, dealing with pests? Would he wear his shiny cowboy boots? Thomas laughed, too. They laughed so hard that Rose's sides started to ache.

"And there's more," said Thomas. He pulled a wad of money out of his pocket. "Everybody gave some money, Rose—not for seeds, but for the cello deductible. They said the pumpkin project had given them all so much, and they wanted to give back in some small way. Mrs. Kiyo gave me two twenties, Mrs. Jacobi gave a ten, and Kirk gave thirty. Wanda and Stanley said they're good for another thirty. . . ." He sorted through the bills. "Dr. Clare gave me fifty dollars, and Jane's tap teacher threw in a ten. . . . Will Stringer gave a twenty, too—I guess that's kind of a discount, huh? Anyway, I think we've almost got the five hundred dollars for the deductible, Rosie— not even counting our seed money!" He laughed. "*Seed money.*"

Thomas handed her the bills. "You better hold on to it so I don't lose it," he said. Then he took off up the yard to see what else had to be done for cleanup.

Rose folded the money carefully and slipped it into her back pocket. She looked around the neighborhood. Mrs. Kiyo had turned on her big porch light, and it lit the new bright-red geraniums down in her Listening Garden. Mr. Pickering had planted his window boxes on the Fourth of July after they'd pollinated the pumpkin plant's flowers—and several houses on the block had followed suit, Rose realized as she looked up and down the street. The Jacobis had a big pot of yellow flowers from Señor Ocampo's store on their stoop. Gram called them mums. There was a pot of reddish-orange ones on Wanda and Stanley's steps. The whole street was brightening up. They should get some mums for their porch, too, add a little more color to Library Lane. Maybe they could use some of their "seed money"—and the money their neighbors gave—to spiff up the neighborhood with more flower boxes, or maybe even start a community garden. She'd talk to Thomas about it.

Rose walked over to Bessie in Señor Ocampo's truck. She just needed a minute to herself. She was a little overwhelmed by everything that had happened at the party.

She was all the way up to the tailgate before she saw what was waiting there: Mrs. Holling's periwinkle case. There was a note attached to it in Mrs. Holling's familiar handwriting. Rose unfolded the paper. It smelled faintly of lemon and mint.

Rose, my sweet . . .

This cello is for you to keep. I know you fixed it for me to take to London, but I never intended to do that. It is an honor to pass this instrument on to you. I can't wait to hear you play it. I took it for a spin, and although it still has to "settle into itself," as Will says, it has a fine sound and feel. He really is an exceptional artist. As are you.

> *All my love,*
> *Mrs. Holling*

Rose opened the case, and her heart caught in her throat. The cello was gorgeous—even as the sun went down and the street darkened to twilight, she could see that it glowed. She'd known that Will Stringer was going to "shine her up and get the scuffs out," but she had no idea it would look so beautiful.

She ran the fingers of her left hand up and down the silky new neck. She traced her right hand over the body where the crack had been. She could not feel the repair at all. What she could feel was that this was her cello — and she couldn't wait to play it.

Rose tucked Mrs. Holling's note in with the cello and fastened the clasps on the beautiful periwinkle case.

Someone had brought a big flashlight out now that the sun was going down. Rose climbed into the bed of the truck, stuck the flashlight in the hole in the top of Bessie, and turned it on. The pumpkin glowed. She looked down into the great golden inside of the summer's pumpkin project. Bessie really was big enough to crawl into. Thomas would love it. She turned to call to him, and then she stopped.

She would love to crawl inside the pumpkin. How many people had ever sat inside a pumpkin? She glanced around. Most of the partygoers were gone. Jane and Thomas were carrying chairs back to Mr. Pickering's garage. Several neighbors were busy cleaning up, sweeping, saying good night. She should probably be helping them, but . . .

Before she lost her nerve, Rose lifted one long leg

and put it inside Bessie. Then she folded the other one in and sank down into the pumpkin. She moved the light around the walls of the pumpkin. It was magical—like being in a lantern or a bubble of light. The color of the inside of the pumpkin was like nothing else she could think of—the words *yellow* and *orange* didn't begin to describe it. There was a warmth, a radiance, to it that she almost *felt*. Rose sighed with happiness and rested her chin on her knees. She was surprised she could do so; all the bending in the pumpkin patch must have made her long legs more flexible.

What a crazy summer! School would start tomorrow. Math at the university the following week. She was ready for all that. She would move the *kintsugi* bowl somewhere else tomorrow, perhaps, because she would need the cello chair as she got to know her cello again. Maybe she could put it on the bookshelf in the living room—then she could see it when she practiced. She was so ready to practice again—even if she had to start slowly, which surely she would. But if things went as well as Dr. Clare hoped, maybe she would join the quartet. They could call themselves *Kintsugi*. She laughed, thinking about proposing the name to the maestro. Maybe she'd take the bowl to their first rehearsal and tell the others the stories it held.

She looked up and out the top of the pumpkin. The night was clear, and she could see a big round moon over her house. As she turned her head, something hard scratched her through her curls. She reached back with her right hand: it was a seed Thomas had missed. She dug it out with her fingernails. Her right hand worked almost as well as her left for some things now.

One seed. So much potential crammed inside it. She tucked the seed in her pocket; she would keep it as a reminder of unexpected possibilities. Her fingers brushed the now-worn sticky-note scraps in the same pocket. She knew what they said without looking: ORGANIZE THE PUMPKIN PROJECT. HAVE FUN. *BE* FUN. She'd pretty much accomplished all that. She smiled — it was good to have goals. Good to meet them. What should she do next?

From inside Bessie, Rose heard the distinct sound of tap dancing. She smiled and wriggled her way up and out of the pumpkin.

Jane tap-danced down the driveway. She stopped when she saw Rose.

"Rose! You're beautiful! You look like Cinderella stepping out of her pumpkin coach!" She paradiddled over to the truck.

Rose laughed. "Thanks, Jane." Rose took a big

breath and called up a little Bach to steady herself. "Ummm . . . Jane. Do you think I could try your tap class this week?"

Jane stopped tapping.

"Really?"

"I just want to try it," said Rose. "I'm not promising I'll sign up or anything. Your teacher brought me some tap shoes to borrow."

"I know—I told her to," said Jane. "She's got big feet, too. And yes, you can come! Of course you can come! Tap class is on Thursday—six thirty. Mrs. Lukashenko will take us."

Jane executed a couple of fancy steps, then skipped across the street.

As she stepped out of the pumpkin, one long leg at a time, Rose realized she was humming. What was it? Not Bach. Not Cole Porter or any of the jazz riffs she'd surrounded herself with the past few weeks. Something from *My Fair Lady*? No. It was a simpler song. . . .

She hummed a bit more and realized that the words behind the notes were about a good girl who loved her mama and Jesus. And Elvis. She laughed out loud. Of all the music from the summer—Tom Petty?

She turned and looked across the street. The Jacobi twins sat with Mrs. Jacobi on their porch, enjoying the evening, their Jesse James guitar case leaning up against the porch post. Jane paradiddled up the steps to join them. Both twins tweaked her ponytail in greeting.

Rose hopped down from the truck and walked across the street. It was almost dark. Mama would call her in soon—tomorrow was a school day, after all.

But there was time to tune the guitar for Jesse and James. It was the least she could do. They had shaved for the pumpkin party.

AUTHOR'S NOTE

I first learned about giant pumpkins during the North American growing season of 2008. One of my lunch partners at work told fantastical tales of enormous plants and fruits grown at specific latitudes around the world. He himself was not a grower, but he was part of the village surrounding a grower—his young adult son, Alex, was quite involved in giant pumpkins. Alex was, in fact, hoping for a prizewinner out of his tiny urban backyard that year—one plant, one pumpkin. I was rather immediately smitten with the whole idea of giant pumpkins—and especially the idea of one plant, one pumpkin in a limited space. Most competitive growers have fields of these giants and pick their biggest one at weigh-off time.

I don't remember discussion about trying to hit the one-ton mark in 2008, but there were probably whispers. The half-ton mark had been reached in 2000. Certainly by 2010, growers around the world were wondering and working to see if a one-ton pumpkin *could* be grown in one growing season from seed. And if it could, would such a heavy pumpkin be able to hold together structurally?

Well, it happened in 2012. A two-thousand-nine-pound pumpkin was weighed in at the Topsfield Fair in Massachusetts—a crazy new world record. But the one-ton mark has been surpassed several times and in several places around the globe in subsequent years.

I started this book in August 2010, and it is set in that 2010–2012 time frame—on the cusp of someone breaking that once seemingly impossible barrier. In 2016, the first pumpkin over 2,500 pounds was weighed in Germany. There is now talk about breaking the *three-thousand-pound* barrier. Perhaps as you read this, it has already happened.

INSPIRING MATERIALS

How-to-Grow World Class Giant Pumpkins: The All-Organic Way by Don Langevin. Norton, MA: Annedawn, 2009.

My soundtrack: *The Cello Suites: Yo-Yo Ma Inspired by Bach.* Sony Classical B0000029YB, 1998, two CDs.

The Cello Suites: J. S. Bach, Pablo Casals, and the Search for a Baroque Masterpiece by Eric Siblin. Toronto: House of Anansi, 2009.

ACKNOWLEDGMENTS

It takes a village, a team, a family to grow a giant pumpkin. Something like that is also needed to write a book, I've found. Alex Bogie, my pumpkin expert, has been with me the longest, answering questions about giant pumpkin growing, clarifying and advising, resourcing and checking. That he helped with such good cheer and such a generous heart for so long helped to keep *me* going.

Experts in other "fields" (pun intended!) joined along the way. Inga Banitt answered my first cello questions and both provided and checked the tiny little details around practicing the cello. Kirk McKinley told me what it was like to stick your hand into a snow blower and not know if you'd ever play cello again. When I needed someone who knew how to build and repair cellos, Will Richardson entered the fray and patiently assisted me in coming up with a fictional cello injury that could be repaired in a meaningful way. I am so grateful to these artists—they allowed me to bring my (totally-uninformed-but-not-lacking-in-enthusiasm) love of cello and Bach's cello suites to the page in an authentic way.

When I needed a hand surgeon to consult with, Dr. Clare McCarthy graciously talked to me on her way home after long days of surgery, helping me to understand *exactly* what can happen with "just one cut." She invited me to her office and drew pictures, put *me* through Rose's hand therapies, and willingly clarified details over and over again.

Satomi Niki taught me so much about Japanese history and culture, as well as the Japanese tea ceremony, that exquisite, beautiful art. She helped me to get the details right without making "The Way of Tea" chapter sixty pages long. I grew to really love Mrs. Kiyo, the latest of all the characters to arrive in *Giant Pumpkin Suite,* and I have Satomi to thank for that.

These good people generously gave of their time and expertise. Any mistakes that remain in this book are entirely mine — they did their very best to help me get it as right as can be.

My deep thanks to the generous readers — teachers, family and friends, writing partners — who read the very many drafts of this book and gave such excellent feedback. I am especially grateful to my young readers. Thank you to Cassie Ahlgrim, Anna Long, Lola Ruff, Ruby Stillman, and their wonderful mothers — the continued enthusiasm of our mother-daughter book club has been inspiring. Thanks also to Alex Hannigan, Anna Nguyen, and Corinne Sidebottom. And to my daughter, Marta, who read more drafts than anyone — thank you, thank you, thank you!

Copious love and thanks to Carrie Hannigan, my agent, who believed in this book with such energy, sweetness, and *vigor* from the start. And to Kaylan Adair, my editor, who understood immediately and exactly what I was trying to do and helped make it so. Many thanks to the entire Candlewick team, as well. I could not have asked for a better experience making a book.

And last, but certainly not least . . . thank you to my husband, Burke, who said yes when I said I wanted to write books for kids. He always asks how the writing is going, and that in itself is a gift.